7/14

the summer i wasn't me

JESSICA VERDI

sourcebooks
fire

Published by Sourcebooks Fire, an imprint of Sourcebooks, Inc.
P.O. Box 4410, Naperville, Illinois 60567-4410
(630) 961-3900
Fax: (630) 961-2168
www.sourcebooks.com

Library of Congress Cataloging-in-Publication Data is on file with the publisher.

Printed and bound in the United States of America.
VP 10 9 8 7 6 5 4 3 2 1

To Amy
For all the reasons

Chapter 1

My mother drives right past the New Horizons sign.

"Um, Mom?" I touch her arm gently.

She doesn't respond. She's zoning out again. But these moments have been happening a lot less often lately. Maybe soon they won't be happening at all.

"Mom," I say again, louder. "You missed the turn."

She finally snaps out of it and glances in the rearview mirror, where the New Horizons sign is still slightly visible.

"Oh!" She pulls a sudden U-turn, and my insides do somersaults. I knew I shouldn't have let her drive. She glances at the clock. "Sorry, Lexi."

She makes the correct turn this time around, and I manage a reassuring smile. "It's okay."

The narrow road up the mountain is so winding and bumpy that we're forced to creep along at a measly ten miles per hour.

A thick forest surrounds us. The trees are dark and plush and reach up and over the rocky road like a fringed canopy. As we inch forward, the amorphous blob of green foliage comes into focus and I can see each leaf and branch in perfect clarity. I roll down my window and take a deep breath. It's so quiet here. I rest my chin on the window jam so that all I see is the forest slowly rolling by. My mind takes me back in time, where I'm riding in a horse-drawn carriage through untouched woods.

But as we progress up the mountain, hints that this place is not quite as natural as it first seemed begin to emerge. The tree branches above us have been pruned back from the road. The narrow strip of grass that buffers the road from the tree line has been neatly cropped. Flowers sprout in patterns too perfect to be accidental.

Someone has gone to a lot of trouble to manipulate the raw landscape into some preconceived idea of what nature *should* look like. Goosebumps trickle across the back of my neck as I realize that's exactly what they're going to do to me too.

About halfway up the mountain, the signs start popping up. They line the edge of the road, sticking up out of the perfectly manicured ground.

You are on the road to truth.

Help is on the way.

God's love heals us all.

I look down at my lap and run my left thumb over the tiny lightning bolt tattoo on the inside of my right wrist. Everything this tattoo means is about to change.

Salvation waits just around the next bend!

Almost there.

With no warning, a deer leaps out of the woods and sprints across the road in front of our car.

"Look out!" I shout.

My mother slams on the brakes, and the car skids forward on the gravel, missing the deer by mere inches. It scampers off into the woods unharmed, but we're still too stunned to move. My knuckles have gone ghost white from my death grip on the dashboard, and my chest stings from where the seat belt jerked too tightly against my skin—but it's my mother I'm worried about.

"Are you okay?" I ask once I've regained control of my voice.

Mom is facing me, her brown eyes wide, red splotches on her fair face and neck. The simple gold cross around her neck sways gently back and forth.

Though my heart is still thrashing around wildly under my ribcage, I unbuckle my seat belt and grab her shoulders. "Mom, talk to me. Are you all right?" She nods, and I exhale in relief. "Okay, I'm driving the rest of the way. Switch places with me."

"I'm fine, Lexi—" she begins, but I'm already out of the car and opening the driver's side door. She sighs and scoots over to the passenger seat.

I readjust the seat and the mirrors, make sure my mother is buckled in, and we resume the final leg of our journey. After rounding the next bend, the hill levels out and the woods open up.

Ahead is a palatial log cabin with a wraparound porch. A woman waves to us from the front steps, her smile so big it looks painful.

I park the car, and the woman rushes over to help with my bags.

"Hello! You're right on time," she chirps. "I'm Brianna." She's in her midtwenties and dressed in head-to-toe pink, from her pink New Horizons T-shirt and sparkly pink capris to the bright pink elastics holding her pigtails in place. I tune out her perky words of welcome and stare up at the giant banner hanging over the log cabin's entrance, a prominent lump developing in my throat.

Welcome to New Horizons, it reads in tall, imposing block letters. And beneath that, *Say good-bye to homosexuality; say hello to your new life!*

I take a deep breath and follow Brianna and my mom up the path.

Here we go.

Chapter 2

"Right this way, Alexis," Brianna says, leading the way up the front steps.

"It's Lexi," I correct her.

She eyes me up and down, her gaze lingering distastefully on my vintage Doc Martens/black romper combo and the way my dyed-black choppy hair contrasts with my pale skin. I'm used to getting this look from people. But my style is one thing I don't want to change about myself.

"I'd prefer to call you Alexis," Brianna says.

My parents gave me my nickname when I was little. But the way Brianna says it, it's like she thinks my nickname has something to do with why I like girls. It's really weird. But as much as I would like to snap back at Brianna and her know-it-all judgy-ness, I don't say anything. If this camp has any chance of working, I need to cooperate.

"Did you have a nice trip?" Brianna asks my mom.

"Oh yes, thank you. Virginia is beautiful country," Mom says.

"The Blue Ridge Mountains are lovely. But it was a long drive. About five hours."

"It was worth it." Brianna smiles knowingly at me.

We cross the threshold, and crisp air-conditioned air caresses my skin. The log cabin-esque exterior was entirely misleading; the inside is modern and spacious, with high ceilings and track lighting. We're in a large lounge-type area, with leather couches and armchairs and glass coffee tables with books and New Horizons brochures neatly laid out on them. The space is really comfortable and inviting. I don't know why, but I'm surprised.

"Lexi!" Mom says, staring around the room in awe. "Look how beautiful this place is! Oh, you're going to have such a wonderful time here!"

I nod, but what I don't say is that whether my time at New Horizons is wonderful or not doesn't matter. The only thing that matters is the grin on my mother's face. She's *happy*. Right now, in this tiny moment in time, she's the woman she used to be. And I'm going to do whatever it takes to keep her that way. Because she's all I have left.

The only other people in the room are a handful of New Horizons staff; no other campers are in sight. A middle-aged, balding man has his blue shirt tucked so tightly into his pants that his bulging belly looks about ready to burst through the fabric. He comes over and extends his hand to my mother.

"Welcome!" he says a bit too jovially. "I'm the director of New Horizons, Mr. Martin."

"Christine Hamilton," my mother says. "And this is Lexi."

Mr. Martin wraps his large hands around mine and smiles down at me. "We are very happy to have you, Lexi. You have taken the first step to inheriting the kingdom of God."

"Um…thank you?" I say for lack of anything better. I pull my hand away.

"You are very welcome! Now, we just have a few business matters to attend to. If you'll follow me." He leads me and my mother into an office with a cherrywood desk and lots of pictures of his family.

I study a framed photo of him with a blond woman and two little boys. The boys are wearing little league uniforms and Mr. Martin's hand is resting on the woman's shoulder. It looks like it was taken at one of those department store photo studio places. Mr. Martin catches me staring.

"Aren't they beautiful?" he says and picks up the frame. "Nancy and I will be married ten years this October. The twins just celebrated their eighth birthday. Big party at the bowling alley." He chuckles.

"They're lovely," Mom says with only the slightest hint of sadness in her voice.

I look back and forth between Mr. Martin and his family photo. They're happy and smiling and perfect—like the fake family that comes in the frame, only real.

Jealousy twists in my heart. But all I say is, "Cute kids."

"Now, Mrs. Hamilton," Mr. Martin continues, changing the subject, "we just have a few documents to go over." He slides a stack of papers across the desk to my mother. Insurance, liability, emergency contacts, medical information…He goes through each one with her, and she signs my life away on the dotted lines.

"And finally, payment," he says as he gets to the last page. He points to some figures. "After your one thousand dollar deposit, your balance is eight thousand five hundred dollars. This covers the entire summer program: the proven New Horizons reparative therapy system, room and board, and incidentals."

My mother nods and reaches into her purse for her checkbook. I'm stunned. $9,500?

"Mom," I whisper. "That's a lot of money."

"It's fine, Lexi, I've got it covered."

"But how?" Money's been tight lately. We don't have Dad's salary anymore, Mom only recently started back at her job, and what money they had saved for my college had to go to Dad's medical bills. I got a job waiting tables at the Hard Rock Cafe in Myrtle Beach to help out—a job I had to quit to come to New Horizons for the summer.

Mom lowers her voice, even though in this small room there's no way Mr. Martin won't hear. "Your father's life insurance disbursement finally came in."

I feel sick. There was no way Dad could have imagined when he took out that policy that this is what the money would go toward: the de-gayifying of his only daughter.

My father died without really knowing me. I mean, he knew me in lots of other ways—he knew that I love shopping at thrift stores and like to experiment with my hair and that my favorite food in the world is the pad thai from Bangkok Delight. We listened to the same kind of music and went to see Radiohead and Death Cab for Cutie together. He knew that I love English but hate science and that it's my dream to go to fashion design school in Paris.

But I never told him I was gay. I wanted to, I really did. If anyone was going to know, I wanted it to be him. But how do you tell a dying man something like that?

Here's the thing: where I come from, people go to church. *Everyone* goes to church, actually. Including my family. We get married and have kids young, and the biggest scandals revolve around the Cardwells' divorce or whether or not Becca Simpson got a boob job before the Miss Dillon County beauty pageant. In my small town in South Carolina, no one is gay. It just. Doesn't. Happen. To the people in my town, homosexuality is something that happens on TV, not in real life.

When Pastor Joe gives his sermons about protecting the sanctity of marriage, heads bob in agreement. When someone does something dumb in school, they get called *fag* and everyone laughs. The word of choice for all things uncool is *gay*.

It goes way past homophobia. It's the norm. It's our way of life.

So what if I told Dad the truth and the shock was so big it made his already-weak heart stop beating forever? What if the last time I saw his eyes, they were filled with disappointment?

"Mom…" I begin as she writes out her check. But she looks at me, her eyes brimming with hope, and I clamp my mouth shut. *It doesn't matter*, I tell myself again. *The money doesn't matter. Dad's life insurance doesn't matter.* The only thing that matters is keeping what's left of my family together, doing whatever it takes to make sure Mom doesn't go back to the dark place she lived in for so long after Dad died. If I lost my mom too, I'd officially have no one. And it would be no one's fault but my own. "Okay," I say finally.

"Okay," she echoes and signs the check.

"Wonderful!" Mr. Martin says, clasping his hands together. "Now, I'm afraid that this is the point where you must say your good-byes. We've got a full day planned for our campers, and we need to get Lexi settled in."

When I see the tears in my mother's eyes, I throw my arms around her and hold her tightly. "I left a list of everything you need to remember on the refrigerator door," I tell her. "Trash pickup is on Wednesdays, so you have to bring the can out to the curb on Tuesday nights."

She nods.

"And I already arranged for Robbie across the street to mow the lawn, so you don't need to worry about that."

"I know."

"And—"

"Lexi. Don't worry about me—I have the church, I'll be fine. You just focus on getting better."

I swallow back my tears. "I love you, Mom."

"I love you too, Lexi."

And then she's gone.

Chapter 3

As Brianna shows me upstairs to the girls' dorm, we pass another camper being led downstairs by a counselor in a blue shirt. He seems about my age and has shaggy, dark-blond hair. His lips are pressed tightly together, but his eyes reveal a glimpse of something. Anger? No. Fear. He doesn't even glance at me as we pass each other. He just looks straight ahead, following the counselor down the stairs and out of sight.

I suddenly feel strangely hollow.

I'm really here. This is really happening.

I run my hand along the polished wooden banister and drift back to the moment that led me here.

It was May, just about two months ago. I came home from school to find Mom balled up on the sofa, surrounded by used tissues, sobbing.

In the six months since Dad's death, Mom hadn't been doing so well. For that first month or so, it seemed like all she was able to do was cry. But I had days like that too, so I understood. We were both a mess. We spent a lot of time just hugging each other or holding each other's hands and letting it all out. But then, slowly, I started to come out of it. I had school and work and a mourning mother to take care of. I missed Dad more than I could ever put into words, but I was starting to move on.

My mom's grief, on the other hand, took a different turn. She stopped crying so much, but then she started doing this thing where every time something reminded her of him—which was almost always—she zoned out, unable to concentrate on anything happening around her. It was like instead of staying in the moment and being sad and working through the pain, she chose to live in her memories, in a place where the love of her life was still alive and everything was happier.

And I guess I couldn't blame her. If I had been able to separate my mind like that, I probably would have too. The pain sucked. The memories were far better. The three of us used to have so much fun together. When I was little, we went to the beach every single weekend, swimming all day and burying each other in the sand and laughing at the tourists who seemed to bring everything they owned with them for just a few hours at the sea. On Saturday mornings, Mom would blast the country western radio station throughout the house, and Dad and I would make fun of her for her clueless taste in music, but she would just laugh and say that if she had to suffer through our music, we had to suffer through hers. After they bought me my first sewing machine, Mom and I made

Dad an apron (he was the best cook in the family) that said *Real men bake cupcakes*. He wore it proudly.

So yeah, the memories were better than the now. I got it. But soon, half a year had gone by and Mom's spacing-out thing still wasn't getting any better. One night she made us a frozen pizza for dinner but forgot to remove the plastic wrapping. I came home after work to a kitchen filled with smoke, an oven rack dripping with melted plastic, and a mother sitting in front of the TV, completely unaware of the wailing smoke detector. And another day I got a call from someone at the electric company who wanted to know why we had sent in a stack of supermarket coupons in our payment envelope instead of actual money.

The worst part of it all was that Mom never laughed anymore; she never even smiled. I missed her.

But it had been a while since I'd seen her crying so uncontrollably like this. I dropped my bag and went to pull her close, to try to console her. But she shrank away from me. That's when I knew: whatever was wrong, it didn't have to do with Dad.

"What's going on?"

Mom blew her nose loudly. "Lexi," she whispered, "do you have anything you want to tell me?"

I stared at her, my mind racing. Did one of my teachers call her about something? Did she find out Vinny Palmer's older brother bought us beer on the weekends? Did I forget her birthday? "What do you mean?" I said hesitantly.

She picked up a book off the floor. I hadn't seen it before now, because it was halfway hidden under the couch and I'd been distracted. But I recognized it right away—it was one of my sketch-books, *the* sketchbook, the one with an adorned *Z* on the cover. The one I'd thought was safely tucked away in its hiding place in the back of my closet. But then I remembered that I'd been feeling particularly sorry for myself last night and taken it out for the first time in months. And I'd forgotten to put it away.

"What were you doing in my room?" I whispered, because I really didn't know what else to say.

Mom didn't answer. Instead, she flipped through the book. Sketches of Zoë filled every page—some in pencil, some in color, some full body, some just her eyes.

"This is Zoë Green, right?" Mom whispered, staring at a sketch of Zoë laughing.

"Yeah," I whispered, but it was barely audible. I cleared my throat and tried again. "Yeah."

Mom nodded, her tears landing on the pages, causing the ink to run. She already knew it was Zoë, of course—everyone knows everyone in our town. Plus, I had stared at Zoë so much over the past year and a half and knew her face so well that every line of her was perfectly reproduced on the pages of the book.

"Are you…in…love…with her?" It took her a long time to get the question out between the sobs, and each word was like another knife being jabbed into me.

She knew. My mother knew. All I had to do was confirm it.

"Not anymore," I said. Those two words said so much—I did love Zoë once; I've been hiding so much from you; I'm gay.

And once the truth was out there in the ether, an amazing calm came over me. There were no more secrets. Maybe her finding the Zoë book was actually the best thing that could have happened. Maybe she would understand. Maybe we could finally move forward.

The truth was, I had never felt sad about being gay. It was just another part of who I was, no different than my size-seven feet or 20/20 vision. The part I hated was the hiding; the pretending to be someone I wasn't; the steady, tormenting harassment that came in the form of Bible scripture and church sermons; the constant fear that if people found out, they would hate me, ridicule me, possibly even hurt me. *That* stuff sucked.

But if Mom knew, and she understood, well…that would just be the best. The barrier between us would vanish, and it would be me and her against the world—instead of always me vs. them.

But then she looked up at me, for the first time since I came in, and my world came crashing down.

The broken expression she'd been wearing for the last six months was now completely shattered. That look in her eyes told me everything I needed to know: she was mourning my loss now too. I had just killed the rest of her family. Because Mom felt exactly the same way about gay people as everyone else did: gay people were abominations. Gay people went to hell.

The barrier between us hadn't vanished; it was raised even higher.

"Why does God keep punishing me?" she said, her voice low and emotionless.

"He's not," I whispered.

"He is."

"But…" I didn't know how to finish the thought. I wanted to talk to her about it, to have a conversation, to tell her that I was still her daughter, that I still had all the same likes and dislikes and opinions as before, that nothing had changed. But I'd known I was gay since I was nine years old. (I mean, I'd definitely had certain *feelings* before then, but the first moment I was actually fully cognizant of what those feelings probably meant was the day I begged Mom to take me to see *The Devil Wears Prada* so I could look at all the pretty clothes—and realized about halfway through the movie that I was paying far more attention to Anne Hathaway's eyes than the costume design.) I'd had eight long years to live with that truth in this town, in this church, in this school, in this family. And I knew that, for my mom, *everything* had changed, and there was no point in trying to convince her otherwise. So all I said was, "I'm sorry."

For the next few days, Mom spent a lot of time at church. She went there early in the morning and came home in the evening. She wouldn't even look at me.

I tried to go on with my days as usual, but all I could really do was turn the whole thing over and over in my mind. Amid the endless, shapeless swirl of pain and confusion and worry and regret, there were two distinct thoughts that kept circling back to me.

One: *"Why does God keep punishing me?"* That was how my mother saw me now: as a punishment. In her mind, I was unholy, worthless. I would never see Dad again in heaven.

Two: *Thank God Dad never lived to learn the truth about me.* I hated myself for even thinking it. But the thought of hurting *both* my parents in this way was incomprehensible.

If only I'd kept that book hidden better. If only I hadn't admitted the truth when she'd asked. Because of my carelessness, my selfishness, Mom had no one. *I* had no one. There were no grandparents anymore, no aunts or uncles, no siblings. I had friends, but no one I was really close with. Not since Zoë anyway.

I was all alone. And it was all my fault.

And then, three days after Mom learned the truth, everything changed again. She came home, sat at the kitchen table where I was failing miserably at focusing on my homework, and said, "Go to the church tomorrow. Speak with Pastor Joe. He's expecting you at three."

Not only was she looking straight at me, she was actually…was that a *smile*? Her eyes were alive. My muscles began to relax. "Does this mean…are we okay?" I asked.

"We're going to be," she said confidently, and for just a half second, I saw a flicker of the woman she used to be before Dad got sick. I didn't know what Pastor Joe wanted, but I knew there was no question of where I would be tomorrow at three.

I do believe in God, no doubt about it, but going to church had changed for me since Dad's death. I hated listening to all that "God needed another angel" crap the church people were always spouting. It was such a cop-out, a convenient way for them to avoid the reality of our tragedy while puffing themselves up and convincing themselves that they were being oh-so-supportive. And it was getting harder and harder to listen to everyone talking about me like God didn't love me quite as much as he did them. They didn't know they were talking about me, of course, but that didn't make it hurt any less.

None of that was on my mind though as I marched up the church steps and entered Pastor Joe's office; that day, I had bigger concerns.

The pastor paused the YouTube video he was watching of a guy giving a sermon about graduations.

"Lexi, welcome," he said. His bushy eyebrows shot up toward his hairline, and he looked at me appraisingly over the top of his glasses. There was no doubt that he knew. Mom had told him everything.

Yesterday, there'd been only two people in the world who knew the truth about me: Mom and Zoë. But now Pastor Joe made three. Would the whole church know by the time Sunday morning rolled around?

Don't think about that right now, I told myself. *Think about Mom.*

"Um, my mother said you wanted to see me?"

Pastor Joe crossed his arms, deep in thought. So much time went by in silence that I began to wonder if he'd fallen asleep with his eyes open or something. But finally he said, "Yes."

He rummaged through a drawer in his desk and came out with a brochure. He pushed it across the desk toward me. *New Horizons Reparative Therapy Summer Program.*

"What is this?"

"They call them 'ex-gay camps,'" Pastor Joe said. "They teach young people to resist *those* kinds of urges."

I gaped at him.

"Marilynn Chaney's grandnephew in Little Rock had a similar… problem. He went to this camp, and they fixed him up right."

Problem? Fixed him?

"The feelings you've had for other girls don't mean anything," he continued. "You're young, Lexi. You don't know who you are yet. The only thing set in stone is that you are a child of God. Everything else is a matter of choice."

My heart was racing so fast that I was starting to get light headed. "I don't understand…" was all I could say.

"You will. Read that," Pastor Joe said, pointing to the brochure in my hands. "And think about it."

Apparently that was my cue to leave. I sat in my car in the church parking lot and read the New Horizons brochure cover to cover. There wasn't much in there about *how* the de-gayifying actually worked, just that it did. But how could you change someone's sexuality? The whole concept seemed crazy. Ridiculous.

But when I got home, Mom was waiting for me on the front porch. She was practically bouncing up and down with excitement.

In the time it took to walk up the porch steps, it all finally clicked: she hadn't been able to fix Dad, but now she believed she had a chance to fix me, before it was too late and she lost me forever too. She needed me to do this. She wanted me back, just like I wanted her back.

And what do you do when you've lost everything? You either give up, or you fight.

I had to fight for my family, for my mother. It was terrifying and confusing and completely surreal, but I knew I had to at least try. I wasn't ready to give up just yet.

Mom watched me, waiting.

"Okay," I said. "I'll go."

She didn't ask anything more—not if I *wanted* to go or *why* I was going or if I thought it would work. I was going, and that was all she needed to hear. She pulled me close and held me tight. "Thank you, Lexi." She took my hand and led me into the house, where dinner was waiting—hot dogs on the grill, sauerkraut, and a homemade salad. It was the first real meal she'd made since Dad's death, and there wasn't a single sign that the smoke alarm had gone off. New Horizons was already changing our lives.

Over the next two months, as we waited for the day I was to

leave, Mom's mental state kept getting better and better. She still zoned out every now and then, and of course she still missed Dad terribly, but she was doing well enough to go back to work part-time and begin socializing with her friends again. She even went grocery shopping regularly, so we always had food in the house. She was happier than she'd been in a very, very long time. I'd given her something to hope for.

But the closer the summer loomed, the more freaked out I became. What were they going to *do* to me? Would it work? Did I even want it to?

I didn't have a single answer, but I kept going forward, one foot in front of the other, telling myself to do it for Mom. For me. For our family.

And things started to piece together. As I sat in church, listening to Pastor Joe, I slowly began to feel less resentful about his teachings of homosexuality being sinful and more optimistic that, maybe by the end of the summer, when I heard talk like this, it would no longer be personal. It would just be another church teaching, holding no more significance than the rest. Maybe that teeny tiny chorus on my shoulder, the one that said, "Deny it all you want, but you *know* you're disappointing God, Lexi," would finally take up residence elsewhere. Because it would no longer have anything to taunt me about.

Junior year came to an end. I went to the prom with Josh Webb. Zoë was crowned prom queen. She looked amazing in her silver gown with her hair lifted off her neck, and I couldn't stop myself from staring at her as she danced with the prom king, her body pressed against his, laughing like she didn't have a care in the world, like she wasn't perfectly aware that I was watching.

I turned away, brushed my thumb over my tattoo, and found myself thinking that I really *did* hope the de-gayifying worked—not only for my mom and my church, but for me too. So I could forget about Zoë once and for all.

And then the day arrived, and Mom and I were loading up the car and programming the GPS for the drive from South Carolina to Virginia, and the window for backing out was officially over.

I was going to go get fixed.

Chapter 4

Whoa, I think as I take in the girls' dorm. *That's a lot of pink.*

The nine twin beds are dressed in identical pink bedding; the carpet is pink; the wallpaper is white with pink flowers. The curtains are pink lace, and the wooden furniture is stained a pinkish hue. I have never seen so much overt girlyness in one place in my life, and that includes the time my friend Anna dragged me to Princess Palace for makeovers when we were seven.

Beside each bed, a flowery sheet hangs from the ceiling. They're pushed back against the wall right now, but they look like they can be pulled closed for privacy, like in a hospital. Each area also has a mirrored vanity and a dresser, and the dressers are labeled with girls' names: Elizabeth, Olivia, Carolyn, Sarah, Melissa, Rachael, Jasmine, Alexis.

There is a crucifix the size of a car windshield on the wall and a shiny new New English Translation Bible is neatly placed in the center of each bed.

The ninth bed is perpendicular to the others and positioned

against the opposite wall, in the middle of the room. It doesn't have a name label. "Who's that bed for?" I ask Brianna.

"The female counselor on dorm duty. We're on a rotating schedule." Brianna points back to the camper side of the room. "That's your area, over at the end of the row."

Some of the spaces are already strewn with personal items, while others are still as empty as mine. "Where is everybody?"

"Every camper has his or her own arrival time. It's important to begin the summer in a place of solitary introspection, with no distractions. The campers who arrived before you have already begun the healing process. You'll meet them soon." I get the feeling she's said this many times before.

I wonder how long Brianna has been working here. She's probably seen dozens of girls come through this room and sleep in these beds. What happened to those girls? Could they really be straight now?

I head over to my spot with Brianna close behind. She sits on my bed and watches me carefully as I begin to unpack.

"What?"

"Don't let me distract you," she says. "I just need to make sure you haven't brought any contraband with you."

"Contraband? What, like drugs?"

"Drugs, alcohol, sure. But we tend to have a much bigger problem with campers sneaking in things that will directly hinder their therapy."

"Such as?"

She shrugs. "Homosexual pornography, gay propaganda, cell phones used to communicate with people back home."

I stare at her.

She stares right back, her eyes narrow and suspicious. "You don't have any of those things, do you, Alexis?"

"They told me I had to leave my cell phone at home."

"Good. And the other stuff?"

I shake my head. "All I have are clothes and toiletries. And this." I hold up my copy of *The Great Gatsby*, my favorite book.

Brianna snatches the worn paperback from my hand. "Mr. Martin will have to approve this. Until then, you won't be permitted to keep it. I'm sorry." But she doesn't sound sorry at all.

"I don't understand," I protest. "That book is a classic, and there aren't even any gay characters in it." Well, that's not entirely true. I've long suspected Nick's infatuation with Jay Gatsby is something more than platonic, but I'm not about to tell Brianna that. "Why wouldn't I be able to keep it?"

"You might be able to. I just have to check with Mr. Martin first."

I suppress a groan of annoyance and go back to unpacking.

"There's also a closet if you need to hang up any dresses," Brianna says after a few minutes.

I glance at the motley assortment of clothes coming out of my suitcase. I like my clothes to reflect my mood, so I've got a variety of pieces, mostly one-of-a-kind items from secondhand stores and eBay—various band tank tops, off-the-shoulder sweatshirts from the '80s, stone-washed skinny jeans, dark red cropped cargo pants, a couple of skirts of varying lengths and flowyness, flip-flops and Converse in every color of the rainbow. Except pink.

And no dresses.

"I'm good," I say and open the dresser drawers. But I'm brought up short when I see that three out of the five drawers are already filled. With pink. I look at Brianna.

"Those are your New Horizons uniforms and sleepwear," she says. "You'll be required to wear them beginning tonight."

What? I can't wear a *uniform*. When people see my clothes, they're getting a glimpse of who I am inside. It's all out there— there's no room for secrets or not saying what you mean. It's not me being the girl who likes girls or the girl whose father died or the girl who doesn't know where she fits in. It's not about being different or edgy or challenging authority—for once, it's just me being me. What you see is what you get. It's honest. It's freeing.

A uniform? No way.

"I can't…I mean, I don't—" But I stop. Brianna's pinned me with a challenging, almost bored look that says *Go ahead. Fight me on this. See what happens.*

I could fight her on it—I *want* to fight her on it—but the words won't come. And suddenly it hits me—I'm scared. Like that boy on the stairs.

Up until right now, I've had tunnel vision: *do what you have to do. For Mom. For you. Get through the summer and everything will be better.* But now I'm here. I'm in it. And I've got no phone, no car, no options. I'm stuck.

Holy crap.

Somehow, all that comes out of my mouth is, "So why don't you let us know that ahead of time? You know, so we don't pack as much?" I cram my folded clothes into the remaining drawers and try really hard not to think about the uniforms awaiting me in the rest of the dresser.

Brianna presses her mouth into a hard line, as if she's remembering something unpleasant. "We've found that the fewer details that are given out about our reparative therapy process ahead of time, the more open-minded our campers are when they arrive."

It's true. I tried to find out more about New Horizons online, but their website was just as vague as their brochure—another reason why it was easy to ignore the big questions about this summer and instead focus on the "coming home and everything being fixed" part.

"One more thing," Brianna says as she opens the drawer of my vanity. She pulls out a long, skinny, velvet box and hands it to me. "This is our gift to you, Alexis."

Inside is a thin gold chain threaded through a small cross with a tiny diamond chip in the center. Not exactly my style. I look up at Brianna. "Um…you shouldn't have?"

Brianna beams, suddenly all sunshine and roses. "Of course we should have! It's just a small reminder that Jesus will be with you, guiding you, every step of your journey this summer." Without asking, she lifts the necklace out of its case and loops it around my neck.

Once the cross is in place, I slide my empty suitcase under my bed and study my area. This is it—home, for the next two months. A knot forms in my stomach. I know I'm here for change and everything, but still, it would be nice to have *one* thing here that's mine, one small thing to keep me grounded, a reminder that when I leave here at the end of the summer, I'll still be me. At least in some ways.

And since I don't have my clothes to do that anymore…

An idea strikes me. "Do you have a pen?" I ask Brianna.

She walks over to the room's only desk and produces a pen from one of the drawers. "Here you go. What do you need it for?"

I answer her by using it to scribble out the *A* and *S* on my name label. "That's better. Thanks."

Brianna looks put off but luckily she doesn't comment. Instead, she says, "Are you ready to begin?"

I know from the seriousness in her voice what she's talking about. She's asking if I'm ready to begin the de-gayifying.

I think I am—I mean, I want to be. I'm really trying to keep an open mind. Who knows, maybe if I do what they tell me to do, it will work. It worked for Marilynn Chaney's grandnephew, right?

I'm here for a reason. It's time to get my head in the game.

And so with the sunshine and the great bursts of leaves growing
on the trees, just as things grow in fast movies, I had that familiar
conviction that life was beginning over again with the summer.

It's one of my favorite lines from *Gatsby* and so true right now.

I take a deep breath and say, "Yes. I'm ready."

We leave the big log cabin with its cool, comfortable recycled air and walk back to the gravel road. I didn't realize it as Mom and I drove up here earlier, but the road actually continues past the building and through more trees, gradually narrowing into a walking trail. The only sound in these quiet woods is the crunching of my boots and Brianna's sandals over pebbles and dead leaves.

After a few minutes, the path opens up into a massive, sunny field. Staggered on either side of the path are five more log cabins, though these are much smaller than the main building.

Four of the cabins have a counselor standing stoically out front.

"Alexis," Brianna says, breaking the silence. "I will leave you here. You must continue the rest of the journey alone."

She sounds like she's sending me out on a vision quest or something. I slowly walk the fifty or so feet to the first counselor, a woman with thousands of braids all over her head, streaming down her back and curling at the ends. Her lips are dark red and shiny.

Even though I'm standing right in front of her, she doesn't speak. Her face is blank, and I wonder if she even sees me at all.

"Um, hi," I say awkwardly. "I'm Lexi?" I don't know why it comes out sounding like a question.

"What is a woman?" she asks suddenly.

"Excuse me?"

"What is a woman?"

I don't know how to respond to that. But she's waiting for an answer, staring me down in that emotionless way of hers.

"Um, a woman is…a female adult?"

"What is a female adult?" she shoots back immediately.

I get the feeling that there's a right answer here, something she wants me to say, but I have no idea what it is. "I guess…a human with female body parts? Who has reached the age of maturity?" This is so weird.

"And what is the purpose of the female body parts?"

Several not-so-G-rated answers cross my mind, and I blush. But I try to think reasonably here. I know the counselor doesn't want me to mention sex, and I'm pretty sure she isn't talking about peeing. So I say the only other thing that comes to mind. "To have children?"

She stares me down a moment more as if evaluating me and then says, "You may continue to the next station."

I guess I passed the test. I walk to the next cabin and stop in front of another counselor. She's young, maybe only early twenties, and though she's wearing the requisite pink shirt, she seems cooler than the rest of the counselors somehow. She's wearing a cute denim skirt and ankle-high cowboy boots, and her hair is dyed a brilliant red and cut into a sleek, angled bob. Her earrings dangle past her hair, and they're silver and jangly and funky—definitely something I would wear.

"What is the role of a woman?" she asks.

"The role of a woman is exactly the same as anyone else's," I say with a shrug. "To live and learn and love and be happy."

The counselor just clears her throat and repeats her question. "What is the role of a *woman*?"

Clearly this isn't a very feminist bunch. I sigh and repeat my last answer, since that seemed to work last time. "To have children."

"And?"

"And…take care of the children?"

She inclines her head a tiny bit. "And who else?"

I take a deep breath. It's not hard to catch on to the general theme of these questions—I know what I'm supposed to say here. I make myself say it. "And her husband."

"You may proceed."

But I don't move. Not yet. "Wait," I say quietly. "Not everyone has to get married, you know." I'm not trying to start a fight. I'd just like to talk more about this, and there's something about this counselor that makes me think she'd be open to that. Yes, I signed up to become straight, and I'll do whatever it takes, but everything I've seen so far—the uniform, the questions—is making me wonder if they're trying to turn me into someone else completely.

Some Stepford version of what a woman should be. I think I have the right to question it.

The counselor seems surprised. She's probably used to people bailing the second she gives them the go-ahead. After a couple seconds, her face softens, and for the first time, I feel like she's actually looking *at* me, not through me. "Most people get married," she says.

"Sure. But I don't see how being a woman equals being a wife. Or what getting married has to do with being gay or not gay."

"It's about gender," she says simply.

Her eyes focus on something behind me. I turn and see the woman with the braids watching us. I doubt she can hear our conversation, but she still doesn't seem happy. I turn back to the redhead. "Gender?" I repeat.

"Yes. A big part of our process here is clearing up the confusion you kids have about your proper gender roles. We have to start at the beginning and undo everything you've learned incorrectly. So, for our purposes, it *has* to be very cut and dry. We can't have any gray area. That's how you learn."

So she's agreeing there *is* a gray area but admitting they ignore it. It doesn't make much sense, but the fact that she's at least acknowledging the incongruity makes me feel better, like the counselors aren't actually set on turning us into brainwashed clones after all, despite their tunnel vision about what a woman is. They're just doing their job.

I nod, thank her, and move on.

The next counselor is a blue shirt. He's got freckles all over his face and arms. He asks a question I can actually answer confidently. "Are you a woman?"

"Yes."

"How do you know?"

Really? "Um…because…I have all the corresponding parts…" I can't *believe* I'm talking about my "womanly parts" with some guy I don't even know.

"How else do you know? Other than the physical?"

"It's just…something I know."

He looks unsatisfied but waves me on anyway. "Go ahead."

The final counselor, a young man with his blond hair neatly parted and slicked to the side, doesn't ask about my womanliness. Rather, he says, "Why are you here?"

To get my mother back. To forget about Zoë. To finally fit in with everyone back home. To not be alone anymore.

"To learn to change," I say. And I mean it. I really do want this to work. I don't know if it can or will, but I want it to. It would solve everything.

He smiles and steps aside to open the cabin door for me. "Please make yourself comfortable while we wait for the other campers to arrive."

• • •

There are four girls and seven boys already inside. They're seated in folding chairs arranged in a circle in the middle of the large, carpeted room. I notice the girls are all wearing the same cross around their necks as I am. The boys are wearing their own version—silver, slightly larger, and more masculine. New Horizons must buy these things in bulk. No one is talking, but they all look up when I enter, surveying me with interest. I dodge their scrutinizing stares and take in the rest of the room. The carpet is dark blue and soft under my feet—it looks brand new. Stacked up neatly against three of the walls are what look like props of some sort. I spot dolls, baseball mitts and basketballs, a chalkboard, an assortment of hats, a punching bag, cooking utensils, and Nerf baseball bats.

There's a fireplace built into the wall on my right, but there's no fire going—probably because it's about a hundred degrees in the cabin.

"Hi," I say as I sit down in an empty chair. I push my bangs back from my suddenly sweaty forehead. "I'm Lexi."

The shaggy-haired guy from earlier is sitting next to me. "Matthew," he says and shakes my hand. His face has been wiped completely clean of any of the emotion from before, and only now do I notice his bright-green eyes and fitted tee with Ellen DeGeneres's face silk-screened onto it. That shirt is amazing. I want it.

"I love your shirt," I say.

He beams. "Thanks! My boyfriend got it for me. But the Nazis here made me cover it up." He gestures to a wadded-up blue New Horizons T-shirt under his chair.

"Shouldn't you put that back on before they come back?" I glance at the door.

"What for? I'm not scared of them." And despite what I thought I saw earlier, I believe him. He seems completely relaxed.

"Oh yeah, me neither," I say, not even close to as convincingly.

There's a long, significant pause.

"So, you have a boyfriend?" I ask Matthew finally.

"Going on two years." I swear his eyes twinkle when he says it. He looks so happy and in love. He doesn't look at all like someone who wants to change his sexuality.

"So why…" I begin. But I don't want to be too nosy.

"Why am I here?" Matthew finishes. I nod, and he rolls his eyes. "Long story."

I want to know more, but our conversation is interrupted by the arrival of another camper. She's tall and has very long, very straight, very blond hair. Her eyes are lowered, but I think I catch a glimpse of blue through her lashes. She's wearing a pink-and-white sundress that I'm sure Brianna approves of, and her skin is tanned, like she works as a lifeguard or on a farm or something. She smiles shyly and slips into an open seat without saying a word.

She's the most beautiful girl I've ever seen in my life.

Chapter 5

I can't stop staring. There's something about this girl, something stronger than just her looks, that's reeling me in. Maybe it's how she folds her lower lip nervously under her front teeth. Or it could be the way she holds her shoulders, a pose that tells me she's shy but also strong.

She looks up and meets my eyes. I was right—hers are blue. Big and bright and blue and as clear as the view of the moon from the beach back home. I should look away. But I can't. She holds my gaze, and my heartbeat kicks into a sprint.

Somewhere in the back of my mind, warning bells are sounding. *Remember what happened the last time you felt like this, Lexi?* But my brain must be disconnected from the rest of me, because my heart keeps pounding and my eyes keep staring.

The door swings open again, and our connection breaks—the girl looks away quickly, her cheeks flaming. Another camper joins the circle. I don't notice if it's a boy or a girl.

I wait a long time for her to look at me again, but she keeps her gaze away.

Even so, I can't help the little buzz of anticipation that's going through me. *She likes girls too.*

"Hello, everyone, and welcome to New Horizons!" Mr. Martin says loudly, and I'm yanked back to reality.

The circle is now complete—I guess I missed the other camper arrivals while I was off in la-la land—and Mr. Martin is breezing through the door, his army of pinks and blues behind him.

Shame heats my face. What is *wrong* with me? I come here, desperate to do anything, try anything, to put my family back together, and that all goes out the window the minute I see a pretty girl? The only way this is going to work is if I give it my all. No more daydreaming.

The counselors hover along the fireplace wall side-by-side, and Mr. Martin strolls around the middle of the circle. His eyes land on each of us as he passes. "We are so happy to have you all here. By the end of this summer, you will be healed from this sickness that lives within you and your lives can begin anew. 'Create in me a pure heart, O God, and renew a steadfast spirit within me.' Psalm fifty-one, verse ten."

Sickness? The word jumps out at me. I don't *feel* sick. But in a weird way, thinking of it in those terms actually opens this whole de-gayifying thing up to possibility—most sicknesses can be healed, can't they? You just have to catch it in time and be aggressive.

I glance at the blond girl. She's watching Mr. Martin almost reverently. It seems she wants to change too. That's good. If we're both on the same page, it will be easier to ignore what I feel when I look at her.

Mr. Martin continues. "Now, who can tell me what SSA is?"

No one speaks.

"SSA stands for 'same-sex attraction,'" Mr. Martin says. "You will be hearing and using that term a lot this summer as we work together to rid you of your SSA. Make no mistake—the work will be challenging and often uncomfortable for many of you. It's a difficult process, but it can and will work. It worked for me and it will work for you."

My head snaps up. Mr. Martin used to be gay?

He smiles. "Yes, you heard that correctly—I am on your side every step of the way because I used to be one of you. I understand you in ways no one else can—not your parents, not even *you*, since you haven't yet reached the other end of the journey like I have. So please, feel free to come to me with any questions, fears, thoughts, or concerns. If there's anything you need—anything at all—please let me know." He takes the time to look at each one of us again. "We are a team, you and I."

I find myself instantly relaxing, knowing that a man like Mr. Martin is in charge of the camp. He understands us; he's *one* of us. He wouldn't lead us astray.

"Allow me to introduce our wonderful staff of counselors," Mr. Martin continues. He introduces Brianna as the head of the girls' program, his second-in-command. I guess I'm going to be seeing a lot more of her. Great. I learn that the clean-cut blond man's name is Arthur, and that an older woman with a tight, gray perm like my grandmother used to have is named Barbara. "And some of our counselors have sat exactly where you're sitting now," Mr. Martin says. "Deb, John, Kaylee, will you step forward, please?" The braid woman, the freckle guy, and the young redhead emerge from the line and smile at us. "Deb, John, and Kaylee here, like myself, used to struggle with SSA. But they have taken control of their lives. Let them serve as inspiration for you as you embark on your work here at New Horizons."

Everyone here is so open and honest about their past! And the de-gayifying worked so well for them that they've actually dedicated their *lives* to helping others go through the same thing. It's inspiring. And look at Kaylee—she's so cool. She clearly hasn't had to give up her style or who she is in order to become straight. I decide in this moment that I'm going to be just like her.

"Now," Mr. Martin says, "we are going to split you up into groups of four. Two boys, two girls. The group you are assigned to will be your group for the entire summer. Apart from the exercises that require the boys and girls to be separated, your group of four will spend every waking moment together. You will have meals together, participate in the majority of reparative therapy exercises together, and spend your leisure hours together."

"Why?" Matthew asks. He's the first camper to speak since the counselors entered the room.

Mr. Martin's smile melts away. "To keep each other accountable. It's easy to give in to the feelings and desires caused by your sickness. Your group members are there to make sure you don't relapse." He picks up the crumpled, blue New Horizons shirt and holds it pointedly out to Matthew. His demeanor emanates friendliness, kinship, but I can't help but feel this is a challenge. Matthew crosses his arms and glares stubbornly back at him. But Mr. Martin isn't going to budge. He stands there, shirt in hand, waiting.

The thickening tension in the room makes the cabin even hotter. No one moves. No one says anything.

I can't stand this. "Take it," I whisper to Matthew, and, finally, he does.

"Remember," Mr. Martin says, "there will always be eyes on you."

"Super," Matthew mutters so low that I think I may be the only one who hears him. He slips the shirt over his head.

Brianna steps in and begins dividing us up, seemingly at random. I sit very still in my chair and watch as she picks us out, one by one. I'm not in the first group. Neither is the blond girl. Brianna comes very close to her as she chooses people for group two, and I hold my breath, but she picks the girl sitting next to her instead. I exhale. I know I'm not supposed to, but I want to be in a group with her. There's no harm in being friends, right? Maybe we can even help each other with the de-gayifying stuff.

As they're assigned their groups, the other campers start dragging their chairs over to their designated corners of the room.

Brianna taps her sparkly fingernails against the corner of her mouth as she decides who should be in the next group. "Matthew… Daniel…" she says. She points at the girl. "Carolyn…"

Carolyn. That's her name.

"…and…"

Me! Pick me!

"Alexis."

Yes!

The four of us slide our chairs into a little cluster. Carolyn is right next to me, but she still doesn't look at me. I'm trying to come up with something not stupid to say when counselor Deb joins us.

"Hello," she says. Even though the creepy "what is a woman" trials are over, she still has that distant look about her. I can't tell if she's acting like this on purpose, or if that's just how her face is. "Please introduce yourselves to each other. Remember to state your age and where you're from." She gestures to Matthew to go first.

"I'm Matthew," he says. "I'm sixteen years old, and I don't need a governess!"

We all stare at him.

"*The Sound of Music*? Liesl? No one?" He sighs, disappointed. "Okay, actually I'm seventeen, and I live in San Diego. Better?"

"Much," Deb says flatly. I grin at Matthew across the small circle.

A skinny boy with rimless glasses goes next. "I'm Daniel. I'm fifteen." His hands are shaking. "Um…what else am I supposed to say again?"

"Where you're from," Deb says.

"Oh yeah. West Virginia."

My turn. "Hi, I'm Lexi." Deb, Matthew, and Daniel are all looking directly at me, but Carolyn's hair has fallen forward in a sleek sheet, blocking her face. "I'm from South Carolina, and I'm seventeen."

Carolyn pushes her hair back. "I'm Carolyn." God, even her voice is pretty. "I'm sixteen. And I'm from Connecticut."

Deb rattles down a list of camp rules.

No touching a camper of the same sex at any time for any reason unless at the direction and in the presence of a counselor.

No using profanity.

Be supportive of your fellow campers and help them stay accountable. Report any questionable behavior to Mr. Martin immediately.

Obey the counselors at all times—insubordination will not be tolerated.

No unsupervised phone calls.

Campers must remain in approved camp areas at all times unless specifically directed otherwise by a counselor.

Designated meal, sleep, and prayer times will be observed by all campers.

No unsupervised meetings between campers of the same sex. Improper fraternizing carries the penalty of immediate expulsion.

She says that last one with added emphasis, giving me the impression that that's the most important rule of all.

When Deb is done with her lecture, Mr. Martin saunters over. "I'll take over here, Deb," he says. "Why don't you go see if Barbara needs help with her group?" After Deb has left, he pulls up a seat. His hands thread together and he leans forward, elbows on knees. "The first step in battling any addiction is admitting you have a problem. And that's a good way to think of your SSA—as an addiction."

"I thought it was a sickness," Matthew counters.

"They're one and the same. Haven't you ever heard addiction described as a disease?"

Matthew just shrugs.

"So," Mr. Martin continues, "like any addiction, you may feel that it is out of your hands and that you are dependent on it. But that's not true. It's *not* part of you. You can work to control it. And you will be better off without it." The soothing, certain way he forms his words makes it impossible to not believe him. He gives us a warm smile. "Don't worry; we'll start slow. Today's session will simply be about sharing your individual stories with your group. What is your experience with SSA? When did you first start having these feelings? What brings you to New Horizons? Be honest with each other—it's the only way to build the trust that is absolutely essential for your therapy to thrive."

That's starting *slow*? Oh yeah, just tell a bunch of people you just met your deepest, most private thoughts. No biggie.

"Who would like to go first?"

There are a few moments of edgy silence, like when a teacher asks who wants to be the first one to give a presentation in front of the whole class.

But then Daniel speaks. "I will," he says, his voice faint.

We all whip our heads around to look at him. Even Mr. Martin looks surprised that this timid, young boy is the first one to volunteer. "Excellent!" he says, pleased.

"I hate who I am," Daniel says. "That's why I'm here."

Mr. Martin nods thoughtfully. "Remember, Daniel, your SSA is not *who* you are. It's something that's been done *to* you. It's not your fault."

"Well, I want it to stop."

"When did you first become aware of your SSA?"

He thinks for a moment. "I don't know. But I know the first time I acted on it." He pauses again, and I wonder if that's all he's going to say.

"It's okay, Daniel. This is a safe space," Mr. Martin says, his voice warm.

Daniel takes a deep, wavering breath. "I was eleven. My friend Colin fell and cut his knee in gym class, and the teacher asked me to help him get to the nurse. The nurse was busy with another student when we got there, so we had to wait. Colin's knee was all bloody and he was crying, and I didn't want him to be hurting, and I didn't know what to do, and before I could stop myself, I just leaned over and kissed him. On the lips. I don't know why I did it," He breaks off as his eyes fill with tears. When he speaks again, his voice is even quieter. I have to strain to hear. "It was like I'd given him an electric shock. He jerked away and hit me—hard—across the face. I ran away and prayed to God for days and days, begging him to make me normal." He turns his body toward Mr. Martin but keeps his head down. "I would have come here sooner, but you have to be at least fifteen."

Mr. Martin reaches over and places a large hand on Daniel's forearm. "Well, you're here now. And you are going to prove to God that you can live by his laws and are worthy of his love." He keeps his hand on Daniel's arm and just…waits. Finally, Daniel looks up. Mr. Martin smiles. So does Daniel.

Mr. Martin in this moment inexplicably reminds me of a grandfather, even though he's father aged. There's something gentle, wise, trustworthy about him. Like if you tell him everything that's hurting you, he'll impart some remarkable wisdom, make you some soup, and everything will be fine.

Then Mr. Martin turns to Matthew, and his supportive face transforms into something just a bit more like disdain. "Why don't you go next, Matthew?"

Matthew raises an eyebrow. "Why don't *you* go next?"

"I'm sorry?"

"I don't think it's very fair that we're supposed to sit here and tell you all this personal stuff about ourselves and listen to you tell us we're sick or dirty or whatever, but not know anything about why *you're* here."

Mr. Martin looks at Matthew levelly. "Like I said earlier, I used to struggle with SSA too. But I have overcome, and I have received the calling to pay it forward."

Matthew snorts, as if he doesn't believe for a second that Mr. Martin has overcome much of anything. "Whatever."

"Now, please, share your experience with the group," Mr. Martin says.

"Fine. I've known I was gay since I played house with Tim MacFarlane at Happy Land preschool when I was four. I had my first kiss when I was thirteen, and I've had a serious boyfriend for the past two years. His name is Justin. Anything else?"

"What brought you to New Horizons?" Mr. Martin asks, not even a little bit fazed by Matthew's bluntness.

"More like *who* brought me to New Horizons," Matthew mumbles. "My father, who else? He walked in on me in a rather… inventive position with Justin and lost his shit. *No son of mine… disgrace to this family…as long as you're under my roof you will do what I say…*blah blah blah. It's so ridiculous—he *knew*. I came out to him when I was fourteen. But then he sees me with Justin and suddenly he's the captain of Team Homophobe. He actually said he'd thought it was a *phase* and that I should have *grown out of it* by now. What the hell, right?"

All Mr. Martin says is, "No profanity, Matthew."

"I want to get married," Carolyn blurts out.

Matthew blinks. "To me?"

She laughs. "No. Just in general."

"Please, say more about that, Carolyn," Mr. Martin encourages.

"That's why I'm here. It's not for my parents—or for God." She looks at Matthew and Daniel. "It's for me. I've dreamed about my wedding day since I was a little girl. I want a husband and kids and a house. I always have." There's something practiced about her words, like it's a line she's recited in front of a mirror many times before.

"And you will have that!" Mr. Martin says, beaming.

She smiles. "I hope so."

I can't stop myself. "But wait," I say, "that doesn't make sense."

Everyone turns to look at me.

"What doesn't make sense?" Carolyn asks. It's the first time she's spoken directly to me.

"If you've dreamed about marrying a man your entire life, then wouldn't that make you straight? I don't understand."

Her eyebrows pull together, and she looks like she's choosing her words carefully. "When I was little, I would dress up Barbie and Ken and walk them down the aisle and imagine the day when I'd get to wear a big white dress like that. I knew that someday I was going to have a husband who looked at me the way my dad looked at my mom. I'd watch romantic comedies and read Jane Austen novels and put myself in the place of the heroine."

A tiny smile forms on my lips as I remember my own Jane Austen-era fantasies, like the horse-drawn carriage one from earlier today—something else we have in common.

She's met my eyes and, for just a moment, the careful, practiced tone is gone.

"But then as I got older, the pictures in my head started feeling…

off. They were still beautiful, but I couldn't see myself in them anymore. And eventually I realized why. I didn't want to marry Mr. Darcy. I wanted to marry Elizabeth Bennet."

For the length of one heartbeat, Carolyn and I just look at each other, understanding each other.

But then her wall goes back up, and she's back to the script. "My whole life, those dreams weren't just something I thought about; they were who I *was*. And I want them back." She pauses. "Does that make sense?"

I can't help but feel as if there's something she's not saying, as if this isn't actually her real story. Or at least not her *whole* story. But all I say is, "Yeah. It does."

A smile brightens her face—and I was the one who put it there. I smile back.

"So that leaves you, Lexi," Mr. Martin says.

"Okay, um, I guess…in a way, I always knew I liked girls more than boys," I say, feeling my way through what I want to say as I go. "I felt more comfortable around them, but, you know, I didn't know what it meant."

It feels strange to say this out loud. I've never told anyone this stuff before—of the few people back home who know my secret, none of them ever asked for details. It's funny to think that the fact that I like girls is the first thing everyone here at New Horizons knew about me, even before they knew my name. The thought is surprisingly liberating.

"When I was about seven or eight, I started getting really into fashion. I would watch movies and fixate on the actresses, studying their outfits and watching the way the fabric moved over their bodies. Eventually I realized that it wasn't just the clothes I was captivated by; it was the women in them. And then..."

I clamp my hand tightly over my lightning bolt tattoo in hopes that it will stifle the memory that's already on its way to the surface.

"And then..."

It doesn't work—the memory comes blasting back. But at least I manage to stop myself from speaking it aloud.

And then Zoë Green happened.

• • •

It had been raining for four days straight—the effect of Hurricane Shauna, which didn't hit our town directly but flirted with us just enough to be really annoying. Sophomore biology was first period, and Zoë came in after the bell, completely drenched. I'd met her for the first time on the first day of school a few days earlier. The only things I knew about her were that she was from Tennessee, she had a brother who was a senior, and she looked a little like Emma Stone.

"You're late," Mr. Buckley said.

"Sorry. Car trouble," she said with a shrug.

"Would you like to go to the ladies' room to get cleaned up?"

"Nah," she said, and instead of going to her seat, she sloshed over to the windowsill and wrung her hair out over Mr. Buckley's collection of plants. "Might as well turn my bad luck into something useful, right?" She grinned.

And that was all it took. I was in love.

It was what I imagined getting hit by lightning would feel like—unexpected, startling, a sharp, white-hot dagger piercing me in one acute point—my heart—and radiating outward until every cell in my being had been altered.

My gayness wasn't just an abstract personality trait anymore—suddenly, I wanted to be *with* someone. I wanted Zoë to be my *girlfriend*. I wanted to kiss her and hold her hand in the halls and invite her over for dinner with my family and call her whenever something funny happened.

The force of it all was so strong that I actually had to gasp for air.

"You okay, Lexi?" the guy sitting next to me asked.

My face flamed and I stared down at my notebook, forcing myself to pull it together. "Yeah, I'm fine," I lied.

I had been hit by lightning, and no one could know.

• • •

"And then?" Mr. Martin prompts me back to the present.

Everyone's staring at me, waiting for me to finish my story. But I can't tell them about Zoë. I just…can't. Not after everything that happened. Besides, the sun has begun to set outside, and the room is getting dimmer, and if I start that story now, we won't get out of here until the middle of the night.

I scramble for something else to say. "And then…my mom

found out. She and the pastor of our church are the only ones who know." Well, besides Zoë. But no need to mention that right now. "My friends all think I'm at a pre-college fashion program in New York this summer." I let out a strained little laugh.

"Mine think I'm visiting my grandparents in Boca Raton," Carolyn says.

I look at her. "So you haven't told your friends either?"

"About New Horizons? No way."

"I told *everyone*," Matthew says, laughing. "And they all think this whole thing is as insane as I do."

Mr. Martin ignores him. "Lexi," he says, "what brought you to New Horizons?"

"I'm here for my mom," I say.

Mr. Martin looks like he's about to ask me to elaborate on that, but I'm saved by a sudden high-pitched dinging sound piercing the air. I whirl around to find Brianna standing near the cabin door ringing a bell.

"Dinner time, everyone! Please stack your chairs and make your way to the dining cabin."

Wow. A dinner bell. I feel like I'm in *Little House on the Prairie* or something.

Mr. Martin and Brianna lead the sixteen of us out of the carpeted cabin and across the field to the dining hall cabin. The rest of the pinks and blues bring up the rear.

Already the groups seem to have gelled. We walk in packs of

four, sticking with the people we know, the people who went from strangers to our closest confidantes in the span of an afternoon. A short girl with thin eyebrows and rosy cheeks—Rachael, I think—starts sobbing uncontrollably, and Mr. Martin drops back to tend to her. I can't hear what they're saying—though I imagine she's probably homesick or scared or upset over whatever was discussed in their group—but Mr. Martin's arm is around her, and he's patting her back as she wails into his side. She seems grateful to have him there, someone strong and sturdy and comforting, holding her up and talking her down, like that grandfather thing again.

As we walk past them and trudge up the path like sheep being herded by T-shirt-wearing border collies, I turn to Carolyn. "So you like Jane Austen?"

She smiles. "Yeah. You?"

"Yeah. What's your favorite?"

"*Pride and Prejudice*. It's cliché, I know…"

"It's cliché for a reason," I tell her. "Because it's freaking amazing."

She laughs. "What's your favorite?"

"*Persuasion*, I think. I don't know, I guess I can relate to it. Everyone I know always seems to think they know what's best for everyone else."

Carolyn lets that sit for a moment and then leans toward me. "Hey, Lexi?" she whispers.

"Yeah?"

"I'm really glad you're in my group."

Another little thrill goes through me, but this time I stop myself before I get too carried away. Carolyn and I are friends. That's all.

I smile. "Me too."

Chapter 6

The dining cabin is a lot different from the cafeteria at school. It's smaller, the lighting is warmer than the buzzing fluorescents I'm used to, and instead of a window where you line up to get your food, there's a simple table set up with a yellow plastic tablecloth and one large woman named Mrs. Wykowski heaving food out of square-shaped pans onto people's plates. We don't get a choice—tonight it's macaroni and cheese, fried chicken, and sweet tea. The four of us get our food and sit at the end of a long table.

When everyone is seated, Mr. Martin leads the saying of grace. I sit with my head down and listen.

"Dear Lord, we thank you for the bountiful gifts we are about to receive, and we thank you for sending these sixteen young people to spend their summer with us here at New Horizons. We ask that you shed your light on them and guide them as they work toward inheriting your kingdom and following your righteous path. Amen."

"Amen," we echo, though I notice a few campers, including Carolyn and Matthew, stay silent.

I wonder what Mom's doing right now. I hope she got home okay. She's probably sitting alone at our kitchen table, saying grace of her own, echoing Mr. Martin's plea for God to guide me along his righteous path.

I pick up my fork but barely even have time to dig into my dinner before Matthew jumps right back into our conversation from the carpet cabin.

"Daniel, don't you realize that you *are* normal?" he says. His words come out in a rush, and I can tell he's been itching to say this since Daniel told his story. "There's nothing wrong with you."

"Yes, there is," Daniel says, staring at his plate. His voice cracks a little.

"No, there isn't."

"You're wrong. I don't want these feelings. I want God to take them away."

"But *why*?"

"Because I'm a Christian," he says. "That's why."

"But then shouldn't you believe that God made you this way for a reason?"

"I think he's testing me."

Matthew rakes his hands through his hair in frustration as Daniel's words linger in the air. The two boys look to me and Carolyn, wordlessly asking us to back them up. Carolyn pushes a piece of macaroni around on her plate with her fork, obviously not wanting to get involved.

I feel like I should say something, but I don't know what. I don't agree with Daniel that this is all some big test, but I can't side with Matthew either. How can I, when I want to change just as much as Daniel does?

Before I can come up with something to say, Matthew redirects his attack. "And I don't get you either, Carolyn."

She looks up, surprised. "What do you mean?"

"You want to get married? You want a family?"

Carolyn nods.

"Great, so do it," he says. Carolyn looks at Matthew like she's not sure what he's getting at. After a moment, he elaborates. "Get the white dress and the wedding cake and the photographer and everything, move to New York or Massachusetts or any of the other states where gay marriage is legal, and marry a girl. You can still have everything you want, and you'd be a lot happier."

She purses her lips. Matthew's argument is a good one, and it seems like she knows it. "But what about children?" she says finally.

"What about them? You've got a uterus. All you need is a sperm donor."

She shakes her head. "You don't get it," she says quietly.

Matthew sighs. "I think I'm the only one here who *does* get it actually." He wraps his arms around his head like we're giving him a migraine or something.

"Guys," I jump in, trying to sound lighthearted, "it's only our first day here. Maybe we can just agree to disagree?"

"But—" Matthew clearly isn't ready to give up, but I cut him off.

"Look around," I say, gesturing to the dining cabin at large. In one way, it does look like a school cafeteria—divided up into cliques. Some of the campers are deep in conversation with their group members; others are awkwardly silent. The counselors are sitting at their own table, talking quietly, keeping their watchful eyes on us. "The four of us are going to be spending a lot of time together this summer. I'm thinking the next eight weeks will be a lot easier to get through if we stick together."

"I agree," Carolyn says.

Daniel nods. "Me too."

Matthew isn't convinced though. "Hellooo, that's exactly what I was trying to do! I was *trying* to be a friend." He looks me in the eye. "I know you know that, Lexi."

I deflect his gaze, suddenly uncomfortable. What makes Matthew think I'm on his side? Does he think he sees something in me? I might not have been so sure about this whole de-gayifying thing at first, but I'm more convinced after meeting Kaylee and the other counselors and seeing Mr. Martin's family photo and listening to his analogies about sickness and addiction. I'm beginning to think I can really do this. Not just for the summer, but for real.

And anyway, even if I did understand where Matthew's coming from, it doesn't matter. It doesn't matter what *I* think about any of it. I just shake my head.

Matthew sits back in his chair. "Whatever. Let's just talk about something else, okay?"

I shoot him a grateful smile. "What do you want to talk about?"

He shrugs. "Anyone seen any good movies lately?"

• • •

It's weird being in the dorm with all the other girls. The room felt a lot bigger when it was empty. Now it's a frenzy of chatter and curtains being dragged along their metal rods and girls hurrying to claim the two bathrooms before a line forms.

I watch them in awe. I've never known anyone who was openly gay before. Until today, I was all alone. And now I'm part of something.

New Horizons is all at once terrifying and thrilling.

With four beds between ours, Carolyn and I are nearly on opposite sides of the room.

Brianna is on dorm duty tonight. "Lights out is at ten p.m.!" she announces. "So you have thirty minutes to get changed and ready for bed."

"But it's barely even dark outside!" a girl with curly strawberry-blond hair whines.

"Designated sleep times will be observed by all campers, Melissa," Brianna responds sharply.

Melissa mumbles something else, but I don't catch it.

"You should close your curtains for privacy while you change, but you must keep them open at all other times," Brianna says to everyone. "You'll find your sleepwear in your top drawer."

I pull a pink thing from the dresser and have to clamp a hand over my mouth to stifle the shriek that is trying to force its way out. It's a nightgown. I haven't worn an actual nightgown since I was about three. I usually sleep in ratty old T-shirts and boxer shorts. And this monstrosity is not only bubble-gum pink, but it also has frilly ruffles around the sleeves and neck and a cinched waist. And it's *polyester*. I feel itchy just looking at it.

"Oh, *hell* no," a girl's voice carries over the top of my curtain. "You expect us to wear *these*?"

My thoughts exactly. I'd rather sleep in a straitjacket. I peek around the curtain. It's Jasmine, the girl whose bed is next to mine. She's got very short, dark hair and tiny earrings up the entire length of her ears. She's standing with her arms crossed, the nightgown dangling by her side.

Brianna steps closer to Jasmine but makes no effort to lower her voice. "Yes, I do."

"I don't understand why we can't just wear our own pajamas."

"It's not your job to understand, Jasmine. It's your job to follow the camp rules." Her gaze travels down to Jasmine's neck and she sucks in a breath. "Where is your cross?"

"I took it off. I can't sleep with anything constricting my neck like that."

"Put it on. Put it on *right now*." Brianna's face is as pink as the room's décor, and there's a vein protruding from her forehead that looks like it's seconds away from bursting. All the other girls have stopped what they were doing and are watching now.

Jasmine just stares at Brianna like she's suddenly sprouted gills. But after a minute, her face goes slack, like she's decided it's not worth the fight, and she yanks the curtain closed. She reemerges a few moments later, dressed in the nightgown, the bottom hem grazing her shins. The cross shimmers under the nightgown's ruffly collar.

"Ah! See how lovely you look?" Brianna says, instantly calmer, her face breaking into a pleased grin. Jasmine looks like she's ready to punch somebody out.

I retreat behind my curtain and pull on the nightgown as quickly as possible. I keep my own necklace on—it's clear now the cross was less of a gift and more of a requirement. Then I crawl into my small bed and slide under the covers before anyone sees me in this getup.

"Everyone, please open your Bibles," Brianna says once we're all in bed. "The last thing we do here at New Horizons each night is read a verse from the Bible together. It gives us something to think about as we drift off to sleep and something to unite us as we look forward to tomorrow. Let's start at this end of the room." She points to me. "Alexis, will you please read Matthew nine, verse twenty-two aloud?"

I flip through the pages until I find the right passage. "But when Jesus turned and saw her he said, 'Have courage, daughter!

Your faith has made you well.' And the woman was healed from that hour."

"Very good. Thank you, Alexis. Good night, ladies." Brianna turns the lights out, and soon after, the sun's final remnants fade away.

I stare into the darkness, feeling…well, weird.

I'm in a new bed, in a new state, surrounded by new people, wearing something I never would have agreed to wear just yesterday. I'm already changing. After just one day.

I have about a million feelings about that, and they're too new and confusing and formless to be able to break down into any sort of coherent order right now. So I just focus on the one thing that I know for sure: Mom is going to be so happy. I did the right thing in coming here.

I turn over and face the wall. The room is quiet. No one dares speak for fear of being yelled at by Brianna, who is lying in her own bed, in her own nightgown—though hers is white—just feet away from us. The only sounds are the songs of the frogs outside the dorm window, soothing us, serenading us to sleep as if they know how trying today was.

I slowly drift away into a restless sleep, where I dream that Carolyn and Zoë are getting married. They stand in big white dresses and recite their vows before Pastor Joe as I sit in the front row of the church, dressed in the pink nightgown, holding hands with a boy.

Chapter 7

When I wake up the next morning, Carolyn is gone.

It's really early and everyone else is still asleep. But Carolyn's bed is empty and neatly made. I get out of bed and tiptoe to the bathrooms—they're both vacant. I look out the window, but all that's out there are woods and a rabbit hopping across the grass. Could she have left? Did something Matthew said make her change her mind so drastically that she couldn't even wait till morning to get out of here? Or did something bad happen? Maybe she was rushed to the hospital with appendicitis or had to go home suddenly because of a death in the family.

I'm about to wake Brianna up to see if she knows anything when Carolyn comes in. Her hair is pulled back into a ponytail and she's wearing workout clothes—sports bra, cropped leggings, running shoes.

For a moment, I'm speechless. She's sweaty, her face is bright red from exertion, and she's slightly out of breath. Her ab muscles pulse as she takes a swig from her water bottle. She smiles at me, her lips wet from the water or sweat or both, and something strange happens—I feel like a hand has clenched around my insides and is tugging, urging me toward her, and I suddenly feel very warm. Hot, even. Like I've been hit with a fever. I have to remind myself to breathe.

She's even more beautiful now than she was yesterday.

And here I am, in this ridiculous pink sack, probably with major bedhead.

I snap out of it and immediately step away from Brianna, suddenly aware of what a terrible idea waking her would have been.

"Hey, Lexi," Carolyn whispers.

"Hey," I say, attempting to discreetly smooth my hair. "Where, uh, were you?"

"Running," she says, as if it's obvious. Which, of course, it is.

"I thought we weren't supposed to leave the group."

"I got special permission from Mr. Martin yesterday. I was so glad when he said we could come to him with any special requests. I couldn't go a whole summer without running—I'd go crazy."

So she's an athlete. It makes sense. She doesn't have an ounce of fat on her. That's even more evident now, looking at her in her form-fitting workout clothes, than it was yesterday—and it explains her tan. "Wow, so you run every day?"

"Yeah. I do about seven miles every morning. I went easy today though because I wasn't sure of my route." She checks the pedometer that's clipped onto her sneaker. "Five point three miles. Not so bad."

"Not so bad?" I say. "That's amazing. I can't even run one mile in gym class without stopping to walk."

Carolyn laughs. "Okay, well, I guess I should go shower. See you later, Lexi."

As soon as she's out of sight, sanity cascades over me like an ice-cold rainfall. I *can't* keep getting so unnerved around her. So she looks hot in her workout clothes. So what?

I figure I might as well use this time while everyone else is asleep to claim a shower of my own. When I emerge from the bathroom twenty minutes later, the scene is a lot different from when I left. The girls are all up now, some of them already dressed for the day (in pink, of course) and some still in their night-gowns. Deb, Barbara, and Kaylee have joined the group, and each counselor is assisting two campers, giving them what looks like style advice. There's a lot of miming and gesturing to hair and clothes and stuff.

I go over to my end of the room, where Kaylee and Jasmine are midconversation.

"But *why*?" Jasmine says. But it doesn't look like she really wants a response to whatever her question was about, because her hands are clasped tightly over her ears, like she's trying to shut out the noisy room.

Kaylee reaches a hand up and tries to gently pry one of Jasmine's hands away. "Because it's all part of the process, Jasmine," she says. "It's important."

"What's important?" I ask.

"Lexi! I'm glad you're here!" Kaylee says, whirling around to face me. But then her face changes as she sees what I'm wearing: cutoff shorts that have been spray-painted silver and an off-the-shoulder white T-shirt with a black bra strap peeking out. "Where's your uniform?"

"Oh, um, I didn't know what we were supposed to wear, so I thought I'd just put on my own clothes for now." I don't add that I was kind of hoping that once I was dressed, no one would say anything and just let me stay in my own stuff for the rest of the summer.

The corners of Kaylee's glossed mouth turn down. She goes to my dresser and pulls out a few things. "Please change into this. This is your day uniform."

I pull the curtain closed and spread out the items on my bed. It's the same thing the other girls are wearing, and no better than the nightgown. A baby-pink lightweight cap-sleeved sweater, a white tank with an eyelet lace collar to go underneath, and a matching light-pink skort with white pinstripes. Plus white strappy sandals with a little heel—a non-pink version of the ones Brianna was wearing yesterday.

My first thought is, how the hell did they know what size I wear? But I guess my mom must have told them when she signed me up.

My second thought is, skorts? Really? Shorts that look like a skirt. Probably invented by the same genius who came up with the spork.

"Lexi?" Kaylee calls through the curtain. "Are you almost done?"

"Just a minute!" I say. With a deep sigh, I change into the New Horizons outfit. At least we get to wear our own underwear.

When I pull back the curtain, Kaylee and Jasmine are still arguing. "It's not gonna happen," Jasmine says, shaking her head, her ears still covered.

"We aren't leaving this room until you take them out." Kaylee turns to me. "Her earrings," she explains.

"Why can't she just wear them?" I ask.

"Girls are allowed only one earring in each ear," Kaylee says, her own hoops shimmering through her hair.

I look around the room and pay closer attention to the conversations between the campers and counselors this time. The discussions are all versions of Kaylee and Jasmine's—girls wanting to wear one thing, counselors insisting on another. Brianna and Elizabeth are actually engaged in a tug-of-war over a pair of black Toms.

Under different circumstances, I would join in the fight. But I look down at my Laura Ashley-on-crack tennis ensemble and know there's no point. We don't stand a chance of winning. This place is a well-oiled machine.

"Is this okay?" I ask Kaylee, gesturing to my outfit. If she's going to harp on my appearance too, I'd rather just get it over with.

She appraises me for a moment, and then reaches into the plastic cosmetics case on Jasmine's bed. "Here," she says, handing me a few small items.

Two barrettes and a thick, white, plastic bracelet.

I look at her.

"Pin your hair back so we can actually see your face, and cover that up"—she points to my tattoo—"with the bracelet."

The bracelet actually isn't so bad, but I don't like being told to cover up my lightning bolt. Even though I'm fully aware that what New Horizons stands for and what the tattoo stands for are entirely conflicting ideals, the lightning bolt is still a part of me. "What do you have against tattoos?"

Kaylee gives a conspiratorial smile. "Personally? Nothing." She looks around the room and then quickly lowers her white ankle sock. I catch a glimpse of a small ink daisy at the top of her foot before the sock slips back into place. "But it's a camp rule."

Yet another camp rule. I'm starting to get the feeling that the New Horizons rule book is longer than the *Lord of the Rings* trilogy.

But Kaylee's gesture proves that, at least in some ways, she's one of us. I give her a half smile to let her know I understand and slide the bangle onto my wrist. I'm pinning my bangs away from my face in the most stylish way I can manage when I hear Jasmine let out a relenting sigh. I turn from the mirror to see her miserably removing the dozens of silver studs and tiny loops from her ears. I guess she realized the same thing I did— Kaylee doesn't make the rules, but she has to follow them, same as us.

My curiosity gets the better of me again, and I ask, "So you were a New Horizons camper once?"

Kaylee nods. "I was. Seven summers ago."

"And it…worked, obviously?"

"Yes. It really did. You just have to think about it in the right way—no one's going to wave a magic wand and change everything for you, but we *will* teach you how to think differently and make better choices and get on a new track. It's like…" She thinks for a minute. "It's like going gluten free or vegan! It's hard work and involves a *lot* of self-discipline, and you have to keep making the choice to stick with it every day. But once you're educated about it and your mind and body become accustomed to it, you know you'll never go back to the way you were because you feel so much better."

"So I guess you're glad you came here then," Jasmine says.

Kaylee grins. "Best decision I ever made. I've never been happier."

"That's really good to hear," I tell her.

"Oh, and listen," Kaylee says, her voice almost at a whisper now. "These next few days are going to be pretty intense, but just stick with it. I promise it will get easier."

Jasmine and I exchange a look. That sounds ominous.

• • •

Half an hour later, we're all in the main room downstairs waiting for the boys so we can go to the dining cabin in our groups. For all the different heights and sizes that we are, the eight of us look eerily similar. It's like we're adopted siblings whose parents are trying to pass us off as twins—same pink and white outfit, same shoes, same cross, neat hair, simple accessories.

Carolyn, Jasmine, and I are leaning against the back of one of the leather couches, side by side, and I'm flipping through a New Horizons brochure. The pictures were all definitely taken at the camp—I recognize the main cabin exterior, the dining cabin, and the big open field—but the people in them have got to be models. And not one of them is wearing anything even remotely resembling the standard-issue pink and blue New Horizons gear. If the words had been covered up, I might have mistaken the brochure for a J. Crew catalog. The phrases "false advertising" and "propaganda" crop up in my mind, but I push them back and toss the brochure back onto the table.

Now that I don't have the brochure to distract me, I notice that the couch behind me is shaking gently but steadily. Carolyn's jiggling her leg nervously. "You okay?" I whisper.

She blinks out of whatever thought process she was lost in. "What?"

I nod at her leg, and the shaking stops.

"Oh." She laughs softly. "Yeah, I'm fine. Just ready to get started." Her eyes dart toward the stairs. "Who would have thought it would take the boys longer to get ready than a bunch of girls?"

I smile. "If their uniforms are anything close to as bad as ours, maybe they're staging a revolt."

But a few moments later, the eight guys plod down the staircase, and I have to bite the inside of my cheek to stop from laughing. They're dressed in light blue polo shirts tucked into pale blue and white seersucker shorts, accessorized with brown belts and brown loafers. It's the perfect outfit—if you're going as a "young Republican at a polo match" for Halloween.

Poor Matthew. He looks even more uncomfortable in his outfit than I do in mine. "Don't say it," he says as he and Daniel join us. "Don't even think it."

I hold up my palms in a surrender gesture. "I wasn't going to say anything." But I can't help grinning.

He shoots me a look, and the four of us follow the rest of the group out of the cabin and down the path.

"They took my Ellen shirt," Matthew mumbles. "That was the only thing I had here to remind me of Justin, and they took it. I'm never going to get it back."

"I'm sorry," I say.

"It's not your fault."

"They took my book yesterday. *The Great Gatsby*."

"Assholes," Matthew says.

"I've never read that book," Carolyn says. "Is it good?"

"It's amazing," I say. "It's about a guy who will do anything for love—including change his entire identity."

There's a long stretch of silence.

"Plus, there are some really awesome parties."

• • •

After breakfast, Brianna leads the sixteen of us on a tour of the camp, since we pretty much just jumped right into things yesterday and didn't get much of an introduction to the place. In addition to the main cabin for the offices and dorms, the dining cabin, and the carpet cabin, there are three others I haven't seen the inside of yet.

One is set up like a classroom. Brianna tells us it will occasionally be used for lessons and "may be utilized by campers for quiet study." On each desk are a marble notebook and a ball-point pen.

"Please find a seat," Brianna says. Once all the desks are occupied, she says, "The notebook in front of you will be your reparative therapy journal. We'd like you to use it to share your feelings about your experiences here at New Horizons. Keeping a personal journal is a very effective tool in helping to organize your thoughts and maintain perspective. It will also serve as a tangible way to track your progress this summer."

I uncap the pen and write *Lexi's Journal* in the blank space on the notebook's cover. Then I add little embellishments—a shooting star up in the corner, a mushroom growing out of a patch of grass down at the bottom.

"And don't worry, you won't have to share your journals with your groups, so you can be as open and honest as you'd like," Brianna adds.

We gather up our notebooks and continue on the tour.

The next cabin is the smallest—the infirmary. It's pretty bare bones, with a cot, a sink, and a tall cabinet filled with first aid supplies. Brianna explains that Barbara is a registered nurse, so if we ever need medical assistance, she'll be able to help. I think that she must be a *retired* registered nurse—she's got to be in her seventies, at least. I hope I never need medical attention.

The final cabin is the rec cabin. It's got several worn couches, a TV, a shelf filled with books, a game table, and an arts and crafts corner.

"Like Mr. Martin said yesterday," Brianna says, "there will be periods of downtime where you will be able to participate in leisure activities. You may play board games or work on arts and crafts with the other members of your group, or you may read approved books or watch approved movies." From what I can tell, the DVD shelf consists mostly of animated Disney movies and other innocuous G-rated titles, and the books all seem to have been published by the same company—one with a cross in their logo. "You may also spend time outside if you prefer, as long as you stay within sight of the rec cabin. During downtimes, your time is your own. But just remember that even if you are doing a solitary activity like reading, you should always be in close proximity to your fellow group members."

Matthew raises his hand. "Sorry, I just want to make sure I've got this straight. You're saying that we have to spend all our time together and only do the things you tell us we can do, even during our free hours." He says it so innocently that even I wonder if he's genuinely just asking for clarification.

"Yes, that's correct," Brianna says.

"So how, exactly, is our time our own?"

I can almost see Brianna's brain jolting into overdrive as she tries to come up with an answer. But Matthew's pinned her own words against her. He smiles benignly, waiting for her response.

"Because…well, because you get to choose which activities you do," she says finally. "Now if you'll all follow me…"

Brianna brings us past the athletics field and the nature trail, and then we all go to the carpet cabin. The chairs have been arranged in rows, and some of the props have been brought out into a stage-like area.

"Good morning, campers!" Mr. Martin says. "I hope you all got a good night's sleep because today we begin the real work. The exercise we are going to be working on for the next several days is called Addressing the Father Wound."

Matthew and I look at each other. *Father Wound?*

"We won't be splitting you up for this one because you may find something in someone else's story that will help you with your own, so we'll be working through this all together, in one big group." Mr. Martin smiles. "Now, do we have a volunteer to go first?"

Chapter 8

Unlike yesterday's session, no one volunteers. Not even Daniel. But Mr. Martin's smile doesn't crack.

"Perhaps it will help if I explain the purpose of the exercise a bit more," he says.

Several of us nod.

Mr. Martin walks back and forth across the makeshift stage. "Despite what some pop singers and the mainstream media would have you believe, you were not born with SSA. You were born clean and pure, just as God intended you to be." He stops walking and gives us a sad, almost pitying smile. "But somewhere along the way, someone or something corrupted you. It may have been intentional or it could have been unintentional. But something—your Father Wound—brought you into this lifestyle." When he says the word *lifestyle*, his nose crinkles up like he's smelling something bad. "You see, the SSA isn't the problem; it's the *symptom*. For other people with Father Wounds, it may have resulted in drug abuse or a tendency toward violent behavior. For you, it manifested into

SSA. Once we are able to identify and address the deeper-seated problem, we can begin to heal it."

I consider what he's saying. I quickly flip back through a lifetime of memories, but for the life of me, I can't imagine what might have happened to make me gay.

"So. Any volunteers?" Mr. Martin asks.

Still no one raises their hand.

Undiscouraged, Mr. Martin scans the crowd. "Let's start with the boys today." He points to a boy with a round face and a crew cut. "Gabe." He holds out a hand in invitation to join him.

Gabe makes his way to the front of the room, stumbling slightly on the leg of a chair as he maneuvers through the rows of seats. When he's standing next to Mr. Martin, the difference in their height is striking. Gabe looks like a child; he's probably not even done growing yet.

Mr. Martin drags a chair to the center of the stage and positions it so it's facing the rest of us. Gabe sits, and Mr. Martin tells him to close his eyes. "Tell us about your childhood," he says in a calming, gentle voice.

Gabe's eyes fly open. "What do you mean? What about it?"

"Please keep your eyes closed. Just tell us whatever comes to mind about what it was like growing up in your family."

Gabe sits there for a while, his eyes squeezed shut, the rest of us watching him. The room is deadly silent. At one point, the stomach of someone sitting behind me gurgles. I don't turn to see who it is.

Then, finally, Gabe speaks. "I live in Orlando," he says.

"The most magical place on earth!" Mr. Martin says, delighted.

"I guess." Gabe shrugs. "I've never actually been to Disney."

Mr. Martin's face falls and he nods. "Who lives with you?" he asks.

"My father and my mother and my four younger brothers."

"What does your father do for a living?"

"He works the night maintenance shift at the airport."

"As the eldest son, there must be a lot of pressure on you to help take care of your family."

"I guess," he says again, his voice trembling slightly. "I don't mind it though."

"Remember, Gabe," Mr. Martin says. "This will only work if you are honest with us." He gives Gabe a meaningful look, which is probably more for our benefit than Gabe's since he can't see it with his eyes closed.

Gabe takes a shallow, wavering breath. "Well, we don't have a lot of money, you know? Even with my father working overtime and my mother cleaning houses. Sometimes my father goes drinking after work, and when he comes home and looks at the state of our apartment, he gets…"

"He gets what?" Mr. Martin nudges.

"Angry. But anyone would," he says quickly. "There's this broken window that won't close all the way, so we have to stuff the hole with towels, and there're always rats in the kitchen. And there aren't enough beds for all of us, so we have these mattresses that we prop up against the wall during the daytime and then put on the floor at night."

"What do you mean by 'he gets angry'?"

"I don't know," Gabe mumbles.

"I think you do know."

Gabe's eyes are still closed. He doesn't say anything.

I quickly glance around the room. Everyone has their eyes fixed on the boy in the chair. No one makes a move or a sound. Matthew's eyes are cold and hard. I look away.

"Gabriel," Mr. Martin says, "I spoke with your mother." Each word is heavy and revealing.

Gabe sucks in a surprised, tremulous breath. "He hits me," he says finally, reluctantly. "He gets drunk and he gets mad and he beats me up."

Mr. Martin nods; he was expecting this all along. He *knew*. This whole thing has been choreographed. He purposely called on Gabe to go first because he already knew his story—the perfect illustration for the rest of us of what a literal and figurative Father Wound looks like.

What else does Mr. Martin know? I wonder what my mother told him about me…

"How long has this been going on?" he asks Gabe.

"For as long as I can remember."

"Is that what this is from?" He touches a dark mark on Gabe's jawline. I'd dismissed it as a shadow, but I can see now it's a bruise.

Gabe nods.

"Does he hit your mother too? Or your brothers?"

Gabe shakes his head and squeezes his eyes tighter so that deep creases spread out from them like reaching fingers. "*No*. Only me. I won't let him hurt them."

"Are you saying that you let him hurt you so he won't hurt them?" Mr. Martin asks.

"It's the only way." There's a pause. "I'm worried about what he'll do while I'm gone."

"Don't think like that, Gabe," Mr. Martin says. "Your church is sponsoring your summer at New Horizons, as I recall?"

"Yes."

"Well, then the best thing you can do for them right now is to let those worries go and instead focus on your work here and making your family and your congregation proud."

Gabe nods. "Okay."

Mr. Martin asks Gabe to open his eyes. He blinks several times, like he's having trouble adjusting to the room, and then looks down at his lap. I can't imagine what he must be feeling right now.

"Everyone, please give Gabe a round of applause for so bravely sharing his story," Mr. Martin says. We clap for him, but there's a solemn timbre to it. Mr. Martin stands behind Gabe and rests his hands on his shoulders. "Gabe's Father Wound is the most straightforward kind," he says to us, "because it has been inflicted by his actual father. Gabe's father is the one person who was supposed to show him what it means to be a man, but instead, he has made sure his son remains a wounded boy with a confused sense of right and wrong."

Tears are spilling down Gabe's cheeks and landing in his lap, and his body is heaving with silent sobs. But I can't shake the icky feeling that Mr. Martin did this to him just to make a point.

"This lifetime of abuse is Gabe's Father Wound," he continues. But suddenly his face brightens. "And now that we've identified it, we can move on to the second half of the exercise—Healing the Father Wound!"

It's like he's just said, *Guess what everyone! There's free cake in the dining cabin!* But there's a broken, abused boy sitting right in front of him—doesn't he feel bad? Shouldn't we take a break or something, so Gabe can have a moment to himself?

Mr. Martin gestures to Arthur, and Arthur drags out some props: a standup punching bag and a Nerf baseball bat. Mr. Martin calls on a tall boy named Ian to come join him and Gabe at the front of the room.

"One of the best ways to work through our Father Wounds is to use role-play," he says. "Ian, you are going to play the role of Gabe's father in this scenario."

Ian's face pales.

"Gabe, please stand up and face Ian."

Gabe does as he says, and Arthur removes Gabe's chair from the stage.

"You may begin the scene, Ian," Mr. Martin says.

Ian looks at him, panicked. "I don't know what I'm supposed to do."

"Remember Gabe's story. You're his father, and you're coming home drunk."

Poor Ian. He looks like he wishes he could vanish into thin air or do anything or become anything to get out of this. Gabe doesn't look much different.

"Please, begin," Mr. Martin says again, firmer this time.

Ian starts walking around in a jerky line and mimes a swig from an imaginary bottle. "Hello, son," he says, in a deep voice.

Gabe looks to Mr. Martin, and Mr. Martin nods encouragingly. "Hello, Dad," he says, unsure. "How…uh, how was work?"

"Same as it always is," Ian says. Mr. Martin makes a keep-going gesture, and Ian adds, "Don't be stupid." Mr. Martin points to the rest of the stage area, coaching Ian. Ian looks confused for a moment, but then his face clicks. "Look at this place! I work hard every night and have to come home to this dump? You need to start pulling your weight around here, boy!" Mr. Martin hands Ian the Nerf bat and nods in Gabe's direction.

Ian's face crumples like he's in pain. He turns to Mr. Martin and speaks in his normal voice. "I can't."

Mr. Martin's brow furrows. "Yes, you can." Ian shakes his head, and a shadow crosses Mr. Martin's face. "Don't you want to help Gabe, Ian? He's in your group; he's your friend. Do you really want to let him down like this?"

Ian looks back and forth between Mr. Martin and Gabe, as if he's trying to decide which is worse—hitting Gabe or defying Mr. Martin. Finally, he lifts the foam bat and brings it down onto Gabe's head.

"Harder," Mr. Martin says.

Ian repeats the action, with more force this time, swiping Gabe across the chest and arms and shoulders with the yellow bat. Even though the Nerf material couldn't possibly cause real injury, the thick, dull sound of the foam meeting Gabe's body over and over again makes me shudder. Gabe shrinks to the floor, cowering in the fetal position, wailing out, "No, Dad! Please, no."

A cry sticks in my throat, and I know that the moment I unclench my jaw, it will fly out. This isn't right. Gabe has been through enough in his life. He shouldn't have to relive it like this. I look to my right—Matthew's face is now red and severe. He's gripping the sides of his chair as if to keep himself planted in his seat—much like how I'm keeping my mouth shut to trap my protest.

I look to my left—Carolyn's face is smooth, unreadable, her eyes unfocused. She looks like she's not even watching the scene at all—instead, she's lost in some faraway memory of her own. It's a familiar sight and makes me feel even more uneasy.

Daniel's face is hidden behind Carolyn's, but his hands are folded securely around a small wooden cross, his thumb steadily grazing the engravings.

"What do you want to do, Gabe?" Mr. Martin shouts over the

wailing and repeated *thwack* of the bat. "Now's your chance! You can say whatever you want! You can do whatever you want to do! You can tell your father what you think of him once and for all! Trust your instincts!"

Gabe lies there a moment more and then slowly pushes himself up to a sitting position. Ian is still hitting him, but there is a look in Gabe's eye now that wasn't there before. It's something like determination. So quickly I almost miss it, Gabe reaches an arm out and snatches the bat from Ian's hand. He stands up and pushes his shoulders back. His face and neck and arms are red where the foam touched his skin.

"I am not your punching bag!" Gabe shouts. "I am your *son*. You aren't supposed to treat me this way! You aren't supposed to hurt me!" He lifts the bat and hits Ian with it as hard as he can. Even though the foam is soft, Ian flinches at the impact. Gabe hits him again and again, and Ian cowers to protect his face. "You're supposed to *love* me, Dad. Why don't you love me?"

Mr. Martin slides the punching bag toward Gabe. "Use this, Gabe. Get it all out!"

Gabe drops the bat and begins tearing into the bag, punching and kicking it so hard that the sound it makes reminds me of thunder. Ian escapes to the far wall, as far away from the action as he can get. Gabe is lashing out at the bag, tears streaming freely from his bloodshot eyes, shouts and cries fleeing from him in a muddled jumble. He punches until his hands are raw and his knuckles are bleeding, and then with one final wave of energy, he tackles the bag so that it crashes over and lays defeated on the carpet.

There is a stunned silence as we watch Gabe stare at the obliterated punching bag, gasping for breath. "Screw you, Dad," he whispers.

Mr. Martin steps forward and puts his arm around Gabe. "Well done, young man! Well done indeed! You did it. You took control and stood up to your father. You are no longer that helpless boy lying on the floor." He gestures to the general place on the floor that Gabe had been curled up. "You are now a strong man, standing tall. How do you feel?" He beams proudly down at Gabe.

"My hands hurt," Gabe says.

"Yes, we'll get them fixed up right away. But how do you feel *inside*?"

"I don't know. Different, I guess."

Different. *Good different or bad different?* Mr. Martin doesn't ask. Instead, he simply says, "Excellent!" and gives an accomplished grin. "You are going to be just fine, Gabe. You may return to your seat."

Gabe makes a beeline to the back row of seats, where Barbara is waiting for him with a first aid kit, and we give him another hesitant round of applause.

What the hell did I just witness?

It was horrible. It was cruel. But…Gabe said he feels *different*. And he undeniably went through some sort of emotional transition;

anyone could see that. Maybe Mr. Martin really does know what he's doing.

But then he repeats the process with two other campers, and I'm less sure. Same as with Gabe's session, it's a mess of crying and screaming and violence. For hours, I am forced to be a spectator, and for hours, I have to fight to remain silent.

Gabe is the only one whose story involved physical abuse, but the other stories are just as painful to listen to—Chris's father left his family out of the blue when Chris was six, never to be heard from again, and for years, Austin had to spend his days after school with a babysitter, a cruel old woman who called him stupid and ugly and made him do menial chores around her house. And when he told his parents what was going on, they refused to believe him.

At first it's shocking to me that everyone who has been called up for a Father Wound session so far has such specific incidences of abuse or trauma in their past. But the more I think about it, the more it doesn't seem so strange. Everyone has something, right? I have my dad's death and my mom's mental instability and my broken heart. None of those things has anything to do with me being gay because they all happened *after* I already knew I liked girls, but still. Everyone has something.

I think about how Mr. Martin mentioned that some people who've experienced trauma didn't become gay but instead turned to drugs or violence. The idea of all of this stemming from a tragic or damaging place in someone's life makes sense when you think about it.

And if Gabe's and Chris's and Austin's stories are any indication, maybe most people's "something" happened a lot earlier in their lives than mine did. Maybe *they're* not the exception. Maybe *I* am.

But still. There's got to be a better way to go about all this.

The midday lunch break is just as uncomfortable as the Father Wound sessions themselves. The dining cabin is quiet, and no one will look directly at the three boys who were forced to give away their most painful memories and beat their caretakers to death in effigy.

Matthew, Daniel, Carolyn, and I sit together, but we are worlds apart, adrift in our own distant thoughts.

Since it's so quiet, it's not hard to hear what Gabe's saying when he goes over to Mr. Martin's table and asks to speak with him.

"Of course, Gabe," Mr. Martin says. "How can I help you?"

"I know you said we should come to you if there's anything we need," Gabe says softly.

"Yes, absolutely."

"Well…I know we're not supposed to use the phone too much, but I'd really like to call my mother if that's okay. I just want to make sure she's all right."

Mr. Martin says he understands completely and asks Counselor John to bring Gabe up to the main cabin so he can use the phone. Fifteen minutes later, Gabe and John return, and Gabe's face looks a lot more relaxed than it did before he left. Guess everything's okay at home. Even I feel happy knowing that—I can't imagine how relieved Gabe feels.

We reconvene in the carpet cabin after lunch, emotionally and physically exhausted. But Mr. Martin shows no sign of slowing. "Now that we've all refueled," he says, patting his oversized stomach, "let's give a female camper a chance, shall we?"

What? No! He said today was the boys' turn! I inch down in my seat and try to hide behind the girl in front of me. I know I'll have to go up there eventually, but I'm hoping my turn will come later rather than sooner.

"Lexi!" Mr. Martin's voice booms. "Why don't you go next?"

Chapter 9

I've never hated the sound of my own name until this moment.

I slide further down in my chair and pretend I didn't hear him. I'm staring at the floor, but even without looking, I know that there are dozens of pairs of eyes on me. My face burns.

"Lexi," Mr. Martin says again. "Don't be scared. Gabe, Austin, and Chris got through it, didn't they?"

Barely.

"Please come up here, Lexi."

Matthew places a hand on mine and gives it a quick squeeze. "Just get it over with," he whispers. "He's not going to back down."

I take a deep breath.

I walk to the stage.

I sit in the chair.

I close my eyes.

Mr. Martin begins the same way as always: "Tell us about your childhood."

"It was good," I say. "Normal."

"You were raised by a mother and a father?"

I nod.

"Any siblings?"

I shake my head.

"Why not?"

I shrug. "They tried, but it never happened."

"What was it like growing up as an only child?" Mr. Martin says.

"I don't know. Fine, I guess. My parents were always nice to me."

"What about your other family members? Grandparents, aunts and uncles…"

"My mom's parents were normal and boring too when they were alive. I don't have any aunts or uncles, and my dad's parents died before I was born."

"Do any unpleasant memories stand out? Maybe something that happened at school, with a friend or a teacher?" Mr. Martin presses.

I hate this.

"No," I say. "My childhood was fine. I don't have a Father Wound."

"Of course you do. We just need to uncover it."

I press my lips together. I'm not going to be bullied into making up some lie about how awful my parents were to me just so Mr. Martin can feel better.

But then he surprises me.

"You know," he says, and from the way his voice carries, I can tell he's pacing around behind me, "when I met your mother yesterday, I couldn't help but notice the way she was dressed."

I open my eyes and turn to face him. "What's wrong with how she was dressed?"

He points a finger at me and rotates it in a circular motion, indicating I should turn back around. I do, but I don't close my eyes this time. "Her clothing wasn't very *feminine*, was it? Jeans, hiking boots, hair almost as short as a man's."

"So what? Lots of moms dress that way."

"Does your mother work, Lexi?" he says. But I know he already knows the answer.

"Yeah," I say. I don't know where this is going, but I don't like Mr. Martin's tone. "She's a teacher. Why?"

"I'm just putting the pieces together," Mr. Martin says.

"What pieces? What are you saying?"

"I'm thinking about your story yesterday during our first session. I recall you saying you became interested in fashion because you liked watching women in pretty clothes on television. And then you started to become more interested in the women than the clothes. Is that correct?"

"Yeah…"

"It seems to me that your unfeminine, working mother wasn't setting an appropriate gender example for you, and therefore you were left to seek that example elsewhere." His voice is cutting, accusatory. "Your mother's demonstration of improper womanhood completely warped your understanding of gender roles, Lexi."

The impulse I've been feeling all day to fight is suddenly

unlocked. "Why are you attacking my mother like this?" I say, my voice betraying the emotion bubbling up inside me. "You don't even know her!" He really thinks that because my mother has short hair and works as a schoolteacher that's what made me gay? It just doesn't make any sense. Plus, for someone who loves stereotypes, it seems like he's going with the wrong one here—he's conveniently ignoring the fact that traditionally, most teachers are not only female but *nurturing* as well. His argument holds absolutely no water.

"I'm not attacking anyone, Lexi," Mr. Martin says calmly. "I'm just trying to help you. Let me help you."

I open my mouth, about to tell Mr. Martin exactly what I think about his whole Father Wound exercise, when I catch Kaylee's eye. She's standing off to the side of the audience area, looking directly at me. She holds up one palm in a tiny, calm-down gesture, and I remember what she said earlier: *Just stick with it. I promise it will get easier.*

I take a few deep breaths and give her a little nod.

I look at the other faces in the crowd—they're riveted. With a few exceptions, everyone is focused more on Mr. Martin than me, and they all have that same expression of reverence that I saw on Carolyn yesterday as she listened to him speak. Already, my fellow campers have so much faith in this man.

I need to too. It's like Kaylee said yesterday—they're doing a job. They have to be harsh and direct in order to get their message across, to cut into fifteen, sixteen, seventeen years of our making the wrong choices. Mr. Martin is a good person—he understands us; he wants to help us; he *was* us. He was so kind to Daniel and let Gabe call home and has been nothing but welcoming.

But then he catches me off guard again.

"Where's your father, Lexi?"

I look at him, and the innocent smile on his face confirms that he knows exactly where my father is. Even if he didn't speak with my mother before I came here, he heard her talking about the life insurance payment yesterday.

But he's got me in his stronghold and isn't going to let me go.

"He's dead," I say, as emotionless as I can, but it still comes out sharp. Even through the pain and anger swimming around in my head, I don't miss the gasps. I guess, in this crowd, a dead parent is a lot rarer than an abusive one. "You already knew that."

"But we're not here for me, Lexi. We're here for you. And we're here for them." He sweeps a hand out toward the fifteen other campers. "Saying the words out loud is a very important part of this process. It makes it a lot harder to deny the truth."

"I'm not *denying* anything," I say. "Believe me, I know all too well that my father is dead. I think about it all the time."

"How did your father pass away?" Mr. Martin asks.

I hate talking about this. I hate even thinking about it. And I really don't understand what it has to do with anything.

But I look at Carolyn out there in the crowd and I know that she's listening, waiting, and suddenly I want her to know my story.

I sigh and lower my voice. "He had pancreatic cancer."

"Tell us about it."

"I guess he'd had it for a long time before they actually knew what it was," I say. "He'd been losing weight and was always complaining of stomach and back pain, but the doctors told him it was stress and to take a vacation. He took me to the South by Southwest music festival in Austin, Texas." It's a complicated memory for me—we had so much fun, but knowing now that the cancer was eating at him the whole time we were there, making him sicker, taints the whole thing. I hate that doctor who told him to go on vacation instead of believing my dad that there was something wrong and doing more tests.

"But then he started getting jaundice—his eyes and skin had this weird yellowish tint—and the doctors finally figured out what was causing it. But it was too late. They pumped all this chemo into him, and he lost his hair and he got really weak and had to leave his job…" I break off for a moment. My eyes are filling with tears and my throat is threatening to close up. I blink, and the moisture overflows, spilling down my face. "And then he died anyway. Seven months after he was diagnosed."

Mr. Martin hands me a tissue, and I blow my nose.

"You must miss him," Mr. Martin says tenderly.

"He was my best friend," I say.

Mr. Martin nods. "I'm assuming that during your father's illness, your mother had to take over his role as the head of the household?"

I shrug. "It wasn't like that. He was never really the 'head of the household,' even when he was healthy. He and my mom made decisions together."

"I see. But as his illness progressed, he wasn't able to make those decisions anymore?"

I sniffle. "Yeah, I guess." I don't think it's worth adding that it wasn't my mom who took over as the head of the household; it was me. Mr. Martin, I'm sure, would have a field day with that nugget of information, and I don't see any reason to give him anything else to work with.

Mr. Martin hands me another tissue and squats down in front of me. "Think about it, Lexi. Your whole life, your parents gave you mixed signals about the roles of men and women. Your mother worked out of the home. She dressed like a man. She shared the head of household duties with your father, thereby reducing his masculine identity. He became more of a friend to you than a disciplinarian." He places a hand on my arm. I have to force myself not to shrug it off. "It's clear that your parents loved you very much; I'm not disputing that. But they taught you wrong."

I twist the unused tissue around and around in my hands so it becomes ropelike and cuts into the soft patch of flesh where my thumb and index finger meet.

"You were right," Mr. Martin says. "You don't have an individual incident for a Father Wound. Rather, the overall dynamic between your parents serves as the Father Wound in this instance. Now, the question is, how do we heal it?"

Chapter 10

Mr. Martin walks in slow circles behind me, deep in thought. The continuous *squish* of his shoes sinking into the carpet is loud in my ears.

I look out over the crowded room. My eyes are blurry from the tears that I haven't bothered to wipe away, and the blur of pink and blue before me reminds me of the ocean at sunset. It's even moving like the ocean, the whole picture bobbing up and down faintly with each breath I take.

The seconds tick by, turning into minutes, but Mr. Martin still doesn't provide an answer to his question: *how do we heal it?*

But he doesn't really mean *heal*. He means *negate*. Because, according to Mr. Martin, my Father Wound isn't something bad, like a physically abusive father or an emotionally abusive babysitter. My Father Wound is my entire existence, my entire childhood, my entire relationship with my mother and father. But I refuse to believe my relationship with my parents was somehow bad.

It's all I can do to hope Mr. Martin doesn't make me beat up my "mother" or "father." I really don't think I could do that.

Suddenly Mr. Martin claps his hands together once, loudly, making me jump in my seat. "Of course!" he says to himself. He selects a few items from the prop collection and pulls them over to where I'm seated, a renewed spring in his step now that he's figured out his course of action. They're a fold-up cot, blanket, and pillow. I'm so relieved at the lack of punching bags and baseball bats that I don't really question what the props are for.

"Daniel, will you assist us, please?" Mr. Martin says. Once Daniel's joined us on the stage, Mr. Martin directs him to lie down on the cot with his head on the pillow and the blanket over him. He tells him not to speak and not to get up, no matter what happens or what I say. "Now, Lexi. Daniel is going to be playing the role of your father. In this scenario, your father is in the hospital and on the verge of passing away. This is your last moment with him. What would you like to say?"

"Wh-what?" I squeak out. "I…I don't understand."

"Your last memory of your father is as a friend," Mr. Martin says. "That's where the problem lies. Your perceptions of parental roles are distorted, and because your father has passed, those memories have been frozen. But if you continue remembering him that way, you'll never be able to get on the right track. You need to *change* that memory of your father. You need to let him know that you know what he and your mother did to you, and you need to let him know how that makes you feel."

I stare up at Mr. Martin, horror-struck. Why is he doing this to me?

But he just smiles back.

I look at Daniel, completely hidden beneath the blue blanket save for his face. How am I supposed to pretend that skinny boy is my father? How am I supposed to tell him what Mr. Martin wants me to tell him? How am I supposed to form the words that will supposedly change my last memory of my father? Why would I even *want* to?

But once again, I'm trapped. I have to do what Mr. Martin says. There's no other choice here—there's no way out, literally nowhere to run.

My head is spinning. The only reason I'm even at New Horizons in the first place is because I have to fix my family. And now Mr. Martin is saying that for the de-gayifying to work, I have to reject everything that my family was and is. So what, then, is the point of all of this?

I squeeze my eyes shut and make myself think.

I could just give up now. Tell Mr. Martin I want to go home and forget I even came here at all. Go back to living with a shell of a mother who fears for my soul, hanging out with friends who don't really know me, working overtime to pay my mom back the $9,500. It's just as well. If Mr. Martin has his way, my relationship with my mom will never be the same again anyway. And if I left now, at least I wouldn't have to participate in this whole Dad-deathbed charade *or* wear these awful clothes for an entire summer.

But Kaylee's words repeat in my head. *I promise it will get easier.*

Maybe she's right—it *is* only the second day. And it's a two-month program. And Mr. Martin said we'd only be working on this Father Wound thing for a few days. Maybe the rest of the summer won't be nearly as bad. Kaylee would know—after all, she's sat where I'm sitting now. And she said it was the best decision she ever made. Maybe I could still get something out of New Horizons even if I'm not fully behind this particular exercise. Maybe, if I stick it out, I can find the gray area Kaylee talked about, my own way to make the de-gayifying work and get the life I want but without sacrificing the things that are important to me.

The thought of my mom's inevitable breakdown when she hears I gave up on New Horizons after only two days is what seals it for me.

"Dad…" I say to Daniel. This is by far the strangest thing I have ever done in my life. It's flat-out *wrong* in so many ways. But I do my best to detach myself from the memory of my real dad and his real illness and the real last time I spoke to him, and instead focus on playing the part that Mr. Martin wants me to play. "You've been a good father. But you and Mom…you kind of messed me up."

"Kind of?" Mr. Martin repeats. "Don't be *weak*, Lexi!"

I shake my head. "No, not kind of. You really messed me up. You didn't act the way normal mothers and fathers are supposed to act. You didn't…lead by example. And now I'm confused." I look to Mr. Martin, and he nods for me to continue. "I feel like I don't know how men and women are actually supposed to act around each other. It's affected me in some very big ways."

"So what are you going to do, Lexi?" Mr. Martin says.

"I…um…" I falter. I don't know if I can do this.

"Say it!" One look at Mr. Martin's face confirms what his tone already gave away. This is not a suggestion—it's an order.

"So, Dad, I want you to know…" I swallow. "Before you, um, *go*…that I am going to remember you as a father. I am going to forget all the things you did and said to make me think that we were friends, instead of what we actually are—father and daughter. And I am going to get my life back on track."

"Tell him about the times he was a real father to you," Mr. Martin says. "Concentrate on those memories now."

I think long and hard, carefully choosing which memories to share. "I will always remember the time you came home from work with the swing set in your trunk and how you spent the whole weekend putting it together for me."

I glance at Mr. Martin again—he's moving his hand around and around, waving for me to keep going.

"I will always remember the time I got a D plus on my life science lab and how you took my allowance away until I got at least a B minus. And I will always remember you as the man who never once forgot Mom's birthday or a Valentine's Day or your wedding anniversary. You were a good husband to her."

For good measure, I lean over and kiss Daniel on the cheek. His eyes flutter open in surprise and his face turns a dark shade of red, but he follows Mr. Martin's instructions and doesn't say anything.

"Good-bye, Daddy," I say, and my voice cracks.

"Well *done*, Lexi!" Mr. Martin says, rejoining us at the center of the stage. He stands me up and takes my hands. "How do you feel?"

I put on my most grateful smile and say, "Much better. Really. You were right. That was exactly what I needed."

"I'm so glad to hear it! And thank you so much for your courageous work here today."

The campers and counselors break into applause, and I'm finally free from this hell. But as I make my way back to my seat, the relief is replaced by heartache as the detachment wears off and I am forced to face what just happened. I just told my dad that I would forget him—not him entirely, but our friendship. It doesn't matter that I didn't mean it or that I said it to someone who was only pretending to be him or that I only said it because Mr. Martin forced me to. I said, out loud, that I would never again think about all those times he was so much *more* than just a father figure. The fun times we had together are the best memories I have, and now they're tainted.

I don't know if I believe in ghosts or angels or the idea that the dead watch over us, but just in case, I whisper, so low that no one can hear over the sound of the clapping, "I'm sorry."

Chapter 11

When we get back to the dorms, *The Great Gatsby* is back. It's lying on my bed with a note stuck to it that says: Mr. Martin said this was OK. Brianna. It's a comforting sight—a piece of home that I so desperately need right now. I wonder if Mr. Martin knew I would need the book today, after the difficulty of my Father Wound session, and made sure Brianna got it back to me.

I open to the first page and read the opening line, even though I know it by heart:

> *In my younger and more vulnerable years my father gave me*
> *some advice that I've been turning over in my mind ever since.*

I slam the book shut.

Mr. Martin has officially managed to ruin everything that's important to me.

But then I see Carolyn across the room, already changed into her nightgown and brushing her hair into the same loose, high ponytail

I saw her go to bed in last night, and I know what to do. I go over to her area and give her a little wave in the reflection of the mirror. "Hey."

She spins around. "Hey, Lexi." There are tiny wisps of blond at her hairline, lighter and finer than the rest of her hair, and they give the opposite effect of a shadow, brightening her face instead of darkening it. I notice a tiny birthmark on her temple—it's adorable. "How are you doing?" Her voice is low and concerned.

She, Matthew, and Daniel tried to get me to talk to them all during dinner and the walk back to the main cabin. But what was I supposed to say? After what Mr. Martin made me do and say, I didn't want to talk about it. I still don't.

"I'm good. How are you?" I say lightly, as if I don't know what she's really asking.

"I'm okay. But, Lexi, if you need someone to talk—"

I thrust the book out. "I got my book back," I say, cutting her off. "I thought you might want to borrow it. It's been approved by Mr. Martin. It's not Jane Austen, but…"

"Oh! Um, yes! Thanks!" She takes the book and runs her thumb over the edge of the pages so that a little gust of wind escapes and ripples through her hair. My stomach does a flip-flop. "This is really nice of you."

"No problem," I mumble, repeating *just friends just friends just friends* in my head. "Okay, well, good night." I duck my head and bail.

On my way back to my own area, Rachael stops me. "I just wanted to say that your Father Wound session today was really inspiring," she says. "Isn't Mr. Martin so amazing? I feel so lucky to get to learn from him."

"Um. Yes," I say. "Agreed."

After everyone's in bed, Deb, the counselor on dorm duty tonight, tells us we will have twenty extra minutes before lights out so we can write in our journals.

I spend my time drawing. It feels good to have a blank page in front of me again, waiting for whatever sketch or doodle is ready to break free from my pen. A string of ivy sprouts onto the page and grows wild, first just around the edges of the paper but then gradually invading the center, the vine branching off and grasping every which way, taking over the page like the stubborn weed that it is. When nearly the entire page has been overrun, I add in a figure, a tiny human no taller than a safety pin. She stares out helplessly from behind the ivy, her arms and legs caught in the vines.

I'm trying to place the expression on the girl's face when Deb announces it's time for our nightly Bible verse.

"'For this reason I tell you, whatever you pray and ask for, believe that you have received it, and it will be yours,'" Jasmine reads aloud.

We close our Bibles, and a few seconds later, the room goes dark.

• • •

Day two of the Father Wound exercise. At least I get to relax today. I've done my part.

But then Matthew is called up first, and my stomach is instantly in knots again. Mr. Martin won't go easy on him.

To Matthew's credit, he doesn't lose his cool like I did yesterday. He answers Mr. Martin's questions about his family and life back in San Diego with amazing composure. There's even a smile on his face as he does it.

"What are your parents like?" Mr. Martin asks.

Matthew shrugs. "My dad's a typical guy, watches football like it's his job, owns a pool cleaning business, drinks a lot of beer. My mom stays home with my youngest sister. She's two."

"Wonderful," Mr. Martin says. But the more questions Matthew answers, the more Mr. Martin looks troubled. Matthew's family is the picture of perfection. Parents in appropriate gender roles, no abuse to speak of, three children and a dog, church on Sundays, family trips to Legoland, homemade apple pie, avocado tree in the backyard.

There's absolutely nothing for Mr. Martin to grab on to.

And Matthew knows it. That's why he's so smug.

Hope builds inside me as I watch the scene up on the stage. *Stay strong*, I think to Matthew. *Don't give him anything*.

Mr. Martin asks so many questions I wouldn't be surprised if someone was feeding them to him through an earpiece. When he exhausts one topic, he jumps right into the next without hesitation: school, friends, extended family, past summer camp experiences, his afterschool job at the dog groomer's. Matthew's carefully thought-out responses are the definition of generic. He doesn't shy away from talking about Justin—which Mr. Martin clearly doesn't appreciate—but he gives absolutely no hint of anything that would have caused him to like boys in the first place. I'm not always sure he's telling the whole truth, but it doesn't matter. His performance is masterful.

Just when I think time has got to be close to up and Matthew has actually beaten Mr. Martin at his own game, Mr. Martin asks Matthew what his favorite movie is.

"*Grease*," Matthew answers without missing a beat.

That one tiny word is enough to completely transform Mr. Martin's demeanor. He freezes for a brief second and then straightens up, confidence overtaking him, a knowing smile crossing his face.

Crap. What just happened?

"*Grease*. That's a musical, isn't it?" His voice is different now. Sly. Certain.

Matthew suddenly looks as worried as I feel. "Um, yeah?"

"What other musicals do you like, Matthew?"

"I don't really see what that has to do with anything…"

"Just answer the question."

Matthew grimaces. Mr. Martin is onto him; he knows there's no point in lying now. "I don't know…*Cabaret*, *Evita*, *West Side Story*…I like them all, I guess."

Mr. Martin nods. "Have you ever been in one?"

Matthew mutters something under his breath, but I can't understand it.

"What was that?"

"Nothing. Yes, I have been in musicals."

"When did you do your first one?" Mr. Martin asks.

"When I was seven. I did a community theater production of *The Music Man*. I played Winthrop," Matthew says.

"And since then?"

Matthew sighs. "I've been in a lot of shows, okay? At least two a year for the last ten years. So just say whatever you're going to say so we can end this already."

"Very well. The artistic world is a breeding ground for SSA, Matthew. Theater, Hollywood, the fine arts…anything goes for those people. I'm sure a lot of the people who have been in these shows with you actively engage in the homosexual lifestyle?"

Matthew doesn't say anything.

"That's what I thought. Being exposed to that environment from such a young age is your Father Wound, Matthew. You grew up observing them, being taught that that kind of behavior is okay."

I think back to the first day when we all introduced ourselves to our groups. Matthew said he's known he was gay since preschool. So that was *before* he was in his first musical. Mr. Martin doesn't seem to remember this though, or if he does, he doesn't care. He's just so damn proud of himself right now.

They go on to do a ridiculous role-play where a seven-year-old Matthew tells Carolyn, who is playing his mother, that he doesn't want to be in *The Music Man* and instead wants to try out for the football team.

When Matthew is safely back in his seat next to me, I whisper, "You okay?"

He places a hand on his chest, opens his eyes wide, and whispers back in a dramatic southern accent, "Why, I'm better than *okay*—I'm cured! Praise Jesus!"

I roll my eyes. Same old Matthew.

He grabs my hands. "Dear, sweet Lexi, will you marry me and have lots of sex and babies with me?"

I pull my hands away, laughing. "All right, all right, I get it."

"But I like girls now, Lexi! And I like *you* most of all!"

He leans forward, like he's going in for a big, sloppy kiss, and I bat him away in a fit of giggles.

It's Mr. Martin's resounding voice that brings us to our senses. "Matthew and Lexi, is there something you would like to share with the group?"

We both turn so we're facing forward and sitting rail straight, all traces of humor gone. "Um, no. Sorry," I say.

"Good. Now, I would appreciate it if you would give Olivia the same courtesy that everyone showed you both when you were up here." His voice is soft, but his eyes are hard.

"Yes, Mr. Martin. Sorry, Olivia," I say, my face flaming, and Olivia's session resumes up on the stage.

The last camper to get called up for the day is Daniel. He's the one member of my group who I don't feel any real connection with yet—despite the fact that he was the one who played the role of my dying father—so in a weird way I'm actually sort of looking forward to his Father Wound session, if only to get to know him a little better.

Like the first day, he is very forthcoming with his story.

His father left him and his mother when Daniel was only a baby, and his mother never remarried. "She worries about me," he says after Mr. Martin asks him to describe his relationship with his mother. "She likes me to stay inside."

"Inside?" Mr. Martin asks.

"Yeah, like inside the house. Going outside with the other kids and playing sports and stuff like that is really dangerous."

"Do you want to go play outside with the other kids, Daniel?" Mr. Martin asks gently.

"I did at first. But I stopped asking after a while. Mom needs me at home, where it's safe."

"How does that make you feel?"

He shrugs. "It's okay. She just doesn't want me to get hurt. I understand."

It actually sounds to me like Daniel's mother is less concerned about his well-being and more concerned about her own. Like she's guilted him into being some sort of replacement companion for her or something.

"We hear versions of this story a lot here at New Horizons, Daniel," Mr. Martin says. "Your experience is very common, and there's actually a term for it. We call boys like you Kitchen Window Boys. Have you ever heard that term before?"

"No."

"It refers to boys who sit in their mothers' kitchen windows, watching all the other boys playing ball outside, wishing they could join them. But they can't because of a sense of guilt or responsibility, or even embarrassment that they're not physically developing into a man as quickly as the other boys."

Daniel thinks about that and nods. "Yeah. That's me."

"I'm going to have you do two healing exercises, Daniel, if that's okay with you?"

Hey, that's not fair. Why does Daniel get to say whether it's okay with him or not and none of the rest of us did?

He nods, though he looks a little unsure.

"The first exercise is a role-play." Mr. Martin calls up me and Matthew. "Lexi is going to play your mother and Matthew is a neighborhood boy coming over to see if you want to go play outside."

Mr. Martin hands me an apron, a pot, and a wooden spoon. I guess I'm supposed to be in a kitchen. I put the apron on and stir the inside of the empty pot, feeling utterly ridiculous. Daniel is sitting on the floor next to me, miming peeling potatoes. Matthew enters the scene and knocks on the wall since there's no door.

"Hi, Daniel," he says. "A bunch of us are gonna go play soccer down at the park and we wanted to see if you would come play with us."

Daniel hesitates and then says, "Sure."

I guess that's my cue. I turn and say, "No, sweetie. Mommy needs you to stay here." I try to ignore the pangs of guilt I feel as I say it, but I'm not very successful.

Daniel swallows and raises his head a notch. "No, Mom. I'm going to go play with my friends. I'll be back in time for dinner." He takes a few steps in the direction of the imaginary door and then turns back. "I love you, Mom," he says quietly. And then he and Matthew leave the scene.

"Fantastic!" Mr. Martin commends, and dismisses me and Matthew. "Now, for part two, we need to address what your father did to you when he left. He left you without a male role model, which is one of the worst things a father can do to his son. You need to fight back, Daniel."

And he drags out the punching bag.

It's a very long, violent afternoon.

Chapter 12

"So, what do you guys feel like doing?" I ask.

It's our first official leisure hour, and we're in the rec cabin. A couple of the groups have settled down in front of *The Lion King*, and the other group has made its way over to the arts and crafts corner.

"I guess we could play a game?" Daniel suggests.

I look to Matthew and Carolyn.

"That works," he says at the same time she says, "Sure."

We set up the Monopoly board and Carolyn doles out the money. The colorful pieces of paper are soft and worn, and I think again about the other kids who have come through this camp, who have sat in this very seat and played this very game.

"Do you guys know anyone who's been to a camp like this before?" I say.

Carolyn shakes her head, but Daniel says yes.

We all look at him. "Really?" I say. "Who?"

"This boy at my church named Peter. He came here three summers ago and went home completely changed. He's engaged now."

"To a boy or a girl?" Matthew says, sounding dubious.

"A girl, of course. He used to be really shy—kind of like me, you know? But now he's so confident. He always says how he'll never be able to thank Mr. Martin enough."

"Wow," I say. Kaylee, Mr. Martin, and now Peter—all living proof that it really can work. "What about you, Matthew? Have you met anyone who's come to a place like this?"

"Nope," he says, rolling the dice and moving the top hat nine spaces to Connecticut Avenue. "I'll buy it!" He hands his money over to Carolyn and looks at me. "Why, have you?"

"No. I was just curious. There's this lady in our church whose grandnephew came here once, but I've never met him." I throw the dice and move the shoe to Reading Railroad.

"That's two hundred dollars," Carolyn says. "Want to buy it?"

I actually have a Monopoly strategy, and railroads aren't part of it. My system is to concentrate my money in one place—buy up all the properties of one color and then start piling houses and hotels on them like nobody's business so I can sit back and collect the rent—rather than spreading it thin around the board.

But Carolyn's face is expectant, waiting for my answer, and before I know it, I'm saying, "Sure." And then I immediately feel like an idiot, because this is just a game and it's not like she cares if I buy a stupid railroad or not.

My fingers brush against hers as we exchange the money for the title deed. It's the first time we've ever touched, and a tremor of excitement shoots through me. I can't help it—I look for a sign that she notices too. Her cheeks get a little pinker maybe, but that could be because it's so damn hot in this cabin. Other than that, there's nothing.

Of course. Because it *was* nothing. A half-second-long accidental touch. At a camp where we both came, voluntarily, to learn how to be straight. I really need to stop forgetting that—it's kind of an important detail.

Daniel's Scottie dog lands on St. Charles Place.

I clear my throat in an effort to clear my mind and focus on tidying my money piles. Then I notice Matthew watching me, an amused smile on his face.

"What?" I say. Oh God, he didn't see me getting all stupid over Carolyn just now, did he?

The smile turns into a full-on grin and he shrugs innocently. "Nothing. Nothing at all."

Crap. He saw.

• • •

An hour later, nearly every property Matthew owns is mortgaged, and Daniel keeps landing in jail, but Carolyn and I are at all-out *war*. I have hotels on all the green and yellow properties, and Carolyn has control of Boardwalk and Park Place. She also owns Kentucky Avenue—which I need so I can start building on the red properties.

When it gets to be my turn, I make her an offer. "I'll give you four hundred dollars for Kentucky Avenue."

She laughs and shakes her head. "No way."

"But you don't even need it! You own half the board already. And four hundred is a really good offer—it's only worth two-twenty!"

"Not gonna happen," she says, smirking.

"Okay, six hundred."

"Nope."

"Seven?"

She shakes her head, a twinkle in her eye.

Arrghh! "Seven-fifty plus Baltic and Mediterranean Avenues."

"Those properties are crap."

I study her, sitting there all smug, leaning back in her chair with her arms crossed over her chest. "Fine. Name your price."

She leans forward, her eyes level with mine. "I want all your railroads plus all your properties that have developments on them."

"Are you crazy? There's no way for me to win then."

"Exactly."

I pick up the dice. "Forget it. No deal."

Carolyn shrugs. "Suit yourself."

I roll the dice—and land on Boardwalk, which has four houses on it.

"That will be one thousand seven hundred dollars, please," Carolyn says, holding out her hand.

I glower at her. "You don't have to be so *happy* about it, you know."

Carolyn laughs. "What's the point of winning then?"

• • •

The next morning, I wake up early again. I lie in bed for a while, trying to make myself go back to sleep, but it's no use. I sit up and scratch my neck where the lacy part of the nightgown rubbed against it in the night.

There's nothing to do—I'm not allowed to leave the dorm, I don't have my book anymore, and everyone (except for Carolyn, who is already out on her run) is asleep so there's no one to talk to. I guess I could get up and take a shower, but the sooner I do that the sooner I have to change into the skorts.

I slide my journal off my vanity and flip to a clean sheet of paper. The first few pages are already filled with sketches, but this time, when I put the pen to the page, words come out. I'm usually not much of a writer. I've always expressed myself better with pictures and designs. But so much has happened over the past few days that I need a way to get it all out, and drawings aren't enough right now. So I write.

I fill page after page with the stuff I've been keeping inside since I came to New Horizons: my resolve to be just like Kaylee, how glad I am to have made a friend in Matthew, the guilt I feel over promising to forget my father.

It feels good to get it all out. Like by taking the abstract, wooshy thoughts that have been floating around formless within me and transforming them into words on a page, they become more real. I know Brianna said that no one would ever read this journal, which is why I'm even writing any of it down in the first place, but the simple fact that it exists in the physical world now and that it theoretically could be read by someone other than me makes me feel like all these thoughts and feelings have actual substance and validity.

I hope Mom is all right,

I write.

I wish I could call her. They would tell me if something happened, wouldn't they? If she had a zoning out episode and drove her car into the ocean or something?

Carolyn breezes into the room, fresh from her run. She gives me a little wave and then disappears into the bathroom.

My pen hovers over the journal in suspended animation. I can almost feel it: every feeling and thought I've ever had about her coursing from my mind, down my arm, through my lightning bolt, and into the pen. It's charged with electricity.

The pen lands on the page again, and I let it all out.

Chapter 13

I'd hoped that once I got all my feelings about Carolyn written down, they would stay safely tucked away inside the journal and out of my head. But when I was done writing, I sat back and looked at the pages.

And that's when I knew: I'm in trouble.

I had been spending so much time trying not to pay attention to the things I've been feeling about her that I hadn't realized just how *many* feelings for her I actually have. Writing it all down just made it all so much clearer. And now whenever I look at her, everything I wrote comes flooding back to me and I can't think about anything else.

The worst part is, I've been here before.

After I fell for Zoë, thoughts of her dictated my life. I made a point of sitting next to her at our lunch table every day. I would look forward to parties if I knew she was going to be there. I chose my outfits every day based on what I thought she would like.

And in a way, it worked. We became really good friends. We

took the same classes and went shopping together after school and texted each other during our favorite TV shows. When my dad got sick, she was there, always ready to talk or listen or keep me supplied with fresh tissues.

And the whole time, I was in love with her.

There was never any way for that situation to end well.

I can't let history repeat itself. So I do the only thing I can think to do—I ignore Carolyn.

If I don't talk to her, I won't find myself asking her questions just to hear her answers.

There's this little fluttery thrill that goes through me whenever she laughs or smiles at something I say,

I wrote in the journal.

It feels amazing. I want it to happen more, so I keep trying to think of things to say to her, but I have to remember not to go too far and ask her something too personal, like whether she's ever kissed anybody before. Even though I really want to know.

If I don't look at her, I won't think about how pretty she is. I won't stare at her hands and wonder what it would be like to touch them again, for longer this time.

She's the only girl in this whole damn camp who can make this absurd outfit look good. Actually, I bet she's the only girl in the world who can.

If I don't pay attention to her at all, I won't fixate on the slightly unfamiliar way she forms her words, wondering if everyone from the Northeast speaks the way she does or if it's just her.

I love how patiently she listens to Matthew's rants about New Horizons and reparative therapy and how he thinks we're all crazy for actually wanting it to work. And I love how she's always doing nice things for people, like offering to go get Daniel a new fork when he drops his on the floor or discreetly whispering to Melissa that she has a lint ball on the back of her sweater.

If I just ignore her, maybe all of this will just...fade away.

I spend all of breakfast looking anywhere but at Carolyn and giving the barest, most minimal responses when she talks to me. I'm sure she's noticed the sudden shift in my behavior—I'm not being very subtle about it—but I don't know what else to do. This crush *cannot* continue.

Complicating matters is that Matthew hasn't forgotten what he saw yesterday. He hasn't said anything about it directly, but it's written all over his face. Every time I catch his eye, he's ready with a knowing grin or a teasing eyebrow waggle in Carolyn's direction. My inner torment is *fun* for him. I want to tell him to cut it out, but there's never a moment where we're alone, out of Carolyn and Daniel's range of hearing—Mr. Martin's rules have made sure of that. So I settle for throwing him the severest looks I can muster, but if he gets my meaning, he doesn't show it.

Breakfast seems to last forever.

• • •

It's the final day of the Father Wound exercise. Thank God.

But that means it's Carolyn's day to be subjected to the wrath of Mr. Martin. He calls her name, and I want to reach out and squeeze her hand and tell her it will be okay, like Matthew did for me. But touching her is definitely not part of Operation Crush the Crush.

She sits in the dreaded chair, and Mr. Martin begins rattling off the usual family and childhood questions. But she stops him.

"It was my cousin," she whispers. I can feel the surprise in the room—up until now, no one has interrupted Mr. Martin's interrogation process.

Mr. Martin blinks. "What was your cousin?"

If it's possible for a person to look embarrassed but confident at the exact same time, that's what Carolyn looks like right now. She knows exactly what she's saying, but it's hard for her to say it. "My Father Wound. He did it."

Mr. Martin's face takes on that condescending look that he's so good at. "Carolyn, I appreciate your willingness to jump right into the exercise like this, but I really think we should discuss your immediate family firs—"

The blue of Carolyn's eyes turns icy. "You said we were doing this exercise as one big group so we could maybe find parts of ourselves in other people's stories, right? Well, I've been sitting here for the last three days doing that."

I've never seen her like this, so strong and determined. I like it.

But then her expression becomes less sure. "But…even though I know *what* my Father Wound is, I just…don't know *how* it factors in. To, you know, me being here. I need your help with that."

Mr. Martin thinks for a moment and then nods. It seems being asked for help has appeased his initial displeasure at having the course of his session hijacked. "Very well. Please, tell us about your cousin."

"His name is Kenny." It's like it hurts her to say the name. "He's three years older than me. And…when I was younger, and our parents left us alone together, he would make comments about… well, about my body."

"What kind of comments?"

Carolyn's face turns crimson. "You know…sexual comments. About the way I was developing."

"Did he ever touch you?"

"He tried to. He would snap the strap of my training bra, acting like he was just teasing, but he pulled on it so hard that I knew he was trying to get it off. Or he would accidentally-on-purpose bump into me and rub against my chest. A few times, I saw his erection through his pants." A fresh blush spreads over her cheeks. "Whenever he got like that, I would run to find my mom in the other room or lock myself in the bathroom."

"Did you tell your parents?"

Carolyn shakes her head. "He's my mother's sister's kid. My mother and my aunt are really close. I would never do anything to come between them."

"When did this all start?"

"When I was seven."

"Is it still going on?"

"No. He went away to college in Scotland, so I haven't seen him in over a year. And the last couple of times I saw him, he stayed away." She gives a labored shrug. "Maybe he finally lost interest. Or maybe he realized that I'm strong enough to fight back now."

I'm vaguely aware of Matthew watching me from the corner of his eye, but I can't pay attention to him right now. I can't focus on anything except Carolyn. All I want is to run up there and wrap my arms around her and comfort her and keep her safe and not let go, not ever.

"Well, Carolyn," Mr. Martin says, "it's clear your cousin's treatment of you caused you to hate men."

Carolyn looks surprised. "I don't know about *that*..."

"It's true. You don't trust men. You aren't comfortable around them."

"But I *do* trust some men. My dad and my brother, my friends at school…"

"Your father and brother don't count. And as for your friends at school, have you ever viewed any of them as having the potential to be *more* than just a friend?"

Carolyn frowns. "No."

"That's because your cousin taught you to negatively associate men and sexuality." Once again, he speaks as if he were the absolute authority on everything, as if he were all-knowing—as if he were God.

"Oh," Carolyn says, understanding dawning on her. "So the way Kenny treated me is the reason I don't feel attracted to boys."

"Yes," Mr. Martin says.

She looks up at him with pleading eyes. "Do you think we can fix it?"

Mr. Martin smiles. "I know we can."

The rest of Carolyn's session consists of her beating the hell out of Matthew, also known as Kenny the Cousin, with the Nerf bat. But unlike the other sessions that involved the bat, Mr. Martin never replaces it with the punching bag. Instead, he makes Carolyn hit Matthew until Matthew runs out of the cabin and slams the door behind him. Mr. Martin claims this symbolically represents Carolyn evicting Kenny from her life. Now that the door has been closed on him, it can never be reopened.

She's exhausted and out of breath, and her hair is a sweaty mess, but she actually seems happy, more at peace than any of the rest of us after our Father Wound sessions. She comes back to her seat, and I forget that I'm supposed to be ignoring her. She looks right at me with a huge, contented smile as if to say, *Can you believe it? I'm finally going to have the life I've always wanted! This is the best day ever!*

I hold her gaze, and my brain scrambles to meld everything I've just learned about her with everything I already knew.

Carolyn has been frightened and toyed with and abused; after all that's happened to her, she should have no hope left at all. But she does. Look at her right now—clearly, she does. Somehow, she still sees the good in people.

But her unparalleled optimism is only one half of her. The other half is filled with strength. Instead of feeling sorry for herself and blaming Kenny for ruining her life, she went and did something about it. She became an athlete, tough enough to stand up for herself and fight back if it ever came to that.

God knows I've been staring at her pretty much nonstop since the moment I first saw her, but right now, it's like I'm really *seeing* her for the first time.

I got my tattoo after falling in love with Zoë. Lightning never strikes the same place twice, and I knew that I would never feel that way about anyone else as long as I lived.

But I was wrong.

For the second time in my life, I've been hit by lightning.

Chapter 14

Why do I keep doing this? I've fallen for someone I can't have, in a place where we can never be together. This is *exactly* what happened with Zoë.

Not exactly, a tiny part of me says. *Carolyn likes girls too.*

The thought gives me pause, but I quickly shake it off. We're at a *de-gayifying camp*, for crying out loud. I'm still here for a reason. And so is she.

Luckily, the dinner conversation is dominated by Matthew, who is on some tirade about something called the Kinsey Scale, so I don't have to talk much. I'm a little afraid of what I'll say, given that all I can think about is this impossible situation I've gotten myself into. Matthew is already onto me, but the last thing I need right now is for Daniel or, God forbid, Carolyn to catch on to my recent revelation.

I'm still stuck in my own head when, after dinner, we all walk over to the rec cabin. It takes me a minute to realize everyone's staring at me, waiting for my answer to some question I didn't hear.

"I'm sorry. What?" I say, blinking out of my haze.

"Do-you-want-to-do-arts-and-crafts?" Matthew says, over-enunciating each word like I don't understand English or something.

"Oh. Uh, sure. Whatever." I start in the direction of the crafts corner.

"Actually, guys, I think I'm going to just go read a while. If that's okay with you," Carolyn says. She holds up my copy of *The Great Gatsby*. There's a bookmark sticking up out of it, about halfway through the book. She's been reading it? When? Maybe during our journal-writing time before bed? Or in the mornings before her run?

"Suit yourself," Matthew says, shrugging.

Carolyn curls up on one of the rec room couches, and the rest of us plunk down in front of the plastic bins filled with art supplies.

"If you had to place yourself on the Kinsey Scale, Daniel, where would you be?" Matthew asks, drizzling Elmer's glue across a sheet of red construction paper. "Pass the glitter, Lexi?"

"Um…I don't know," Daniel says. He's staring intently down at his own paper, but whether he's actually trying to figure out something to make or just trying to avoid answering Matthew's question, I can't tell.

"I'm definitely a six," Matthew says.

"What does six mean?" I ask. The charcoal pencil in my hand is moving confidently across the white of my paper.

Matthew gives a sigh of exasperation. "Weren't you paying attention to *anything* we were talking about at dinner?"

"Sorry. I've got a lot on my mind."

"Clearly." Matthew's eyes dart to Carolyn, and I make a point of studying my sketch. What started out as a halter top has morphed into an evening gown. I add some embellishments around the waist. "*Anyway*, the Scale is zero to six. Zero is one hundred percent straight; six is one hundred percent gay. But Kinsey's research showed that most people are somewhere between one and five."

I look up. "Really?"

"Sexuality isn't black and white, Lexi. It's a whole lot of gray. Despite what *they'd* have us believe." Matthew nods his head over at Brianna and John, who are sitting at another table, sipping coffee out of oversized mugs.

"But not for you?" I say.

"Huh?"

"You said you're a six. That's a hundred percent gay, right? Not much gray area there."

Matthew smiles. "Shut up, smarty pants." He blows the excess glitter off of his paper and holds it up for Daniel and me to see. It's a disco ball.

"Oh yeah," I say. "Definitely a six."

Matthew shakes his paper over my head and glitter rains down everywhere. I shriek and push him away, laughing. Then Matthew goes after Daniel with the still-wet disco ball and within seconds, the three of us are hysterical, glitter and glue everywhere, covering our clothing, the crafts table, even pirouetting slowly through the thick summer air. Daniel grabs a container of multicolored feathers and empties it all over Matthew, so that Matthew looks like a psychedelic seagull. Daniel's face is lit up—it's the first time I've actually seen him look happy.

Brianna appears out of nowhere. "What is going on over here?"

"Nothing," I say quickly, brushing glitter off my sweater.

"Just having a little fun," Matthew says, still giggling. "That's not against the rules, is it?"

Brianna stares us down for a long moment. "No, I suppose not. But please clean up this mess." She looks pointedly at me. "You have glitter in your hair, Alexis. Get rid of it before you go back to the dorms—we don't need you tracking that stuff all over the camp."

I remove my hair clips and work my fingers through my hair to dislodge the little flecks of shimmer. "Why do you call me Alexis?" I ask. It's been bothering me since my first day here, and I figure now's as good a time as any to ask. At least it will help me keep my mind off that other thing.

"Because it's your name."

"Technically, yeah. But no one calls me that."

One corner of her mouth turns down slightly. "Alexis is your Christian name, the name you were given at birth. When people change their names, it's just another way to go against what God intended you to be when you were born."

"Like being gay," I say, putting the pieces together.

"Like acting on same-sex attraction, yes."

"But come on, even you have to admit that going by a nickname isn't even close to the same thing as having SSA." I give a little smile.

To my intense surprise, Brianna's stony façade cracks and she actually smiles back. It's small, but it's there. "I guess you could say they're on different levels, yeah."

We share a strange moment of almost laughter, but then it's gone as quickly as it arrived and I wonder if I imagined it. She crosses her arms, the mask back in place.

I sigh. "You're still not going to call me Lexi, are you?"

"No, Alexis, I'm not." And with another hand gesture reminding us to get the crafts area cleaned up, she leaves us.

• • •

On the way back to the main cabin, Carolyn sidles up next to me. "You have glitter on your face," she says with a grin.

I swipe at my cheeks. "Is it gone?"

She shakes her head. "Want some help?"

My heart leaps into my throat, but I manage a small nod.

She looks around to make sure no one is looking, and then her thumb brushes across my cheekbone, leaving a trail of heat behind. She holds her hand out. "Make a wish."

"Like an eyelash?"

"Yup."

"Okay." I stop walking, give my wish a moment to take shape, and blow the specks of glitter away from Carolyn's fingers. I look up to find her watching me carefully.

"What did you wish for?" she whispers, her eyes burning into mine.

And then it's just the two of us, sharing a moment more real than anything I've experienced, maybe ever. She stares at me almost pleadingly, like my answer is the key to some puzzle she's desperately trying to solve.

I don't know what it is that she's not saying, but whatever it is fills me with something pretty damn close to joy.

And then the moment passes, and I pull my eyes away from hers and resume walking. "If I tell you, it won't come true." And I really, really want it to come true.

When we get back to the dorm, Brianna makes an announcement. "Everyone, please collect your journals and bring them up to the front of the room."

Terror tackles me like a tidal wave. What does she mean? What does she want with our journals?

"Are you going to read them?" Melissa asks.

"Yes."

"But I thought you said they were private!"

"I said you didn't have to share them with your group, Melissa. I didn't say anything about the counselors. We don't get much one-on-one time with you, so we use the journals as a way to track your individual progress. We'll be collecting them once a week."

Shit. She did say that. And I misinterpreted it the same way

Melissa did. I don't know why I'm surprised—Brianna probably worded it that way on purpose, trying to trick us.

The girls reluctantly retrieve their marble notebooks and line up to hand them off to Brianna. I grip on to mine so hard that my hands start to shake. Or maybe they're shaking because of the sheer panic that is racing through me right now.

I can't believe this is happening again. What was I *thinking*, writing about Carolyn in the journal after what happened with Mom and the Zoë sketchbook? Stupid, stupid, stupid. Now Brianna and Mr. Martin are going to know everything. Maybe they'll even move me to another group, to keep me as far away from her as possible.

I turn away from Brianna and quickly tear the offending pages from the book. I cough to muffle the sound of the ripping paper, but there's no way to hide the fact that pages have been removed—the sewn binding of the marble notebook doesn't allow for that. They'll know something was torn out. But it's better than the alternative.

"Alexis? We're just waiting on you," Brianna says.

I spin around, the extracted pages crumpled tight in my fist, and hand the book over to Brianna, my heart beating violently.

"Thank you," Brianna says and leaves the room armed with the eight journals. It's Barbara's night to be on dorm duty.

I'm last in line for the bathrooms, but even though the wait is long and my hand is cramping, I don't dare open my fist. Like Mr. Martin said that first day, there are eyes everywhere. All it would take is for one person to ask what's in my hand, and in seconds, the whole dorm would know everything.

When I finally get into the bathroom, I lock the door behind me and pry my hand open. My fingers have gone numb, and creases have been dug into them from the crumpled up ball of paper, but as quickly as my fumbling hands will go, I tear the pages into confetti-sized pieces and flush them down the toilet. Soon it's like they never existed.

I splash cold water on my face and lean against the sink. That was close. Too close.

"What are you *doing*?" I whisper to my pale, dripping reflection.

But the only answer I have to give myself is: *I have absolutely no idea.*

Chapter 15

"Why is no one up?!" a voice pierces through the depths of my sleep.

I squeeze my eyes more tightly shut and pull the blanket up over my head. It took a long time to fall asleep last night; my head was too busy revolving with thoughts of Mom and Dad and Carolyn and Zoë. I couldn't have gotten more than a couple of hours of sleep at the most.

I wish I were back in my bed at home, in my own clothes, wasting my summer vacation by sleeping until noon every single day.

"We're already running late," Brianna says, her voice even more irritated than usual. "Chop, chop." She claps her hands.

I rub my eyes and sit up. Brianna and Carolyn are the only ones up and dressed. I check the time—it's 8:10 a.m., forty minutes after we're usually woken up by the counselor on dorm duty. But I guess Barbara slept through her alarm. Three cheers for old people—I really needed the extra sleep today.

We get dressed in a hurry and head downstairs to meet the boys.

But Brianna asks me to hold back a moment. "I noticed there were some missing pages in your journal," she says once we're alone.

Wow, that was fast. What did she do, stay up all night reading them? I try to stay cool. "Oh. Yeah."

"What happened to them?"

"To the missing pages?"

"Yes, Alexis," she says impatiently. "What happened to the missing pages?"

"I tore them out."

"I realize that. What I would like to know is why."

I use the one lie I was able to come up with last night that didn't sound completely unbelievable. "They were drawings I started, but they weren't coming out right, so I threw them out."

She purses her lips. "That's another thing I wanted to talk to you about. The journal is not a sketchbook. It's for writing and writing only."

"Oh. Why?"

"Because we use the journals to track your progress, and we can't do that if you don't actually write anything."

Actually, you *can* tell a hell of a lot from looking at a drawing— that's how Mom found out about me, isn't it? But I'm so relieved that Brianna's dropped the whole torn-out-pages thing that I'll go along with anything. "Of course." I nod. "I understand."

"Good. Now let's catch up with the others. We have a big day today."

• • •

"Do you guys know what free association is?" Kaylee asks us. We're in the carpet cabin again, but today we're split up into our groups of four. Kaylee's standing in front of an easel with a large white pad on it, an uncapped marker in her hand. There's an oversized beanbag chair sitting in the middle of our circle.

"Isn't it when you blurt out the first thing that comes into your head? Like: Abs! Lube! Ryan Gosling!" Matthew says.

Kaylee sighs. "Sort of. It's a psychoanalytic technique which encourages patients not to censor their thoughts and to say whatever they're thinking based on different prompts. So, for example, if I say 'dog,' what is the first thing that comes into your mind, Carolyn?"

"Um, cat?"

"Good! And, Daniel, if I say 'apple,' you say…?"

"Pie!" Daniel shouts out, excited.

Kaylee laughs. "Nice. So we're going to use that concept as the jumping off point for today's exercise. We'll use the free association to try to access your deep-rooted hopes and dreams, and then we'll take that foundation to build a vibrant, clear picture of what your lives can and will be like after you graduate from the program at the end of the summer. So as the exercise goes on, I may start asking you more specific questions. Sound good?"

Carolyn, Daniel, and I nod. Matthew laughs.

"Let's start with you, Lexi. Go ahead and lie down on the beanbag. Get as comfy as you want."

She doesn't have to tell me twice—I love beanbag chairs. I had a bunch in my playroom when I was a kid. I used to lie there all day long, drawing and painting. Mom and Dad were constantly picking little Styrofoam balls off my clothes.

I fall butt-first onto the beanbag and then shimmy around to get the stuffing to mold perfectly to my body. It feels safe, familiar. I close my eyes.

"So, Lexi," Kaylee says. "I'm going to write down everything you say on this pad, so don't worry about keeping track of your thoughts. Just let your mind roam as uninhibited as possible and then, once we're done, you'll have time to look at what we've come up with."

"Okay," I say.

"Place," she says, beginning the exercise.

"The beach," I say immediately, and I hear the squeak of Kaylee's marker on the easel.

"Which beach?"

"The beach at home."

"How does the beach make you feel?"

"Happy," I say.

"Name three things about the beach that make you happy."

"Sitting in the surf and not being able to hear anything except the rush of the waves; staring at the point where the world disappears off the horizon; watching the fat seagulls scavenge for people food." I've been thinking about the beach a lot lately. I miss it.

"Is the beach where you see yourself living after you're done with school?" Kaylee asks.

"Definitely."

"In South Carolina?"

"Or Florida," I say automatically. But wait—the point of this exercise is to think big, right? I sink further into the chair's squishy beans and let my mind expand. "Or maybe Hawaii. Or the South of France! It would be cool to be fluent in French."

"Where will you learn?" Kaylee asks, a smile in her voice.

"I take French in school already, but maybe I could start taking extra classes on the weekend too." That's not a bad idea actually.

"What kind of home will you live in?" Kaylee shoots back.

"A loft," I hear myself say. Strange that's the first thing I thought of. I've never even seen a loft apartment in real life before. "With lots of open space and four walls of floor-to-ceiling windows and a terrace where you can open the doors and let the ocean air come in."

"When will you move?"

"After college."

"Where will you go to college?"

"Paris." That one I knew already.

"And what will you study?"

"Fashion design."

"What type of fashion design?" The quicker Kaylee's questions come, the more I'm lulled into a rhythm—instead of thinking with my head, I'm answering with my heart.

"Women's street wear, retro eighties meets twenty-first-century technology."

"What will you do with these skills once you graduate?"

"I'll start my own line." Whoa. I hadn't known I wanted to do that until the words popped out of my mouth. I always imagined myself working for an established designer or label. But now that I've said it, it feels right.

My eyes are still closed, but I pick up on Kaylee's slight hesitation before throwing out the next question. Oh right, women aren't supposed to work out of the home. We haven't gotten to the gray area yet. "Let's move on," she says. "What will your family life look like?"

"It's just me and my mom," I say.

"Right now, yes. But in the future, who will be by your side?"

"I would love to have kids," I say. Again, something else I never gave a whole lot of serious thought to—at least, not before New Horizons, not before Carolyn admitted that's what she wants. An image pops into my mind unbidden. "Two boys and a girl. My mom will live with us too, and she'll be happy and laughing all the time and spoil her grandkids rotten. The kids will all have cute little French accents and play soccer and have bright blond hair, like their mo—"

I clamp my mouth shut and propel myself out of dreamland and back to the land of rational thought. I was going to say, "Like their mother." But I'm clearly not blond. In this perfect little fantasy, these kids had two moms, and one of them was blond haired and blue eyed.

"Like their dad," I say instead. Matthew clears his throat, acknowledging my slipup. Does nothing get past this guy?

"What is their dad like?" Kaylee asks.

I go on to describe my perfect man, the handsome Frenchman who owns a five-star restaurant and is an Olympic rower. But for all intents and purposes, the exercise is over. I'm giving Kaylee the answers I know she wants to hear. I stopped being true to myself the moment I forced the image of Carolyn out of my mind and replaced her with some cookie-cutter French dude.

When I finally run out of steam, Kaylee asks me to open my eyes and take a look at the list we made. "This is not just your utopia, Lexi," she says. "If you want it badly enough, it can be your actual future. God gives us the tools to live our very best lives—we just have to use them." She tears the pages off the giant pad and hands them to me.

Daniel, Matthew, and Carolyn take their turns on the free association beanbag, but I only half listen. I stare at the pages in my hands, covered with Kaylee's bubbly handwriting.

Wow. France, a family, my own line…and my mom there for all of it. I suddenly realize this *is* what I want, what I've always wanted, even through all that time back home when all I'd been able to think about was keeping my secret. This is my utopia.

I mean, yes, there's the tiny issue of a husband in the place where I'd rather see a wife, but if having a husband is the key to having my mother back—happy, healthy, and alive—and to living my dream…well, then I just need to work harder at this whole becoming straight thing, don't I? Boys aren't *that* bad when you think about it.

• • •

After lunch, we go to the classroom cabin for Bible study.

People back home quote the Bible like it's a pop song constantly stuck in their heads. And most of it's actually pretty decent: thou shalt not steal; love thy neighbor as thyself; honor thy father and mother; a merry heart does good like a medicine but a broken spirit dries the bones.

But those aren't the passages Mr. Martin chooses to focus on.

"Leviticus eighteen, verse twenty-two," Mr. Martin says. "Luke, would you please read aloud?"

"'You must not have sexual intercourse with a male as one has sexual intercourse with a woman. It is a detestable act,'" Luke mumbles.

"And, Daniel, would you read Leviticus twenty, verse thirteen to us?" Mr. Martin asks.

Daniel does him one better—he recites it from memory. "'If a man has sexual intercourse with a male as one has sexual intercourse with a woman, the two of them have committed an abomination. They must be put to death. Their blood guilt is on themselves.'"

Put to *death*? I thought God was supposed to be all about forgiveness, not the death penalty.

"Very good, Daniel," Mr. Martin says.

While Mr. Martin explains the verses—even though we're already aware of *exactly* what they mean—Matthew passes a note to me. **What do you think would happen if a guy and a girl got caught having sex here?**

I smile and write, Sorry, you're not exactly my type. I pass it back.

His eyes bug out of his head, and I have to stifle a laugh. He scrawls a long response. **That wasn't an invitation, you crazy person. And believe me, I know who your type is.** I glance at him and he nods his head in Carolyn's direction. My face gets hot and I quickly turn my attention back to his note. **I just meant what do you think would happen? I bet they'd give us a hundred gold stars.**

He's probably right. Even though I'm pretty certain that the Bible condemns any kind of sex before marriage, I get the feeling that if a guy and a girl got caught in the act here at New Horizons, the counselors would never be prouder.

"Corinthians six, verses nine through eleven," Mr. Martin says. "Rachael, would you please read aloud?"

"'Do you not know that the unrighteous will not inherit the kingdom of God?'" Rachael reads. "'Do not be deceived! The sexually immoral, idolaters, adulterers, passive homosexual partners, practicing homosexuals, thieves, the greedy, drunkards, the verbally abusive, and swindlers will not inherit the kingdom of God. Some of you once lived this way. But you were washed, you were sancti-fied, you were justified in the name of the Lord Jesus Christ and by the Spirit of our God.'"

"Yes!" Mr. Martin shouts, his palms raised to heaven. Suddenly he's turned into a Baptist preacher. "Yes! That's exactly it! *That's* what we're here for! The homosexuals will not inherit the kingdom of God. But if you wash yourselves clean, if you *reject* those impulses, you will be *justified* in the name of the Lord Jesus Christ!" Mr. Martin sinks into a chair with a deep sigh and wipes his forehead. "You know," he says, talking in his normal voice again, "in many ways, I envy you all."

"*You* envy *us*?" I say before I can stop myself. "But you just said we should all be put to death!"

He shakes his head. "No, no, Lexi, you misunderstand me. The Bible says that those who are sanctified are exempt from that punishment. You're all here for that very reason—to be saved. *That's* why I envy you. You're changing your paths at such a young age. I wasn't so lucky. It took me a long time to find my way."

He seems like he's in a mood to talk, and I'm curious. "What happened?" I ask.

He glances at Brianna. It's almost like he's asking her for permis-sion to continue. But that doesn't make sense. *He's* the one in charge here, not her. But only after she nods slightly does he continue.

"I lived the homosexual lifestyle for a long time," he admits. "I refused to listen to my parents when they tried to talk to me about right and wrong and my responsibility to God. I thought I had it all figured out. I left home when I was eighteen years old and didn't return until I was thirty-five."

Whoa. Mr. Martin was out and proud for *seventeen years*?

"So what changed?" Matthew asks.

"I was saved by Jesus. He spoke to me, and his voice was so clear, it was as though he was right there in the room with me. He told me he had a bigger plan for me. I went home to my family, and they reintroduced me to the church. Two years later, I married Nancy and started New Horizons. I don't want you to make the same mistake I made. Don't wait seventeen years to make the right decision. Make the choice to inherit God's kingdom *now*."

Daniel raises his hand. "How did you do it, Mr. Martin? I want to do exactly what you did."

As Mr. Martin goes off about how he went to church every single night and stopped listening to secular music and started only going to female doctors and hairdressers, I find myself tuning him out and tuning Carolyn in. She's a few desks down from me, diligently taking notes, her hair tucked behind one ear, revealing the birthmark on her temple.

Mr. Martin said we have to make the choice to "inherit God's kingdom," which, for me, means I have to make the choice to not love Carolyn. But I thought I'd already done that. I tried ignoring her. I tried focusing on all the reasons I'm here, all the reasons I need this program to work. I've done everything I'm supposed to. But here I am, fantasizing about pressing my lips against Carolyn's birthmark.

If New Horizons is, like Kaylee said, the tool God gave me to create a better life, I'm pretty sure I'm using it wrong.

Chapter 16

Later that night, Carolyn gives me back my book.

"Wow, you finished it already?" I ask.

"Yeah, I pretty much devoured it." She laughs. "I can't believe I'd never read it before."

"I know, so good, right?"

She nods. "*So* good." There's a pause, and then she says, "So, um, I hope you don't mind, but I marked my favorite part. In pencil, don't worry."

Mind? I'm suddenly giddy—I get to find out what her favorite part of my favorite book is! I begin to flip through the pages. "Which part?" I say, but she stops me. Her hand rests on mine, and this time it's deliberate. And she doesn't move it away. My mouth suddenly goes very dry.

"Wait until the next time you read it," she says. "It'll be like a little surprise."

I just nod, because I'm incapable of speech right now. We're practically holding hands!

She smiles and walks away, her ponytail swinging behind her.

I change into my nightgown, dive into bed, and quickly write some nonspecific crap in my journal about the Bible study day being interesting. I've learned my lesson. From now on my *real* feelings are staying where they should have stayed all along—locked securely away inside my head.

I close the journal and look at the clock—fifteen more minutes before lights out. I grab *The Great Gatsby*. Like a kid who knows where her parents hid the Christmas gifts, I'm faced with a moral dilemma: skip ahead to the big reveal or revel in the anticipation?

I choose option B and start on page one.

• • •

Because my reading time is so limited, I don't get to Carolyn's favorite part until two nights later.

There's a bracket marked around one short paragraph on page 24—a paragraph I've honestly never given much thought to. It's when Daisy is telling Nick about the birth of her daughter. She says she wept when she found out she'd had a girl, and that she hopes she'll be a fool, because a beautiful little fool is the best thing a girl can be in this world.

I read the paragraph over and over, trying to devise some meaning, some clue as to why *this*, of all the amazing moments and quotes in the book, is Carolyn's favorite. I stare at the page, desperate for this clue into Carolyn's mind.

By the time the prayers are said and the lights are turned out, I'm no closer to an answer. Even though I don't know why Carolyn's favorite part is her favorite part, I still love knowing that it's her favorite part. And I want her to know mine. I use the small ration of moonlight shining through my window to underline a passage of my own.

I give the book back to Carolyn the next morning. She takes it but stares at me, confused.

"I thought it would only be fair for you to know my favorite part too," I say.

She grins. "Cool. So what'd you think about mine?"

I try to come up with something smart to say, an insightful literary analysis of what F. Scott Fitzgerald was trying to say by having Daisy wish for her daughter to be foolish, something to show that I completely understand why that line spoke to Carolyn so much…but I fail miserably. "Honestly," I say, defeated, "I have no idea what to think. I don't really get it."

Carolyn laughs and explains as we go downstairs to meet the boys. "I just love how Daisy totally *gets* the whole societal-pressure thing. Like, back in the twenties, a woman could be one of two things: a subservient wife or a carefree airhead. But Daisy isn't either of those things—she's too smart. So she doesn't fit in, you know?"

"Yeah." I'm hanging on her every word.

"But even she knows there's no point in fighting the gender roles that have already been set up by society. So it's all she can do to wish that her daughter fits into the mold, because her life will be a lot easier. Like an 'if you can't beat 'em, join 'em' kinda thing."

I'm nodding like crazy, unable to believe that I never understood that until now. *Especially* now, with all this gender stuff we're being put through. I always thought Daisy was being ridiculous, wishing for her daughter to be stupid. But what she really wants for her daughter is exactly the same thing Carolyn and I want for ourselves—to fit in.

• • •

The next day, I get the book back again. This time I don't wait—I immediately open to page 100, where my all-time favorite *Gatsby* moment is waiting.

Gatsby has been obsessed with staring across the bay at the green light at the end of Daisy's dock, as if that light were the one thing connecting him to her despite their distance. It made him feel close to her, like a part of her was right there with him whenever he gazed at it. But now that he and Daisy have finally found each other once more, the green light has gone back to being just a green light. Gatsby's *count of enchanted objects has diminished by one.*

In the margin beside the words, Carolyn has written, Amazing. Goosebumps. In a good way. ☺ PS—turn to page 56.

Her handwriting is terrible and adorable.

My heart skips a little as I flip through the pages. I feel like I'm on a scavenger hunt or something—searching for an unnamed treasure.

I get to page 56, and when I see what she's written, I laugh out loud. The other campers look at me, annoyed. Before my outburst, the room was silent, the girls scribbling away in their journals. "Is there a problem, Lexi?" Deb asks.

"Nope," I say, suppressing the giggles. "No problem. Sorry."

I glance at Carolyn—she's giggling too. I grin and press a finger to my lips.

Carolyn has underlined the line where Nick admires Gatsby's tanned skin, attractive face, and perfect haircut, and she's written, *Oh my God, Nick, why don't you just marry him already??* in the margin.

I write beneath that, *So you see it too? Nick's in love with Gatsby, right?*

Carolyn's response, the next day: *Oh, big time. Check out page 54.* And on page 54, she's marked the long paragraph where Nick does literally nothing but gush over the perfection of Gatsby's rare, understanding, reassuring, *irresistible* smile.

Jeez, Carolyn has written. *I think somebody needs an intervention!*

I write back, *I've always thought Nick was gay. You know, the way he's always describing the men as effeminate or feminine or handsome, and never paying attention to any girls except Jordan, who's sporty and "small-breasted."* The margins are too small for a comment this long so my note crosses over to the next page. *But I thought maybe it was just me projecting. And I couldn't exactly ask my English teacher! ⌣ Go to page 44.*

On page 44, I bracket off the strangest, most up-for-interpretation passage of the whole book, and write, *Did you notice this?*

…I was standing beside his bed and he was sitting up between the sheets, clad in his underwear, with a great portfolio in his hands.

Oh my God, I can't believe I missed that! Carolyn writes back. *Nick totally had sex with pale, effeminate Mr. McKee! It's all there in the ellipsis!*

Our exchange goes on like this for days. Carolyn and I can't talk about this stuff in the open, so we save these discussions for the book. Apart from that first conversation we had about Daisy's daughter, we never speak about *Gatsby* aloud. As far as everyone else at the camp knows, the only thing we use the book for is reading. No one knows about our secret method of communication.

Over time, the pages of the book become more and more marked up—asterisks, underlines, brackets, dog ears, and a huge mess of notes in the margins. But it just makes me love the book even more—it becomes *more* than just a book; it becomes a symbol of my relationship with Carolyn.

If *relationship* is even the right word. I don't really know what's going on between us. As far as I can tell, she's still fully committed to the de-gayifying and the work we do during the days, and I'm… well, I'm trying my hardest to do the same. I'm still trying to make the "choice" each day to not love her. It just keeps getting harder.

The conversation eventually moves away from Nick's sexuality and into more serious subjects. The eyes of Doctor T.J. Eckleburg, for example, bring up the subject of God.

Do you believe in God, Lexi? Carolyn asks.

Yes, I write back. Though lately I haven't been so into the idea of someone else telling me what my relationship with God should be. You?

I don't believe in anything. Atheist through and through. And churches weird me out.

You know this is a religious camp, right? :‿

If there were such a thing as a secular conversion camp, I would have gone there instead!

I go to church with my mom every Sunday. But it hasn't felt totally right since before my dad got sick. I think now the only church I really belong to is the Church of Art and Fashion.

I like that, she writes back. I guess I belong to the Church of Running. And now the Church of Gatsby. :‿

When I read that last part, an incredible warmth fills me, right down to my soul.

Chapter 17

A week goes by, then two. Each day here is a different reparative therapy session, a different exercise, a different lesson.

There are classroom sessions where we work from workbooks like the ones in French class back home, only instead of conjugating verbs *en Français*, we have to identify Jim and Sally's Father Wounds, dress them in gender-appropriate outfits, and read about them in different social situations and describe how, if we were their friends, we would help them "stay accountable."

There are days where the boys and girls are separated, where they teach us girls how to style our hair and put on makeup in "acceptably feminine" ways, and teach the boys the rules of football and how to do basic household repairs.

And there's lots of praying and there's lots of Bible study.

Some nights Kaylee gets out her guitar and leads us all in singalongs around the campfire. She's amazing—she's got a gorgeous voice and she plays the guitar like Joni Mitchell. Even though we're singing songs like "Here I Am To Worship" and "How Great Is Our

God" (if it were up to me, we'd be singing something by The Swell Season or Mates of State instead), these are some of my favorite moments at New Horizons.

While there's an obvious theme to the way the camp is conducted, the exercises are still, somehow, always surprising. The New Horizons staff has us going from day to day blindly, not knowing what's going to happen from one minute to the next. I feel like I'm blindfolded and lashing out at a piñata—who knows if I'll hit it, when I'll hit it, or what's inside.

I'm even starting to look a little different. Brianna has us giving ourselves manicures and pedicures every other day, so my usually naked nails are now perpetually shellacked in pink, and my hair is getting longer, my boring, light brown roots growing in.

I've been worrying about my mom more and more too. I hate not knowing how she's doing. I'm trying to have faith that she's still riding the high that came with my agreeing to come here and that Pastor Joe and the rest of the congregation are helping her out with anything she might need, but I'd still feel a lot better if I could call or write to her.

So one night at dinner, I finally work up the nerve to ask Mr. Martin if I can use the phone.

"I'd really like to check and make sure my mother is doing okay," I explain.

He studies me, running a hand back over his thinning hair.

"You understand we only let our campers use the phone in case of emergencies, right?"

I nod. "Because too much contact with the outside world can be a detriment to our therapy."

"That's correct."

"But I do think this qualifies as an emergency. My mother hasn't been well since my father died, and I think I would be better able to concentrate on our work here if I weren't worrying about her so much."

Mr. Martin nods. "Very well. Brianna will escort you to use the phone after supper."

A balloon pops inside me and relief whooshes out, filling me head to toe. "Thank you, Mr. Martin."

After dinner, I sit in his office with Brianna, the phone to my ear. It rings and rings, but there's no answer. When the voicemail message kicks on, I hang up and try again. Same thing. Where could she be? I leave a message, asking her to call the camp and let someone know she's okay.

Oh God, please let her be okay.

But soon, twenty-four hours have gone by, then thirty-six, and I still haven't heard anything. I'm praying more than I ever have and on the verge of collapsing into full-on panic. What if she's in the hospital? What if she's dead? What if I'm already all alone in the world and don't even know it?

I don't ask to use the phone again though. And I don't tell

anyone what's going on. Because if I say it out loud and transfer my fears onto other people, it will become way more real. It will go from a series of worries swimming around in my head to an actual possibility.

Passing the book back and forth with Carolyn is the only thing keeping me grounded. It's my lifeline—something to look forward to, something good I *know* is going to happen.

And then, at dinner two nights after I called home, Brianna comes down from the main cabin and tells me I've received a message.

I can't move.

"You mother called," she says. "She said she's just returned from a camping trip and didn't get your message until now, but she's doing fine." She walks away and gets on the food line.

The noise that comes out of me is part sob, part gasp, part screech. My eyes are wet and my throat is bone-dry all in the same instant. She's not dead. She's *doing fine.*

My whole body starts to shake as all the fear and panic I've tried to hold at bay for the past two days is let go and crashes head first into the relief and happiness still trying to grab hold inside me. I start to cry.

Mom is okay.

Carolyn, Daniel, and Matthew are watching me, silent and stunned.

"I'm sorry," I say, gasping for air, desperately trying to calm down. What was Mom doing *camping* anyway? She doesn't camp. She barely leaves the house.

"What's going on, Lexi?" Matthew asks.

And so, when I've finally got myself under control, I tell them about my mom. They've never asked about her—I get the feeling it's because after finding out that my dad died, they didn't want to upset me by asking any more family-related questions. But I want them to know, so I tell them about how she lost it when Dad died and lost it even more when she found out I was gay. "So, when it comes down to it," I say, "this is my last chance. If New Horizons doesn't work the way I need it to, I'm going to end up completely alone."

They all go quiet as they let that sink in. I guess no one knows what to say, but their silence is just as revealing as any words they could come up with. Because no one, not even Matthew, says that I'm doing the wrong thing.

One day the counselors scatter our groups across the carpet cabin so we're not in each other's way, and Mr. Martin joins our group. Even though we can't be any more interesting than any of the other groups, he always seems to find his way over to us. My theory is that it's because Matthew continues to be just as defiant about the whole de-gayifying process as he was on day one and Mr. Martin wants to keep an eye on him.

"We're going to do another role-playing exercise today," he tells us. "I call it Observe and Correct. We don't always realize that our words and body language can have unintended subtext. This exercise will help you become more aware of the subconscious signals you are giving off to others, so you can work on correcting those behaviors. So what we're going to do is play out short scenarios where you will interact with a camper of the same sex while your fellow group members watch. Afterward, they'll point out what you did wrong. Any questions?"

Matthew opens his mouth but I shake my head at him, and he closes it again.

"Carolyn and Lexi, you're up," Mr. Martin says.

Carolyn and I stand, and Mr. Martin tells us to pretend we're in a department store. I'm the shopper and Carolyn is the salesperson.

I start pretend browsing through clothes racks, and Carolyn taps my shoulder.

"May I help you find something?" she asks.

"Um, sure. I'm looking for…a dress for a cousin's wedding." It seems like something Mr. Martin would want me to say.

"I can help you with that. Do you have a color in mind?"

"I don't know…black?"

"Okay." She holds up an invisible hanger and looks at me. "This would look great on you. The sheath style would work well with your figure and the satin material would perfectly complement your skin. Plus, the little rhinestones along the neckline would really make your eyes pop."

Okay, hold on.

My "figure," my skin, my eyes…she didn't have to say any of that. She could have said, "Here's a dress. Buy it. The end." But instead, she said…more.

"Um, yes," I say, trying to stay in the moment. "That sounds good. I'll try it on. Thanks for your help."

"Anytime," she says and gives me a little smile.

"So," Mr. Martin says, "what could Lexi and Carolyn have done differently?"

"Maybe they could have stood further apart?" Daniel says. Carolyn immediately sidesteps away from me.

"Yes. Remember to always respect other people's personal space," Mr. Martin says. "You two *were* a little bit too close."

We were? It didn't feel like it. But then again, I feel like I'm never close *enough* to Carolyn.

"What else?" Mr. Martin asks.

"I think Lexi should have picked a color other than black," Daniel says.

"I agree," Mr. Martin says. "Try to choose something more feminine next time."

"What, like pink?" I say.

"Not necessarily. It could be white or yellow or purple." He turns to Matthew. "What do you think, Matthew? What else could Carolyn and Lexi have done differently?"

"Nothing. I think they did great."

Mr. Martin narrows his eyes at Matthew, but all he says is, "What about what the words Carolyn chose to use?"

"She sounded like a salesperson," Matthew says.

"Yes, she did a very good job taking on the persona of her

character. But the rules are different for people who battle SSA. We need to watch what we say and do much more carefully than those who don't have this struggle. So even though the average saleswoman may have said exactly what Carolyn said, it would have been a wiser choice for Carolyn to stay away from complimenting Lexi so directly."

No it wouldn't! That was the best part!

I sneak a sideways glance at Carolyn and catch her watching me for the tiniest fragment of a second before she whips her gaze away.

"Can I try again?" she asks Mr. Martin. There's a hint of desperation in her voice.

Mr. Martin checks his watch. "Unfortunately, we actually need to be moving on. Matthew and Daniel, please switch places with the ladies."

Carolyn's *noticed* me. She was basically telling me she thinks I'm pretty. And just now, she was staring at me. I'm sure of it.

Is it even possible? Could she be feeling it too? Does she think about me the way I'm always thinking about her?

After dinner, we have free time. It's Saturday night, so we even get a couple of extra hours. But as we make our way over to the rec cabin, Brianna approaches us.

"Matthew," she says, "Mr. Martin would like to see you in his office."

Matthew's brows pull together. "Why?"

"He has a few things he'd like to discuss with you," Brianna says. "It won't take long. You'll be back here with your friends soon enough." Her voice is all business, but her face betrays a hint of something I can't quite place—unease? Regret, maybe? It's strange.

But Matthew just shrugs and trudges off through the trees toward the main cabin.

"I wonder what that was all about," I say once the rest of us are inside the rec cabin. It feels weird with Matthew not here. The four of us are together so often that it feels like we're suddenly missing a limb.

"No idea," Daniel says.

Carolyn doesn't say anything. She didn't say anything at dinner either. She's been getting like this more and more—spaced out, eyes unfocused, lost deep in her own mind. More like Mom.

Daniel chooses a DVD from the shelf and we sit and watch the beginning of *The Wizard of Oz*. By the time Dorothy lands in Munchkinland, Matthew is back.

"What happened?" I whisper.

"Mr. Martin 'isn't happy with the level of effort I've been contributing to our therapy exercises,'" he says, doing air quotes.

I smile. "You've been contributing *zero* effort."

Matthew grins back. "That's what I told him. My dad can force me to be here, but no one can force me to actually *believe* in all this crap."

I stare at the TV screen. The coroner is averring that the witch is really, most sincerely dead, but I'm not really watching it. I still don't know if I believe in all this crap or not. It's all so complicated.

But then Matthew changes the subject and I'm saved from having to come up with a response. "So anyway…" he says, "when I got to Mr. Martin's office, he wasn't there yet. So I thought I'd look around for a bit."

I turn back to him, and he's looking at me with a sly smile.

"What?" I say.

"Look what I found," he says and slips a small bottle of vodka out of his shorts' pocket.

I immediately glance around the cabin. Barbara is dozed off in one of the big armchairs and Kaylee is playing Scrabble with Jasmine's group. The other campers are either watching the movie or off doing their own things. No one is watching us.

"You took that from Mr. Martin's *office*?" I whisper to Matthew. "Are you *crazy*?"

Matthew shrugs. "Probably. But I think it's about time we have some fun around here, don't you?"

"*No.*" I shake my head fiercely. "You're insane."

Matthew just smiles, slips the bottle back in his pocket, and goes over to the snack table. He grabs a few bottles of water and then says, "Hey, Daniel, Carolyn, want to go get some fresh air?"

"Sure," Daniel says, "I've seen this movie a hundred times already anyway."

Carolyn shrugs and follows Matthew and Daniel out of the cabin.

Great, now I *have* to go. If I stay here, people will notice our group has split up, and they'll tell the counselors and the counselors will find out what Matthew, Carolyn, and Daniel are up to, and they'll all get in a lot of trouble. *Damn you, Matthew.*

I locate them around the corner of the cabin. It's a fairly hidden spot, tucked into a little crook of trees. No one will find us here unless they're really looking.

"Are we even allowed to be back here?" I ask.

"All Brianna said was that we had to stay within sight of the rec cabin," Matthew says. He reaches out and taps his palm against the exterior cabin wall. "And we are."

"What's going on?" Carolyn asks.

"Look what I found," Matthew says and reveals the bottle.

Daniel's eyes go wide, and Carolyn whispers, "Where did you get that?"

"Doesn't matter," Matthew says. He transfers the vodka into an empty water bottle and then hurls the vodka bottle so deep into the woods that we don't even hear it land. He takes a big sip and then holds it out to Daniel. "You in?"

Daniel looks like he thinks it's a trick question.

"I'm in," Carolyn says immediately. She grabs the bottle from Matthew's hand and takes a swig. Her face crumples up as she tastes the liquor, but she swallows it like a champ.

God, I'm really giving into peer pressure today. But if my two best friends at New Horizons are going to get drunk, there's no way I'm just going to sit back and watch while they have all the fun.

"All right, I'm in," I say and take the bottle from Carolyn.

"Thought you might say that," Matthew says as I drink. I've never had vodka before, just beer at parties and the odd glass of mulled wine at Christmas. The vodka is warm and tastes like what I imagine lighter fluid would probably taste like. It burns, but once it's down, my belly is warm and my head is light. It actually feels pretty good.

"What about you, Daniel?" Matthew says.

Daniel looks at each of us, the pink light of the sunset catching the lenses of his glasses. "Um…" he says.

"You don't have to if you don't want to," I say. "It's okay."

He hesitates a moment more and then says, "No, I do want to." He takes a small sip from the bottle, swallows, and coughs like crazy.

We sit on the grass floor in a little circle and pass the bottle around. I try to pace myself by only taking a sip every other time the bottle comes around to me and drinking a lot of water in between, but before I know it, I'm drunk. Turns out vodka is a *lot* stronger than beer and mulled wine.

I stretch my legs out in front of me and kick off my stupid sandals. "I hate these fucking clothes," I say, and the three of them burst into laughter.

"Are we a little drunk, Alexis?" Matthew says, in a perfect mimic of Brianna's voice.

"God, don't call me that!" I groan. "And how could you tell?" I thought I was doing a pretty good job of acting normal.

"I've never heard you curse before," Matthew says.

"Curse? What, like cuss?" I say.

"Yes, Miss South Carolina, *cuss*. Swear. Use naughty language. Whatever."

"I actually know Miss South Carolina," I say. "Her name's Patricia."

They all crack up again. What, I'm not *that* funny when I'm drunk, am I?

"I've never been drunk before," Daniel says, slurring his words a little.

"We know," Matthew says and gives Daniel a little pat on the back. "What do you think?"

"It's different than I thought it would be. It feels like…like I'm floating in a river made of honey."

We all laugh. "Not an entirely inaccurate description," I say. "I'm surprised you even wanted to join in on this, Daniel. You know we're breaking the rules right now, right?"

"Yeah, I know. But I'm following the rules in a way too!"

"How do you mean?" Matthew asks.

"I'm not being a Kitchen Window Boy. I'm doing what Mr. Martin said to do—I'm joining my friends in the fun."

There's a momentary silence, and I'm pretty sure we're all thinking the same thing: that's the first time Daniel's described us as his friends. He's one of us now, even if he *is* only drinking because he thinks Mr. Martin would want him to.

Matthew smiles. "So the river made of honey—is it a good feeling or a bad feeling?"

"Oh, it's definitely good," Daniel says. "It's like…if I don't want to think about something, I don't have to think about it. The thought just goes away."

"I know exactly what you mean," Carolyn says and takes another huge gulp.

"What are you trying not to think about?" I ask her.

She squeezes her eyes shut and shakes her head. "Let's talk about something else."

Wait. Does Carolyn have a *secret*? Is it the thing she thinks about when she's off in la-la land? What could be so big that she can't even talk to us about it when she's drunk? She's already told the whole camp about her cousin sexually harassing her—what could be worse than *that*?

I catch Matthew's eye. "Hey, Lexi," he says, making it clear that he's changing the conversation for Carolyn's benefit. "Tell us about your tattoo."

The request catches me off guard, and the first reaction my vodka-delayed senses come up with is to laugh.

"What did I say?" Matthew says, confused.

I just shake my head, still laughing. "You wanna know about this?" I slide the clunky bangle off my arm and hold up my tattooed wrist.

"Um…I guess?" Matthew looks unsure now, after my reaction.

Screw it. Carolyn doesn't want to talk about her stuff? Fine. But I have nothing to hide anymore. "Okay, here's the story. I got this tattoo because of a girl named Zoë Green."

I tell them the about the rainstorm and the plants and the lightning and how I had to keep it all secret.

I run a hand through my hair. "I had all these…these *feelings*, and I couldn't tell anyone, and it was killing me. I had to get it out somehow. So I got this." I hold out my lightning bolt again. "At least I could share *this* with the world."

"So nothing ever happened with you two?" Carolyn asks.

I look at her and a crazy idea takes hold of me. I smile mysteriously and say, "Well, I didn't say *that*…"

I know it's stupid. There's no point in trying to make her jealous. This whole situation is freaking impossible; it's not like we'll ever be more than friends. But I'm feeling loopy and can't help myself.

"Ooh, now it's getting good," Matthew says, leaning forward. "What happened?"

"Yeah, what happened?" Daniel echoes.

Everyone's staring at me, waiting eagerly for the story's salacious conclusion.

Oh God. I should have kept my fat mouth shut. I should have said, *Nope, nothing ever happened with us.* End of story. But I didn't. So now I have to tell them.

"We were at this party…" I close my eyes, take a deep breath, and tell them the rest.

It was last summer. After secretly being in love with Zoë for almost an entire year, I got the chance I never thought I would see. There was a big end-of-summer bash at Vinny's house, and we were playing Spin the Bottle. Most people there were pretty drunk. Except for me. With Dad sick at home, I didn't want to do anything to stress my parents out more, so I volunteered to be the DD. Perfect excuse to stay sober.

I spun the bottle, and in that never-ending moment where all you can do is wait to see where it settles, I wished and prayed and projected every last bit of energy I had into that beer bottle with the torn label landing on Zoë Green.

The rules of the game were that you had to kiss whoever it landed on. The guys seemed to have more of a problem with that rule than most of the girls did. Whenever a guy spun it and it landed on another guy, they would just do a jokey, quick peck on the cheek and then laugh hysterically for about five minutes. I think the only reason they played the game at all was so they could get a chance to make out with the cheerleaders. I didn't blame them. The only reason *I* was playing was to get a chance to make out with Zoë.

It couldn't have been a more perfect situation. This was my one chance to kiss her—the one thing I wanted more than anything—*without* having to confess my secret. In the world of this drunken party game, I could actually have it both ways. Even for just a few precious seconds.

And it actually worked. The bottle came to a halt and was pointing directly at Zoë.

I crawled across the circle, my heart pounding so intensely I thought for sure everyone would hear it, and touched my lips to hers. Her mouth was soft, and she tasted like beer and Starbursts. And it felt so *right*. As if the stars had finally aligned just for me and her, and this moment existed only for us.

And she was kissing me back. She was into it just as much as I was. Her tongue even slipped inside my mouth a few times.

I slid closer to her, our mouths moving in perfect harmony. I completely forgot about the room full of people watching us, and that we were just playing a game, and that Zoë was only kissing me because she was drunk. In that moment, I even forgot about all the reasons why we would never get to be together.

I was just so *happy*.

Zoë finally pulled away, and I came back to the room. She downed the rest of her beer and popped another Starburst in her mouth. The boys were all cheering like the two of us making out was the greatest thing they'd ever seen in their lives, and Zoë licked her lips and grinned at them.

"Now it's a *party*!" she shouted and high-fived a bunch of the guys as a new wave of cheers sounded.

After that, everything changed. Suddenly the world was filled with magic. For days, all I did was think about that kiss—that perfect, life-changing kiss. *She kissed me back.*

A few days later, we were hanging out in her room. School was starting the next day and I was supposed to be helping her find something to wear for the first day of junior year. But I wasn't doing a very good job of staying focused.

"What are you smiling about?" Zoë asked, amused.

I looked up from the elaborate doodle I was working on in one of her notebooks, my cheeks suddenly on fire. "Nothing." I shook my head.

"Tell me!"

"It's nothing."

She flopped down on the bed beside me. "You *like* someone, don't you?"

Her face was bright and her smile was knowing—it was like she knew what I was thinking and she just wanted me to say it aloud. And I wanted to, more than anything. I couldn't get that kiss out of my head and all I wanted was to lean over and close the distance between us and kiss her again, right there on her bed, just the two of us. No cheering crowds this time.

And suddenly all that want and the memories of the kiss and her teasing smile and the year of suffering in silence all got to be too much. I couldn't keep it in anymore.

"Actually, yeah," I said softly. "I do like someone."

Zoë squealed and scooted closer to me. "I knew it! Who? Who is it?"

And before I could stop myself, I leaned forward and kissed her.

She pulled back almost immediately. "What...?" But her question went unfinished. She just looked at me with wide, bewildered eyes.

There was no backing out now. "It's you," I said, ignoring the instinct to flee. "You're the one I like. It's…it's been going on a long time." She was still speechless, her forehead crinkled like a Shar Pei puppy's. "I know it's a lot. I never even considered telling you before this weekend. But after we kissed at Vinny's party, I thought…maybe…you might feel the same way? About me?"

I waited, my heart racing, my fingernails digging into my palms.

Slowly, Zoë's face changed. The surprise and confusion left and was replaced by the kind of look that's usually reserved for watching someone get hacked to death with a chainsaw in a horror movie.

"You thought I was *gay*? That's so gross," she said, effectively slicing my heart in two. "Why would you *think* that?" She backed away from me, not even bothering to hide her disgust.

"I…um…" I stuttered, trying to rearrange my thoughts into something resembling coherence. "I thought…um…didn't you kiss me back?"

Her nose scrunched up in revulsion. "That was a *game*, Lexi. We were drunk. It was a show for the guys. I can't believe you thought it was *real*! Oh my *God*."

Slice, slice. My heart was officially in pieces.

"I can't believe this." She ran her hands through her hair and then looked at me, her eyes hard. "You know we can't be friends anymore."

We stared at each other for a long second, so many emotions zapping between us that it would be impossible to count them all.

"Get out of my house," she said. "Get *out*!"

And then I ran. Out of her room, out of her house, out of her life forever.

See, that's the problem with getting hit by lightning. You get burned.

Chapter 18

Everyone is staring at me. I blink the moisture away from my eyes and take a long pull from the vodka bottle. "So, yeah. That's the story of the lightning bolt."

I can tell they're all trying to come up with something to say, but I'm surprised when it's Daniel who speaks first. "I'm sorry that happened to you, Lexi," he says. He slides next to me and puts his arm around me.

I rest my head on his bony shoulder. "Thanks, Daniel." I sniffle.

"I know how you feel. It's kind of like what happened when I kissed Colin," he says.

I remember his story of kissing the boy in the nurse's office. "Yeah, I guess it is," I say. "But he hit you, didn't he? I can't imagine what that must have been like."

"It's the same though," he says. "Zoë didn't hit you, but she hurt you just as much."

I sigh and thread my fingers through his. "At least we'll never have to go through something like that again, right?"

Suddenly Matthew's on his feet. "Oh yeah, because Mr. Martin and his cute little Jesus camp is going to turn you straight, right?" Crap. He's upset. No, he's *mad*.

"Yes, Matthew," Daniel says, his voice firmer than I've ever heard it. "That's right."

Matthew laughs, but there's no humor in it. "Wake *up*, people! This whole place is a total scam! You can't *pray the gay away*. Jesus Christ!" He kicks a rock and it skids off into the woods.

"Please don't take the Lord's name in vain, Matthew," Daniel says. This kid should really get drunk more often—he's a hell of a lot more confident with an elevated blood alcohol level.

"Fine, sorry." Matthew sits back down, but he's still all worked up. "But come on, you guys *have* to know that you can't change your sexuality any more than you can change your eye color. You really should just get used to it already."

"You don't know that," Carolyn counters. "*You're* the one who always talks about that stupid scale and sexuality being fluid and all that. So maybe we're more *fluid* than you are. Ever think of that?"

"If you were that fluid, Carolyn, you wouldn't need a team of counselors and a whole summer of workbooks and freaking *role-playing* exercises to make you hot for guys."

Carolyn's face goes bright red, and I jump in to defend her. "She's got a point, Matthew. Maybe we're *not* like you. Maybe it can work for us."

He crosses his arms and glares at me. I glare back. I feel bad for ganging up on him, but he's the one who started it.

"Okay, Lexi, let's say for a minute that you're right. Maybe you guys are different. So tell me: how's it going?"

"What do you mean?"

"Well, we've been here for a while now, doing everything they tell us to, saying whatever they want us to. And I know you three have been trying your very hardest to kick that pesky SSA once and for all. So how's it going?"

Our eyes are locked now. His piercing stare says it all: he knows I'm hooked on Carolyn the way I was hooked on Zoë, and he knows I'm not one iota less gay now than I was when I drove up that mountain road with my mom.

I let my eyes soften. *Please*, I beg him silently. *Don't make me say it.*

Either he really does feel bad for me, or my wordless plea is enough of a victory for him, because he lets it go.

"What about you two?" he says to Daniel and Carolyn. "You're two of Mr. Martin's star pupils. So, are you straight yet?"

Daniel's confident demeanor falters. "We've only been here three weeks," he mumbles.

"And it's an eight-week program. So we're almost halfway done. Do you feel almost fifty percent more attracted to the opposite sex than you were before you came here? If you do, then say so. Prove me wrong." He steps back and sweeps out a hand in front of him. "The floor is yours."

Silence.

I look from Carolyn to Daniel, waiting for them to put Matthew in his place. But Carolyn's got that far-off look in her eye again, and Daniel is picking at the sole of his shoe.

"Yep. Didn't think so," Matthew says.

"No," I say. "You don't get to just be right about this." I want to prove him wrong, if not for me, then for Carolyn and Daniel. So I explain it the way Kaylee did back on the second day of camp. "It's not magic. I think we can all agree on that. It's not like a switch can be flipped or a few wires rearranged and everything is different. It's about learning what choices to make, what things to focus on in our lives. It's a long-term process, like a diet."

Daniel is nodding like crazy and giving me a grateful smile. Carolyn isn't doing much, but she seems to be more present than she was a minute ago.

"Sounds like a pretty miserable existence to me, to have to keep denying who you are every second of your life," Matthew mutters.

"I think the point is to keep working at it, every single day, so it becomes *part* of who you are," I say.

The vodka's gone now, and it's pretty obvious the fun is over.

I buckle my sandals back onto my feet, we all brush the grass and dirt from our butts, and we go back inside.

Everything is exactly the same as we left it; no one seems to have missed us at all—which is funny, because so much has changed.

Chapter 19

The next day, we all pretend like last night never happened. I've got a killer headache, and the others don't look so great either, but we don't talk about it.

The exercise for the day is baseball—the boys have to play; the girls have to watch. I have a pretty good feeling that most of the girls would rather be playing and most of the guys would rather be on the sidelines, but I guess it's supposed to be another way to instill appropriate gender roles in us. Girls don't play sports. Boys do.

It's fine by me though. If I had to swing a bat and run around on a field with this hangover, I'd probably puke all over home plate. I don't know how Matthew and Daniel are managing to hold it together.

It turns out Ian, the kid who had to hit Gabe during the Father Wounds, is an incredible baseball player. He hits every pitch that comes his way. By the third inning, the score is 11–0 and the male counselors join in the game—"to even out the teams"—but Ian tramples all over them too. Everyone is rooting for him, even the guys on the opposite team. It's pretty great, watching him put the counselors in their place.

My eyes keep wandering over to Carolyn during the game. She hasn't said much since last night, and I wonder if she's thinking the same thing I am: the reparative therapy isn't working.

I know what I said about it being about choices and the diet analogy and everything, and I do think that can probably work for some people; the idea that the camp doesn't zap us completely free of our SSA but rather gives us the tools to fight back against the SSA and be content choosing a different path in life isn't so hard to believe.

But the thing is, I don't know if it's a diet I can personally commit to. God knows I've been trying to fully entrust myself to the de-gayifying exercises I believe in, and to find the gray area in the others, but I still keep drifting back to Carolyn.

Carolyn, who looks so completely miserable right now. I hate that whatever is on her mind is making her so sad. So, on the off chance she's thinking the same thing I am, I whisper, "There's still five weeks left."

She looks up at me.

"It'll be okay," I say. "You're going to be okay."

She nods. "There's still five weeks left," she repeats.

"Five weeks is a long time."

"Thanks, Lexi." She gives a small smile and goes back to watching the game.

But now that I've consoled Carolyn—or as much as I can without knowing exactly what it is I'm comforting her about—I have nothing to distract me from my own misery.

The reparative therapy isn't working for me. I have all these tools, and I'm trying to use them, but nothing's happening. And I'm pretty sure five more weeks isn't going to change that. I feel it, deep down in my core. This just isn't going to work. Maybe I'm different from Mr. Martin and Kaylee and Peter. Maybe I just wasn't meant to be gluten free after all. Maybe this is what God has wanted for me all along...

But I *cannot* go home to my mother and look her in the eye and tell her it didn't work. It would kill her.

After the game (final score: 21–0), Brianna whisks the girls away to do some gender activities in the main cabin. Today's lesson: laundry.

"Are you *serious*? The boys get to play sports and we have to *clean*? That's not fair!" Melissa blurts out as Brianna presents us with the ginormous pile of pink and blue laundry in the cabin's basement laundry room.

"Melissa, I'm really getting tired of your complaining," Brianna says. "Another word and you'll be on laundry duty for the rest of the summer."

Melissa zips her lips and throws away the key.

That's the best thing a girl can be in this world, a beautiful little fool.

"Mrs. Wykowski usually takes care of the camp's laundry, but we gave her the day off today," Brianna explains. She shows us how to sort the laundry into lights and darks and work the settings on the row of washing machines and dryers. I already know how to do all this stuff, but it seems like a lot of these girls have never had to do their own laundry before.

I'm on hand-wash duty (the girls' sweaters are hand-wash only—yet another reason to loathe them), but I actually don't mind. The repetitive motion of soaking, rinsing, and wringing is conducive to thinking, and I have a lot to think about. The de-gayifying isn't working. So what the hell am I going to do?

By the time the sweaters are all laid flat to air dry and it's all hands on deck for the Great Fold, I've come up with a new plan: I will stick with the program for the rest of the summer. I will do everything Mr. Martin and the other counselors say to do, so they can tell my mom what a model camper I was. And I will spend the rest of my life lying to my mother.

If I'd done a better job of keeping that damn sketchbook away from her in the first place, she never would have known I was gay. Just like if I tell her the de-gayifying worked, she'll never know that it didn't.

I can get married. I can have babies. You don't have to be in love to do those things. You don't even have to be in like. I repeat to myself what I told Carolyn: *it'll be okay. You're going to be okay.*

• • •

The following Sunday marks the summer's halfway point—and brings with it a couple of surprises.

The first thing that happens is that Mr. Martin announces at breakfast that we'll get the chance to call our parents today. My heart immediately swells up—for the first time in a month, I'm going to get to talk to Mom!

We all line up outside Mr. Martin's office and go inside one at a time for a five-minute supervised conversation.

Matthew is in line right before me, and he whispers just before he goes in, "I'm calling Justin."

My jaw drops. "You can't! Mr. Martin said parents only! He's going to be watching you the whole time."

"What he doesn't know won't hurt him," he says and disappears into the office.

I listen through the door. After a few moments of silence, I hear Matthew say, "Hi, Dad, it's me." Pause. "I know, I'm glad to hear your voice too." Pause. "It's not so bad. I've got some friends here so that's good. How's everything at home?" Long pause. "Yeah, I bet!" Laughter. "Okay, well, I have to go, but I'll see you in a month." Short pause. "I miss you too. I love you." Short pause. "Say hi to Mom!" More laughter. "Okay, bye."

The door swings open and Matthew's face is pure joy. I can't help but smile.

I go into the office and sit down. With a quick glance at Mr. Martin, who's sitting behind his desk watching me, I pick up the phone and dial my house number.

As it rings, the excitement I'd been feeling as I waited in line turns to apprehension. What if she's not "doing fine" after all? Or what if she's not home again and I don't get another chance to speak with her for four more weeks?

But she picks up on the third ring—and her voice sounds bright and happy.

"Mom?"

"Lexi! Oh my goodness, how are you?"

"I'm okay. How are you?"

"I'm doing really well. Oh, Lexi, I wish you were here to see it."

"You sound great," I say, relieved—and surprised. "I heard you went camping?"

"Yes! It was such fun, but I am so sorry I wasn't here when you called. I've missed you so much."

"I've missed you too, Mom. I'm so glad to hear you've been keeping busy though."

"I definitely have. I joined this exercise group that goes on long walks and hikes—that's who I went camping with—and I took on a shift at the church daycare center. And I joined a widow support group—it's wonderful. I really should have done it earlier."

I'm stunned. "That's great, Mom. I'm so happy for you." Tears spring to my eyes.

"Well, you inspired me, honey. You knew you had to get help, and you went and did it. I realized there's no reason why I shouldn't do the same thing. How is everything at New Horizons? Are you making good progress?"

Now I'm full on crying, and I'm not even sure why.

I do my best to make my voice sound normal. "It's really great. I…" Deep breath. "I really think it's working." There it was, lie number one in a lie-filled lifetime.

"Oh, that's such wonderful news! I'm so proud of you, Lexi. I *knew* he didn't know what he was talking about."

Wait—what?

"Who didn't know what he was talking about?" I ask. "Pastor Joe?"

There's a pause. "No, no, sorry, never mind. I still get confused sometimes," she says.

"Oh. Okay…Are you *sure* you're all right?"

"I'm great. I promise," she says.

Mr. Martin is making a wrap-it-up gesture. "I have to go, Mom. I love you."

"I love you too, honey. You keep working on getting better, and when I come to pick you up next month, we'll go out for a big celebration dinner. How does that sound?"

"Sounds great." I clear my throat. "Bye!"

"Bye, Lexi."

I hang up the phone and leave the room in a daze. She sounded just like the woman she used to be, the one whose specialty was macaroni and cheese casserole with a black olive smiley face baked into the top, who made her own homemade crayons for her students because she thought they deserved the best. I should be glad that she's doing so well. And I am—I really, really am. My utopia is actually starting to come true.

back to the outside world as seamless as possible. Of course, you won't be wearing your New Horizons uniforms in your regular lives back home, so it's important that we help you practice making good choices in the way that you present yourselves now. Brianna, anything to add?"

"Yes, thank you, Mr. Martin," Brianna says. "I'd like to add that while you'll be getting more freedom in your wardrobe from now on, there *is* a limit to what is acceptable attire. If we see you wearing anything that we don't approve of, we will ask you to remove it immediately, and we expect your full cooperation."

We all nod eagerly. Whatever wardrobe restrictions she has in mind still have to be better than the uniforms.

"We also have a limited reserve of men's and women's clothes in case you find that your old wardrobe doesn't comply with who you are now," Brianna says.

Yeah, there's no way I'm going to wear anything of theirs ever again.

When we get back to the dorms, Carolyn is already in bed, reading *Gatsby*.

"Hey," I say. "Are you okay?"

She nods. "I'm fine. Sorry I got upset."

"It's okay. I think the phone calls put everyone a little bit on edge. Except Matthew." I smile.

She smiles back.

"So, I have some good news," I say and pause for dramatic effect. "We don't have to wear the uniforms anymore!"

But somehow utopia doesn't feel so…well, *utopic*.

At dinner, everyone talks about their phone calls. Daniel is grinning. Over the past week, he's slowly been working past the dejection he felt during our fateful night of drinking, and now that he's finally gotten a chance to check in with his mother, the last of his worries seem to have evaporated, his faith in New Horizons fully restored.

Matthew gabs away excitedly about all the San Diego gossip he found out from Justin. Apparently, someone named José cheated on someone named Diana with someone named Jennifer, which "everybody totally knew was going to happen."

Everyone's glad to hear that my mom's doing so well. I don't tell them the part about me not being as happy about it as I thought I would.

"How about you, Carolyn?" I ask. "How did your conversation go?"

She doesn't look happy; there's a deep crease between her eyes that wasn't there before her phone call. "They miss me," she says, and there's an edge to her tone.

"Well, that's good, right?"

"They want me to come home," she says, picking a biscuit apart with her fingers. "They don't get it."

Matthew, Daniel, and I exchange a look. "They want you to come home?" I say. "Like, *now*?"

"Yup. They didn't want me to come here in the first place."

"So…then…why…" I'm having trouble forming the question. Carolyn's parents *didn't* want her to come here? I know we're all here for different reasons, but up until now, I thought the one common theme among all of us was that our parents were at the very least *supportive* of the de-gayifying.

I don't get an answer to my barely formed question though, because Carolyn suddenly throws down the mangled biscuit and storms out of the cabin, slamming the screen door behind her.

Chapter 20

I want to go after her, but Kaylee is out the door and following Carolyn before I can even leave my seat. And then Mr. Martin calls everyone to attention, so I couldn't leave the dining cabin even if I wanted to.

"I trust everyone enjoyed their phone calls home today!" he says. "And now I have another announcement to commemorate the summer's halfway point—beginning tomorrow, you will all ge to wear your own clothes again."

Oh my God. Finally—*gray area*. And it couldn't have co at a better time. I feel like I've won the lottery. The entire r breaks out in celebration: fist bumps, hugs (between mem of the opposite sex only, of course), cheers, and lots an of applause.

Mr. Martin waits for everyone to settle down before cont "In one month, you're all going to be leaving New Hori the second half of the summer will focus on the real-life tions of what we've worked on thus far, to make that

Carolyn sits up, all traces of melancholy suddenly vanished. "Are you serious?!"

I grin. "Yup. Starting tomorrow. It's so we can practice how to 'make good choices in how we present ourselves' or something."

"Oh my God. Amazing!"

"I know, right?" We stay like that, grinning at each other, for a suspended moment. Then Deb announces fifteen minutes till lights out and Carolyn looks away.

"Here," she says and hands me the book.

I clutch it to my chest.

• • •

The clothes in the bottom drawers of my dresser are like long lost friends. "Hi," I whisper and give them a little wave. I don't care if I look crazy.

I take all my clothes out of the drawers and spread them out on my bed, my heart giving an excited little jump each time I spot one of my favorites pieces. I resist the urge to roll around in them like a pig in mud, but I do pick up a few of them and bring them to my nose, breathing in the smell of home.

I finally decide what I'm going to wear today and then carefully place everything else back in the drawers. But unlike the last time I did this, this is not a good-bye. It's just a see you later.

It takes a little longer than usual to get ready today because the counselors have to survey each camper from head to toe. They make little adjustments—buttoning up a top button here, nixing a studded belt there—but everyone cooperates. Even Melissa doesn't complain.

When Brianna gets to me, she purses her lips, studying my layered tanks, skinny jeans, and black high-tops. "Some jewelry would help," she says finally.

I'm already wearing the cross (none of us pressed our luck with that one), but I grab a long, beaded necklace from my vanity and slip it around my neck too.

Brianna nods and then walks away.

There's a palpable change in the camp's atmosphere today. Everyone's a little extra smiley, chatting a little extra loudly. I think they all understand now what I knew all along—when you're wearing something you love, you get to be confident. Comfortable. Happy. You get to be *you*.

Carolyn's wearing a canary-yellow sleeveless dress with little teardrop earrings and flip-flops. Matthew's in a pair of cargo shorts and a heather gray V-neck tee. And Daniel's monochromatic in denim shorts and a baggy blue T-shirt that is way too big for him.

Matthew raises his glass of OJ. "To our last four weeks at New Horizons!" he says.

"And to no more uniforms!" I add.

"Hear, hear!" Carolyn says at the same time that Daniel says, "Cheers!"

We all clink glasses.

"Are you feeling better today, Carolyn?" Daniel asks.

I put my glass down, my good mood deflating a little. Why would he bring that up now, while we're having such a happy moment?

But Carolyn just smiles and says, "Yes, much. Thanks for asking, Daniel."

Damn. Now I wish *I* were the one who'd asked.

The activity for the day is Avoiding Satanic Influences. It's in the classroom cabin, and we're all in one big group again.

Mr. Martin begins by giving a speech about how the world is filled with evil and how resisting our SSA and resisting Satan go hand in hand. "Book of James, chapter four, verse seven," he quotes. "'Submit yourselves therefore to God. Resist the devil and he will flee from you.'" He looks at us. "What are some ways you can resist the devil?"

Daniel's hand goes up. "Don't do drugs."

"Very good. What else?"

"Go to church," Sarah says.

"Yes, that's very important."

I catch Carolyn's eye and she gives a tiny smile. I know what she's thinking: *the Church of Gatsby.*

"What else?" Mr. Martin asks.

The list keeps growing. Follow the Ten Commandments. Don't join a gang. Dress modestly. Wait until marriage for sex. Don't masturbate.

Matthew rolls his eyes so much I wouldn't be surprised if they got stuck like that. And a few times he actually bangs his head against his desk in frustration. Honestly, I don't blame him. Some of this stuff is so ridiculous. I mean, in what world would I ever join a *gang*?

And I don't really understand how all of these things can be considered on the same level. Joining a gang means *killing* people— obviously that's bad. But dressing immodestly? How is that even in the same conversation?

The group has exhausted its devil-avoiding list, but Mr. Martin still has some ideas of his own to add.

"Halloween, pop music, sex on television…our culture has become so submerged in evil that half the time we don't even realize it. Take *Harry Potter*, for example."

Matthew and I exchange a wide-eyed *can you believe this?* look. Mr. Martin has really lost it now. How could cute little Harry Potter possibly be bad? Things just elevated to a whole new level of crazy.

"*Harry Potter* is luring innocent children to witchcraft and the occult," he explains. "It teaches that you can leave the world of structure, safety, and family and go to a place where the rules don't apply, where you can get whatever you want—as long as you access dark magic." Mr. Martin shakes his head in dismay. "How many of you have read the *Harry Potter* series or seen the movies?"

Almost all of us raise our hands.

"And I'll bet you never realized how it was corrupting you," he says.

No one responds, but there are a few shrugs and headshakes. Matthew's whole body shakes with silent laughter.

Then, suddenly, the silence is broken ever so slightly by Daniel, who whispers something down at his desk. I don't think Mr. Martin hears way up at the front of the room, but those of us near Daniel turn our heads.

"What was that, Daniel?" Matthew asks.

Daniel looks up. His eyes widen when he sees so many of us looking at him. "Nothing." He shakes his head. "Never mind."

"No, you said something," Matthew presses. "If you have something to say, you should say it."

"What's going on back there?" Mr. Martin asks.

"Daniel has something to say," Matthew announces.

Daniel's face is the darkest shade of red I've ever seen it. "No, I don't."

Mr. Martin smiles. "Please, Daniel, if you have something to add, we'd love to hear it."

Of course he wants to hear it—Daniel always agrees with him. If it were Matthew who had something to say though, I doubt he'd be so encouraging.

Daniel stares down at his desk. "Well…I was just wondering… if…" His voice is low, but it easily carries through the small, silent room. "Well, if you've ever read *Harry Potter*."

"No, I must say I haven't," Mr. Martin says confidently. "I practice what I preach, of course."

"Oh," Daniel says. "Well, I don't think it's what you think."

Everyone in the room is rapt with attention now, leaning in a little closer, craning their necks a little further. All eyes and ears are on Daniel.

"Oh? Please, explain," Mr. Martin says, his voice still as sturdy as ever, but his smile beginning to falter slightly.

"Well, I actually think it's a pretty Christian story. There're a lot of parallels between Harry's story and Jesus's."

Whoa. Daniel is standing up to Mr. Martin!

"How so, Daniel?" Mr. Martin says, his tone turning sour.

"It's all about sacrifice and good winning out over evil and finding your faith, you know? And there are even Bible verses on Harry's parents' tombstones: 'The last enemy that shall be destroyed is death,' which is from first Corinthians chapter fifteen, verse twenty-six, and 'Where your treasure is, there will your heart be also,' which Jesus says in Matthew six, verse twenty-one." Daniel's confidence is growing now—he's looking directly at Mr. Martin. "And of course, one of the main themes in *The Deathly Hallows* is resurrection."

Mr. Martin swallows, and the muscles in his neck strain against his skin. "Thank you, Daniel. You've been very informative." He manages a small smile. "That's all for now, everyone. Please proceed to the dining cabin for lunch. Oh, and Matthew, may I see you in my office, please?"

"Now?" Matthew asks, surprised.

"Yes. Now."

• • •

Matthew fills us in on what happened with Mr. Martin during leisure hours that night. The Monopoly board is set up between us, but it's going largely ignored.

"He said that he was trying to give me time to adapt to being at New Horizons, but that by this point, my 'attitude' really should have 'adjusted' by now, and that he's going to be a lot less tolerant of my 'insolent behavior' from now on." He looks at Daniel. "Basically, he thinks I'm a bad influence on you."

"I'm so sorry," Daniel says. "I didn't mean to get you in trouble."

Matthew shakes his head. "Forget it. I can handle that asshole. And anyway, I'm the one who owes you an apology. I shouldn't have put you on the spot like that." But after a pause, he says, "But it was pretty great." He grins at Daniel.

Daniel smiles too, but it doesn't reach his eyes. "I can't believe I did that. Mr. Martin is just trying to help us, and I was so disrespectful."

"No, you weren't," I say. "You were perfectly respectful. You didn't raise your voice or anything. You just disagreed with what he was saying. There's nothing wrong with that."

"But I shouldn't be disagreeing with him in the first place," Daniel says. "I'm here to learn from him. He won his fight with SSA. He knows what he's doing."

"Daniel, I really don't think disagreeing with Mr. Martin about the merits of *Harry Potter* is going to be the thing that stops you from getting what you want," I say gently. And that gets me thinking again about how some of us will get what we want and others won't. I hope Daniel's in the former category. I don't know what category Carolyn's in. I'm in the latter category, but no one will ever know that.

Because really, the only difference between someone who succeeds at the de-gayifying—like Kaylee—and someone who just *pretends* to succeed at it—like me—is the happiness level of that person. The rest of it—the hard work, the commitment, the actively pushing back against your nature—is all the same. It's just that, for me, I imagine the "diet" will be a lot more like starvation.

Well, that's depressing.

I look around the rec cabin. Kaylee, John, and Deb, the counselors who used to struggle with SSA, are all here tonight. Why are they capable of this and I'm not? What do they have that I don't?

Somewhere along the way in my wandering, rambling thoughts, my gaze lands on Matthew as he confidently rolls the dice and gets the Monopoly game started.

There *is* one other possibility I haven't considered…

What if the de-gayifying doesn't work at all? What if the success stories are all lies?

Mr. Martin and his ten-year marriage to Nancy. Kaylee and her decision to work at New Horizons after going through the program herself. Daniel's friend Peter and Counselor John and Marilynn Chaney's grandnephew and the countless, nameless others…have they *all* made the same choice I have? Are they all faking it?

Or maybe they've been telling the lie so long that they've started to believe it themselves.

I lower my head and rest my cheek on the tabletop. The only thing I know for sure is there are a hell of a lot more questions than answers. And when it comes down to it, that's like knowing nothing at all.

Chapter 21

Mr. Martin announces the next morning that we're going to get the chance to leave the camp that night.

"It's just for a couple of hours," he says, but the qualification doesn't matter. Civilization! We're finally going to get to dip our toes back in the real world, where things like cell phones and the Internet exist, and where the adults wear clothes besides pink and blue T-shirts!

"Where are we going?" Jasmine asks.

"You are going…on dates!" Mr. Martin declares.

My mouth falls open.

"Dates?" someone asks. I'm too stunned to pay attention to who it is. "With who?"

"With a member of your group, of course!"

I immediately glance at Carolyn. The second our eyes meet, her face turns beet red and she turns away.

Matthew smirks and shakes his head. "Oh yeah, right," he whispers to me.

"Most of you probably don't have much experience dating a member of the opposite sex," Mr. Martin continues, "so we're giving you a chance to practice. Brianna will pair you up."

An excited buzz spreads across the carpet cabin as Brianna makes her way from group to group, splitting us up into couples.

But the four of us just stare at each other. I look from Matthew to Daniel and back to Matthew again. Which one of them will I be "dating" tonight? I can't imagine going out with either of them. It's just too weird.

Finally Brianna gets to us and she wastes no time splitting us up. "Matthew and Carolyn. Alexis and Daniel." Then she moves on.

I look at Daniel. He's not just my first boy date; he's my first date, period. Somehow, when I used to imagine what my first date would be like, the image of this scrawny boy never came into the picture. But I guess I should know by now that things never work out the way you plan. He smiles shyly at me.

Matthew and Carolyn are dancing around on the carpet arm-in-arm, doing some kind of jitterbug/waltz thing. He dips her and she giggles hysterically. A searing blade of jealousy rips through me. "We are going to have a delightful evening together, my dear," Matthew says in a suave, old-timey movie star accent.

"Okay, everyone, settle down," Mr. Martin calls out once all the couples are arranged. "Here's what's going to happen. There are seven counselors and eight couples, so with the exception of one group of four, each couple will be paired with one chaperone.

Your destinations have been prearranged, and you will each be going somewhere different. You are expected to be on your best behavior the entire evening, and *all* camp rules will still apply."

He runs down the list of rules again and then pairs us each up with a counselor and a destination.

Daniel and I are going with Barbara to dinner at a local Italian restaurant and the 7:00 showing of some PG movie about a high school prom.

At 5:00, we all meet in the main cabin lobby, freshly showered and made up, dressed in our finest date clothes. I'm wearing a floor-length gauzy white skirt and a simple black tank top, with a scarf tied around my hair like a headband. Daniel is wearing khakis and a button-down shirt. His hair is neatly combed, and it looks like he put some sort of gel in it. The poor kid actually looks nervous.

I take his arm. "Don't worry," I whisper as we make our way to the bus. "We'll have fun."

The bus drops off Jasmine and Chris, who are being chaperoned by Kaylee, and then Matthew and Carolyn, who are stuck with Brianna for the evening. Then Daniel, Barbara, and I arrive at Vincenzo's, which, if the sign in the window is to be believed, has the best meatballs this side of the Atlantic Ocean.

Barbara goes to speak with the hostess, and a few minutes later, Daniel and I are shown to a booth. Barbara gets her own table a few yards away. It's 5:30 on a Tuesday, so the only other people in the restaurant are old people here for the early-bird special and families with screaming kids, but it's still amazing to be out in the real world again.

We spend a few minutes looking at the menu and another minute giving our orders to the waitress. She looks at us curiously, and I wonder what Barbara told her about us.

But then she leaves and it's just the two of us. Me and Daniel. Sitting across from each other. On a date. And it's *really* weird.

Daniel keeps fidgeting with his place setting, straightening out his silverware and aligning his napkin and placemat with the edges of the table.

I pick at a piece of bread.

What are we supposed to talk about?

"So…what did you order again?" I say, because the silence is killing me.

"Chicken parm," he says. "What did you get?"

"Spinach ravioli." After another pause, I add, "I guess one of us should have gotten the meatballs."

Daniel makes a face. "There's no way this place has the best meatballs in America."

I laugh. "I know, right? Who are they kidding? They have *crayons* on the table."

Daniel smiles. "And they spelled *lasagna* wrong."

"They did? I didn't even notice that! I was too distracted by the dried glob of ketchup on my menu."

Daniel laughs and reaches for a piece of bread. He smiles at me as he chews.

I glance at Barbara—she's at her table, sipping a glass of red wine, reading a book. "What do you think her deal is?" I ask, nodding my head in her direction.

"What do you mean?"

"Well, she's got to be at least seventy, right?"

"I guess."

"So what do you think she's doing here? Shouldn't she be off spoiling her grandkids or living it up in some retirement community or something?"

Daniel gives me a stern look. "She's here to help us, Lexi."

"Oh. Right." I nod. "I know, I just meant…never mind. It doesn't matter."

Daniel studies me. "You don't agree with all that stuff that Matthew said, do you?" he asks quietly. "About New Horizons being a waste of time?"

I meet his eyes. "No," I say after a minute. "Of course not."

He looks relieved and goes back to sipping his soda.

Time for a change of subject. "So what do you like to do back home, Daniel?"

He shrugs. "I don't know."

"Oh come on, there's got to be something. Some hobby or something?"

"Well…I like to read."

"Me too. Ever read *Harry Potter*?"

He looks up at me, confused. "Don't you remember—"

I burst out laughing at his bewildered expression. "That was a joke. Sorry. I guess it wasn't very funny."

"Oh." His face slowly breaks into a grin. "No, it was funny. I've never been very good at picking up on jokes and stuff."

"That's okay. So, you like to read…?"

"Yeah. Mostly fantasy books."

"Oh, cool."

"Have you ever read the *Flame Hunter* series?"

"No. What's it about?"

"You have to read it, Lexi. It's so good. It's about this world where all the light has been extinguished. The sun has burned out, and there's no such thing as electricity, and the use of fire is regulated by the emperor." He leans forward eagerly. "And there's this band of people called the Flame Hunters who track down the last Sparks left in the world and distribute them to the poor people who can't afford to pay the emperor's prices. But what they're doing is the most illegal crime possible, so they're always on the run from the emperor's henchmen and in a constant state of danger."

"Wow," I say. "Sounds complicated."

"Nah, not really. It's all explained really well in book one."

"How many books are there?" I ask.

"Nine so far, but there's another one coming out in a few months. I pre-ordered it." There's a glimmer of real joy in Daniel's eyes.

I smile.

Daniel goes on and on about the illicit love affair between Princess Thenbie and the Flame Hunter leader Dominic Archer, and I just sit back and listen, happy he's happy.

"So what about you? What do you like to do?" he asks just as the food arrives. It's steaming hot and smells incredible. Maybe we underestimated this place. Or maybe we're just really sick of Mrs. Wykowski's dining cabin food.

I take a bite of ravioli. "Oh my God, that's good," I say through a mouth full of cheese and spinach and sauce. "How's yours?"

"Delicious," Daniel says. "Want to share?"

"Ooh yeah, good idea!" We split our food in half and swap portions. We eat in silence for a while, but this time it's a comfortable silence. It's not until my plate is nearly empty that I remember our conversation. "Oh, so to answer your question, I really like drawing—designing clothes and stuff."

Daniel nods. "I know—I've seen you at the arts and crafts table. You're really good."

"Thanks."

He smiles. I smile back. But then he doesn't take his eyes away. He just keeps smiling and staring at me way past the socially acceptable amount of time, and it's starting to get awkward and I have to look away. I check my watch, just for somewhere to look, and I'm surprised to find that it's already 6:30.

"We have to get to the movie," I say and push my plate away.

Barbara pays our bills and makes a quick phone call. A few minutes later, a taxi pulls up in front of the restaurant and drives us to the movie theater.

The movie is really dumb and the theater is really cold. Daniel notices me shivering and puts his arm around me.

Then about halfway through the movie, just as the kids start doing some big dance that somehow everyone in the school knows the moves to, he reaches over and takes my hand.

This is not just a friendly hand-holding. His hand is shaking—with nervousness?—and he grasps my fingers tightly, giving them a little squeeze every now and then. I don't understand it, and I sure as hell don't like it.

I look at him and I can just make out his smile in the flickering light of the movie screen.

I don't know what to do. I want to pull my hand away, to demand to know what he's thinking and storm out of the theater. But if I freak out, Barbara will know I'm not giving this whole "date" thing my all, and it will get back to Mr. Martin, and then he won't be able to tell my mother that I was a perfect student. Plus, I don't want to embarrass Daniel or hurt his feelings. He clearly *is* giving the date thing his all, and I don't want to ruin it for him.

I'm just *really* uncomfortable right now.

But wait—maybe holding hands is against the rules? Maybe it's considered inappropriate conduct or something. Maybe if Barbara

saw, she would make us sit apart from each other. I turn my head
to look at Barbara in the row behind us, trying to nonchalantly get
her attention, but she's sound asleep, her head tilted back and her
mouth wide open.

So I just stay like that, in Daniel's arms, my hand getting sweaty
in his, counting the seconds until the end of the movie.

I finally get my hand back when the lights come up. Daniel is
still grinning at me, but the best I can do is give him an unsure
eyebrow raise. We stand on the sidewalk outside the movie theater,
a bubble of weirdness surrounding us, waiting for the bus to come. I
never thought I'd actually be looking forward to seeing Mr. Martin
and getting back to New Horizons, but at this point, I'll take it. I
just want this night to be over.

I rock back and forth on my heels impatiently, my arms crossed
over my chest.

"Are you cold, Lexi?" Daniel asks.

"*No*," I say a little too forcefully. "I mean…no. I'm fine." I
muster up a little smile.

"I'm going to go run into the convenience store to see if they
have the candies I like," Barbara says to us suddenly. "Are you two
okay to wait out here on your own?"

No, I try to say with my eyes. *No, please. Stay!*

But Daniel says, "Of course, we'll be fine. Take your time," and
Barbara disappears through the store's automatic doors.

The second she's out of sight, Daniel turns to me. "Lexi, I had such a wonderful time tonight," he says shyly. He grabs both my hands, and I watch in horror as, in slow motion, he closes his eyes and leans toward me, lips puckered.

No no no no no! It's not exactly the word *no* that's going through my head—it's more like every fiber of my being, even the New Horizons–altered parts like the grown-out roots of my hair and my baby-pink manicure, is screaming out the *essence* of no. This is so wrong. I don't want this. I will *never* want this.

Daniel's about an inch away from my face when I finally come to my senses. I yank my hands away and leap backward, putting as much distance between us as I can.

Daniel's eyes are huge, his body frozen in that same going-in-for-a-kiss position. "What's wrong?"

"You were going to kiss me!"

"I know…I…"

Let him down easy, I remind myself. "This isn't a real date, Daniel. I'm sorry, but it's just an exercise."

"But…" His hands start shaking and he nervously folds them under his arms. "But I thought…I thought you liked me."

His face is flooded with hurt, and I immediately feel like a complete jerk. I take a small step closer. "I do like you. As a friend. But that's all."

He shakes his head. "No. You put your head on my shoulder that night outside the rec cabin! And you kissed me during your Father Wound exercise!"

But after we kissed at Vinny's party, I'd said to Zoë. *I thought… maybe…you might feel the same way? About me?*

God, how did things get so turned around?

"Oh, Daniel, I'm sorry. I didn't mean to give you the wrong idea. I kissed you—on the cheek—because you were playing the role of my father. It was all part of the exercise. And I put my head on your shoulder because I was drunk and sad and you're my friend. That's all it was."

Tears are filling his eyes, and his lower lip is beginning to quiver. He takes his glasses off and wipes the lenses on his shirt—I get the feeling he's just doing it so he doesn't have to look at me.

I take another step closer to him and gently place my hand on his shoulder. I quickly check to make sure Barbara isn't coming back yet, and then I whisper, "Daniel, do you really have those kinds of feelings for me?"

He chokes out a sob. "I don't know. I'm so confused."

"I know," I say. "I know. Me too." And at the risk of giving him the wrong idea yet again, I pull him into a hug.

He cries into my shoulder, and I just stand there and hold him and let him get it all out. After a few moments, I see Barbara exiting the store from the corner of my eye. "Barbara's coming," I whisper, putting a safe distance between us once again.

Daniel nods, wipes his eyes and nose on his sleeve, and manages to get a pretty good hold of himself by the time she reaches us.

"Did you two have fun tonight?" she asks, giving us a grandma-like wink.

"Yes," I say, answering for both of us. "It was great. Thank you."

And then the bus pulls up to take us home.

Chapter 22

"How was your date, lovebirds?" Matthew asks at breakfast.

Daniel just stares at his untouched eggs.

"It was good," I say. "The movie was terrible, but the dinner was pretty good. Right, Daniel?"

He nods.

"How was yours?" I ask Matthew and Carolyn.

They grin at each other. "It was so much fun," Carolyn says. "We went to this big arcade place. Matthew won me a little stuffed monkey."

"Well, if there's one thing I know, it's how to treat the ladies." Matthew winks. "And this girl"—he jerks a thumb in Carolyn's direction—"is the best Skee-Ball player I've ever seen in my life."

"What can I say? It's a gift."

For the second time, I feel that irrational surge of jealousy. I want to switch places with Matthew so badly. I want to be the one who played Skee-Ball with Carolyn last night and won her a stuffed monkey and be reminiscing about it with her this morning.

But I laugh along with them anyway.

For the next few days, the girls focus on childcare. We have to carry around these creepy little electronic babies that cry randomly and won't stop until you hold a key in its mouth for a certain amount of time.

Brianna and Kaylee demonstrate how to change a diaper on a dummy, and we each take turns mastering the process. Mrs. Wykowski shows us how to use a food processor to whip up our own natural baby food. And over the course of several sessions, Barbara teaches us the basics of knitting and sewing, so we can make things like baby blankets and booties and stuff. I actually really enjoy that last part. I get permission from Brianna to go to the rec cabin and get some stuff from the arts and crafts corner to add to my booties—sequins, different colored thread for adding colorful stitching around the ankle. They actually turn out really adorable and I get a lot of compliments from the other campers. It might not be high fashion, but for now, it's as close as I'm going to get.

Toward the end of the week, Mr. Martin announces that we'll be leaving the camp again, this time with our group of four.

"We're going to take a day-trip into the city tomorrow," he says. "It's a major step in the reintegration process. You will still be chaperoned, but the plan is a lot less structured than it was for date night. You will be the ones who decide where you want to go and how you want to spend your time."

"I vote for a gay bar," Matthew whispers to us.

I giggle. "Shhh!"

"This outing will be all about experiencing the world through new eyes. Where will you go? What will you do? How will you interact with others? Remember your lessons as you make all of these choices, because the temptations out there in the real world are much, much greater than they are here. As it says in Philippians four, verse nine, 'Whatever you have learned or received or heard from me, or seen in me—put it into practice. And the God of peace will be with you.'"

That night, the four of us hang out in our hidden spot outside the rec cabin. Daniel flips through a Washington, DC guidebook and suggests ideas to the rest of us.

"There are free shows on Saturday mornings at the National Theatre," he says. "Or we could go see the butterflies at the National Museum of Natural History."

"I was serious about the gay bar," Matthew says. "They have ones that are eighteen and over. I bet they wouldn't even ID us."

"Oh sure, I'm sure Kaylee would be totally cool with that," I say.

"There are ways to ditch a chaperone, Lexi. Haven't you ever been on a school field trip?"

"It's not gonna happen, Matthew."

"I've always wanted to go to the Smithsonian," Carolyn says as she practices her purl stitch.

"Which one?" Daniel says, looking it up. "There're so many."

"Oh. I don't know. Isn't there a pop culture exhibit? I heard that somewhere." She scoots over to look at the guidebook with Daniel.

Matthew glances at me. "Can I talk to you for a minute?" he asks and nods his head toward an area of the field several yards away.

"About what?"

"It will just take a minute." He starts walking away and, curious, I follow.

"What's up?" I ask once we're out of earshot of Carolyn and Daniel. He sits on the grass and pats the spot next to him. "Sit."

I do.

"I just wanted to see how you're doing. We never get a chance to talk."

I smile. "I'm doing okay. How are you doing?"

"Oh, you know. I'm fine. Looking forward to getting the hell out of here."

"Yeah."

"So what's going on with you and Carolyn?" There's an eager glint in his eye.

I sigh. "Nothing's going on, Matthew. And you really have to stop looking at me like that."

"Bullshit. You're completely smitten. And who can blame you? She's hot."

I raise an eyebrow. "Mr. Kinsey Six, thinking a girl is hot? Maybe Mr. Martin has gotten to you more than you think."

Matthew rolls his eyes. "I might be gay, Lexi, but I still have eyes. And that girl is gorgeous. And the two of you together…that would be hotness overload."

My stomach twinges a little at the thought. "We're just friends." I tie a blade of grass into knots.

"Why?"

"Why?" I repeat.

"Yeah. *Why* are you just friends?"

"Why do you think?" I tick off the reasons on my fingers. "Because we're here to learn to become *straight*. Because there are more important things in life than having a crush on somebody. Because she doesn't like me like that. Because New Horizons is the *last* place on Earth that we could be together. Because some things just aren't worth the risk."

"I disagree," Matthew says. "If there's *anything* worth any risk at all, it's got to be love, right?"

I shake my head. "I might have thought that once but not anymore."

There's a pause as Matthew lies back on the grass, leaving me to consider what I just said.

"You do know you're not going to leave here straight, right?" he says after a minute.

"I know."

"So why do you keep going along with all of this stuff?"

I tell him my plan to fake being "cured."

He stares at me, bewildered. Then he says, "Lexi, when you first realized you were gay, like really acknowledged it on a conscious level, how did you feel?"

"What do you mean?"

"I mean, what did you think about the whole thing?"

"I don't know." I shrug.

"Think about it," he pushes.

I pick a dandelion and pluck its little yellow petals off one by one, thinking back to fourth grade, when I finally realized why I had never understood my friends' excitement about the first boy-girl parties. Might as well tell the truth while I can. "I was terrified."

"How come?"

"Because all I knew, everything I'd been taught, was that gay people were sinners. I didn't know what would happen if people found out." I still don't know how the town would react, actually, if they all knew. I toss the bald dandelion stem.

Matthew shakes his head. "That's not what I mean. I don't mean what did you think other people would think. I mean what did *you* think? Deep down. Apart from all the small-town bullshit."

Oh. Hmm. I push away the fear of the unknown, the fear I've been living with every day for eight long years, and really think about Matthew's question. The answer kind of surprises me. "I guess I felt kind of relieved in a way."

Matthew smiles. "Why?"

"Because I finally understood why my feelings never seemed to match up with my friends'. Everything finally made sense." I lie down now too. Fluffy cotton-ball clouds drift across the sky.

"Were you ashamed?" Matthew asks.

"No," I admit.

"Were you sad?"

"No."

"Embarrassed?"

"No."

"Did you hate yourself?"

"No."

"You were okay with it?"

"Well…yeah."

Matthew turns to face me. "So what the hell, Lex? You're already so much better off than most of the kids here. Why would you want to go backward?"

I hesitate. "My mom…"

"I know. It's a shitty situation. And I get it, I really do. But Lexi, this is *your* life. It's not your mom's. You have to do what makes you happy too."

I don't say anything.

"What do you want?" Matthew asks.

He wants me to admit that I don't want to change. That I don't want to live a lie. That I'm happier being me, as is, even if it means I have to move away from my hometown and never go back. That I want to be with Carolyn. But I can't. I'm not ready for that.

"I want my family back," I say, sticking with the only part of the truth that I'm comfortable speaking aloud. Then a troubling thought occurs to me. "You don't say this stuff to Carolyn too, do you?"

"Nah."

"Why not?"

"I don't think she'd listen to me," he says. "She's still hoping for a reparative therapy miracle."

I let out a groan of frustration. "So then why the hell would you think it would be a good idea for me to tell her how I feel?"

"Because I think she likes you too. And it would be a lot more effective if it came from you."

I watch as a cloud slowly morphs from an ice cream cone into a pirate ship. A minuscule spark of *what if* has ignited somewhere deep inside me, and I hate Matthew for putting it there.

"You know what I think?" he says after a long stretch of silence. "I think you're scared."

"Of what?"

"Of telling Carolyn how you feel and being rejected. And I think you might be hiding behind the mom excuse so you don't have to put yourself out there again."

I feel like I've been punched straight through my stomach. "You don't know what you're talking about."

"Very possible. But one thing I do know is that Carolyn isn't Zoë. And you'll never know for sure until you try."

Chapter 23

I float through the morning drive to DC; Matthew's words have been branded onto my mind. *You're scared. This is your life. You'll never know until you try.*

But even though the conversation keeps replaying in my head, presenting itself from different angles, I'm still in the same place. Because no matter how good Matthew's points might have been, what he doesn't seem to understand is that my feelings don't matter. It's the circumstances *surrounding* them that hold the power. The way things are back home, both in my town and in my family, the rigid structure of New Horizons, Carolyn's dedication to the process, the scars still fresh on my heart. So maybe he's right: maybe I *am* scared. But if my choices are safety and security versus certain pain, I know which one I'm going with.

The bus drops us off at the Capitol building. "Remember, everyone!" Mr. Martin calls out before we all disperse. "Meet back here at six p.m. sharp! Don't be late!"

Daniel, Matthew, Carolyn, Kaylee, and I set off on foot. Daniel has a whole itinerary mapped out for us. First stop: the Capitol Reflecting Pool, followed by the Jefferson and Lincoln Memorials and the Washington Monument. He reads aloud from the guidebook, telling us all the important dates and facts.

"History is *fun*," Matthew says sarcastically, as we stare up at the giant obelisk that's somehow supposed to pay tribute to our first president.

The big event for the day is the National Zoo, which beat out the Smithsonian after Matthew presented a pretty convincing case against spending our one day of freedom stuck in a museum, so after all the history, we walk to the Metro red line.

As we walk, Matthew whispers to me, "I have a plan."

I give him a sidelong glance. Matthew's plans are *never* a good idea—it's a miracle they haven't gotten us into trouble yet. "Can't you take a break from all the scheming for one day?"

He grins. "No way. This is my best plan yet!"

"But we're having such a nice time—"

"Just trust me. You'll like this one. I promise."

His eyes are bright and excited, and I know there's no talking him out of whatever he's got up his sleeve. "If you say so," I say.

We buy our Metro tickets, and a few minutes later, the train rolls into the station. We all get on, and Matthew starts up a conversation with Kaylee and Daniel about which animals they're looking forward to seeing most at the zoo.

Then, just as the doors are about to close, Matthew turns away from his conversation, grabs me and Carolyn, and pushes us off the train. I trip over my own feet and fall onto the platform, skinning the heels of my hands. By the time I gather my bearings, the doors have closed, Matthew is waving at us from inside the train with the biggest, dopiest grin I've ever seen, and Kaylee is pounding against the door, futilely trying to get to us. The train pulls away, and I look up at Carolyn, who somehow managed to survive Matthew's surprise attack in one piece. She stares back down at me, her eyes huge. We're alone now. In the city. With no group, no chaperone, and no way to get in touch with them.

I'm going to kill Matthew.

Chapter 24

Carolyn reaches down to help me up. My scraped-up hand stings as it comes into contact with hers, and I wince.

"Oh my God, your hands!" Carolyn says, noticing my injury. "Are you okay?"

"Yeah, I'm fine." I brush my palms together to show that it's just a surface wound. "I can't believe Matthew!"

"I know! Why would he do that?"

I try to keep my face neutral. "No idea."

"Me either." She shakes her head, baffled. "So what do you think? Should we wait here for Kaylee to come back for us, or should we get on the next train and meet them at the zoo?"

I don't know where it comes from, but before I know it, I'm saying, "Or we could take advantage of this opportunity away from everyone."

She stares at me, as though she's not sure what I'm getting at. "What do you mean?"

"Um…I mean we could go do our own thing. See the city on

our own and then later say we tried to find them but we got lost or something. We know where and when to meet everyone, so it's not like we'll be stranded forever."

Suddenly her face brightens. "We could go to the Smithsonian! We could see Kermit the Frog and Dorothy's ruby slippers!" She does a cute little excited jig.

I look at her smile, and suddenly I don't want to kill Matthew quite so much anymore.

"Sounds fun," I say.

Carolyn buys some Band-Aids and first aid ointment at a pharmacy, and her hands move delicately across mine as she fixes up my cuts.

"Okay," she says once I'm all bandaged up. "So how do we get there?"

"I have no clue. I was relying on Daniel to tell us where to go. Guess that was poor planning."

"Lexi, neither of us could have predicted that Matthew would pull a stunt like that."

"I should have," I mutter under my breath.

Carolyn asks someone on the street where the museum is. It's actually not that far, and in less than ten minutes, we're staring up at a giant sign that says *The National Treasures of Popular Culture gallery is CLOSED for renovations. We apologize for any inconvenience!*

Carolyn looks crestfallen. "I'm sorry," I say.

She shrugs. "It's okay. At least we tried."

"So what should we do now?" I ask. Then I begrudgingly add, "We can go to the zoo to try to find the guys if you want."

Carolyn nods. "Yeah, we should probably do that."

My heart sinks. We walk back to the Metro, and just as we're about to go down into the station, a guy hands us a flyer. "Free concert today at Dupont Circle," he says. "Just two stops away on the red line."

The flyer lists a bunch of bands I've never heard of, but that doesn't matter. Wherever this Dupont Circle place is, I suddenly desperately want to be there. I look at Carolyn. "I haven't been to a concert since before my dad died."

"Do you want to go?" she asks.

"Yeah, kinda," I admit. "But we don't have to—"

"Let's go," she says decidedly.

I smile. "Really?"

"Why not? We probably won't be able to find Matthew and Daniel and Kaylee anyway, and this is important to you."

It turns out Dupont Circle is a really cute area with restaurants and coffee shops and stuff. A bluegrass band is playing on a small stage set up in the middle of the circle.

"This is amazing!" Carolyn says.

She's right. The band is really good—a girl in a cute floral-print dress and cowboy boots is singing and people are dancing. A group of little kids has joined hands and is skipping around in a big circle. I'd actually forgotten how much joy there really is in the world.

"You hungry?" I ask Carolyn as we pass a sidewalk café within hearing range of the concert.

"Famished," she says, and we get a table.

While we wait for our burgers, Carolyn raises her water glass. "To new friends."

"And a whole afternoon without chaperones," I say.

Carolyn laughs, and we clink classes. "You mean you don't miss Brianna?" she says, mock shocked.

"Not even a little bit." I can't even joke about it. "Do you ever wonder why she's here? I mean at New Horizons?"

"I don't know." Carolyn looks thoughtful. "She didn't go through the program, right? Just Kaylee, Deb, and John?"

"Right. So we know she doesn't have SSA. But then why isn't she off doing her womanly duty and popping out kids?" It was meant to be a joke, but I immediately realize how judge-y that sounded. "Sorry. I didn't mean…obviously there's nothing wrong with having kids. Or…you know, *not* having kids."

Carolyn laughs and says, "No, I knew what you meant. Maybe she's here out of some sort of religious duty."

I shrug. "Maybe. But she's *so* hardcore about the whole thing. Like, she won't even call me Lexi, you know? There's got to be more to her story than she's letting on."

Carolyn's smile fades away. "Not everyone has to share their entire life story with the whole world, Lexi." A biting tone has entered her voice.

Heat rushes to my face, and I instantly feel like a total jerk. Carolyn's been just as secretive about her past as Brianna has. Of course she would take my comment personally.

I open my mouth to say something, but then the waitress shows up with our food and I close it again.

"Can I get you ladies anything else?" the waitress asks.

We both just shake our heads.

When the waitress finally leaves, I quickly say, "I'm so sorry, I didn't mean—"

"No," she cuts me off. "You didn't say anything wrong." She hangs her head and whispers into her food. "I really should be over it by now."

Over it? Over what? I wait for her to say more, but she doesn't.

I take a couple of bites of my burger, but eventually the suspense gets to be too much. And she wouldn't have said that if she didn't want me to ask, right? "You should be over what by now?" I say.

Carolyn looks up at me, her face weary. "My ex. Natalie."

I stare at her. Her *ex*? As in ex-*girlfriend*? I try to keep my composure. "Natalie?"

"Yeah." There's another long pause, and then she says, "We were together for over a year. Thirteen months and eleven days, to be exact."

I'm floored. I don't know why I never considered that Carolyn would have had a girlfriend before. I guess I just assumed she was like me: closeted and utterly inexperienced.

"So what happened?" I ask. Then I add, "You don't have to tell me if you don't want to."

She sighs. "No, it's all right. But just keep it between us, okay?"

"Of course."

She stabs a French fry with her fork. "You remember how when you were a freshman, everything was kinda scary? Like, you were at a new school and there were so many people and so many hallways that looked the same and so many intimidating older kids?"

I don't exactly remember that. My school is so small it's almost nonexistent, and most of us have known each other since kindergarten, maybe even before. But I just nod.

"Well, Natalie saved me from all that. She was a junior when we met. We were on the varsity cross-country team together, and she and her friends accepted me into their group, and suddenly I went from being the nobody freshman to the cool freshman who was hanging out with the juniors and seniors. It was great. And Natalie and I started spending more and more time together and…Well, you know. It became more."

Carolyn glances up at me, but I don't say anything. "She was a lot more experienced than I was," she says. "She'd been out since middle school. She helped me come out to my parents and friends."

"Wait," I say, confused. "I thought you said no one knew about your SSA."

She blinks. "When did I say that?"

"On the first day of camp, when we were telling everyone why we were here. I said almost nobody back home knew about me and you said you didn't tell anyone either."

"No, I said I didn't tell them about *New Horizons*." She looks at me like she doesn't see why this is important. I'm not sure why it is—maybe because I thought it was something else we had in common.

"So how did they handle the news?" I ask to get the conversation back on track.

She looks off into space. "They were amazing. My parents didn't care at all. They said they just wanted me to be happy. And they loved Natalie, so that helped. And my friends were her friends, and they obviously already knew she was gay, so this was barely even news to them."

Carolyn absentmindedly picks the sesame seeds off the bun of her untouched cheeseburger. "I loved her so much, Lexi," she says quietly. "She was my whole life. She told me she wanted to marry me someday. I actually started keeping a wedding planning book." She shakes her head, embarrassed. "I really *do* want to get married, you know. I wasn't making that up. But Matthew's right—I never really had a problem imagining *two* white dresses in that scenario." She laughs, just a little.

Hmm. "So then why…" I want to ask why she said she wanted to marry a man if she really doesn't. I want to ask—if that whole story was a lie—why she's *really* here at New Horizons. But I know

Carolyn well enough by now to know that sometimes staying quiet is the best way to get her to open up.

"She ate dinner with my family most nights after practice and she even slept over sometimes. My parents joked that they had another daughter now."

"Slept over?" I say almost before I realize I'm speaking. "Like, in your room?"

She raises an eyebrow. "Like, in my bed."

"Oh. Right. Sorry, I'm stupid." Okay, envy just got upgraded to full-on, green-eyed jealousy.

"No, actually I am," she mumbles.

"Huh?"

She rubs the back of her neck. "I was so in love with her that I couldn't see what was right in front of my face."

"I don't understand."

"After a few months, she started acting different. She wouldn't come over as much or she would come over for dinner and then have some reason why she couldn't sleep over. A few times I asked her if anything was wrong, but she would say, 'Of course not, baby, why would you even say that?' and smile and kiss me, and I would forget about everything except the way she made me feel. Even after I started hearing the rumors..." She trails off, but I can't let her stop talking now. I need to know.

"Rumors?"

"Yeah. The problem with being friends with Natalie's friends was that they would sometimes say things around me when Natalie wasn't around, almost as if they forgot I was her girlfriend."

"What kind of things?"

"Like, things about her going to the city on the weekends to hook up with other girls." Her voice trembles.

"Oh, Carolyn…"

"But I refused to believe it. She loved me. She cried when I told her about Kenny, and she helped me understand that it wasn't my fault. She told me she loved my family and couldn't wait to officially be a part of it. We went to visit colleges together, but only ones that were close enough for me to visit her every weekend. I never doubted for a *second* that she was as committed to me as I was to her." She's starting to tear up. I hand her my napkin. "Thanks." She blots her eyes.

"If this is too hard for you to talk about—"

"No, it's okay. It actually kinda feels good to get it out."

I understand that. "So what happened?" I ask.

"I borrowed her phone one day at practice and saw text messages from a girl at another school." Carolyn's expression is fragile, like she's just seconds away from crumbling into sobs. "When I asked her about it, she broke down and admitted everything. She said she'd been hooking up with other people—but only because she loved me so much that it scared her and made her do things she didn't really want to do."

I reach a hand across the table. She holds on.

"And the thing was, I stayed with her. Even though I was totally destroyed inside. She promised she wouldn't do it anymore, and I was so obsessed with her that I actually believed her. She'd admitted to being with other girls but still somehow made me feel like I was the only girl in the world."

Her bleary gaze drifts across the street to where the bluegrass band is playing their instruments and stomping their feet. The happy music clashes harshly with the tone surrounding our table.

"It happened again a couple of months later. And I forgave her again. It wasn't until it happened for a third time—the third time that I knew of, at least—that I finally forced myself to admit that I couldn't stay with her. I loved her so desperately, but I wasn't in control of my own life anymore. I felt like a puppet."

I squeeze her hand tightly. I don't care that it hurts the scrapes.

"Breaking up with Natalie was the hardest thing I've ever done in my life. She was sobbing, apologizing, begging me to forgive her. And I wanted to. But I couldn't."

Carolyn takes a deep breath and looks straight at me. "Lexi, if I had to go through something like that again, I don't think I would survive." She lets go of my hand. "If I'm with a boy, then it will never be this bad again. *I'll* be the one in charge of how things go."

There it is. That's why she's here. That's why she wants to change so badly.

"But what makes you think it will be any different with a guy?" I ask. "Have you ever had a boyfriend?"

"No." She thinks for a minute. "I just know it would though. I see my friends with their boyfriends, and yeah, they have their problems, but it's different. Guys are different. They don't get as emotional. There's only one set of stupidly overactive teenage girl hormones in the relationship, not two. It's just easier."

She straightens up and shakes her head quickly as if to shake the sadness away. "Anyway. All that stuff with Natalie is in the past now."

But I don't think it is in the past at all. I think it's very much in her present. "Is that what you think about when you get all distant?" I ask.

She blushes. "I didn't realize I was being so obvious about it."

"You're not," I say. "I just happen to have a lot of experience in spotting that kind of thing, you know? So I noticed that sometimes you aren't entirely *here*."

"I guess it's just that every time something happens at New Horizons that makes me feel uncomfortable or makes me second-guess my reasons for being here, I think about Natalie and what she put me through. It helps me stay determined." She looks at me. "You do that sometimes too, don't you?"

I blink. "I do?"

"Yeah, like with your mom?"

"Oh. Yeah." I wonder how she knew that.

We pay the check and step back out to the sidewalk, trying to figure out which way to go. But this whole conversation has my head spinning. Every time Carolyn's lost in her thoughts, she's thinking about another girl. Natalie. A girl she loved and shared her bed with and surely did stuff with that I've only ever read about. I'm so jealous I can barely even see straight.

The band switches to a bluegrass-y cover of a song that I know I know but can't place at first. Then the singer comes in, and I've got it: "We Will Become Silhouettes" by The Postal Service. It was one of my dad's favorite songs—some sort of sign, maybe?—and this blue-grass version is so weird and unexpected that I'm suddenly inspired to do something else weird and unexpected. I grab Carolyn's sleeve and pull her across the street to the center of the circle. Then I jump into the cluster of kids and join them in their goofy, wiggly dancing.

Carolyn stands just outside the crowd, laughing.

"Come on!" I call to her.

She shakes her head.

"Yes!" I jump around to the beat of the music.

She just watches me, chewing on her lip, her arms crossed over her chest, debating.

I watch her right back, still dancing but looking only at her. I want so badly to go up to her and gently uncross her arms and hold her hands in mine. I want to smooth away the place where her teeth are worrying her lip and share my lip balm by brushing my mouth against hers. I want her to forget all about Natalie and everything bad that's ever happened ever. I want to dance with her.

I skip over to the edge of the circle, clapping my hands to the song along with the rest of the crowd. I stand right in front of Carolyn. Our toes are touching.

I hold my hand out, waiting. "Have fun. Just for today. You can go back to being sulky tomorrow, I promise."

She hesitates for a moment more, and then a grin begins to tug at her lips. "It *would* be a shame to waste this…" She looks around us, taking it all in. Her eyes flicker with the movements of the people dancing and the cars passing by and the wind blowing through the leaves of the trees. And finally, she gives in.

She grabs my hands, and suddenly she's the one pulling me into the circle, and we dance around together, making up our own doofy square dance moves. It's all I can do to try to appreciate every single second—and pray my palms don't get sweaty.

We probably look ridiculous, but nobody seems to care. No one seems to care that we're two girls, holding hands, dancing together either.

Four songs later, we're still not tired. Somehow, this strange, accidental day has become one of the best of my life.

When the band goes on break, we resume our walk.

"Feeling better?" I ask, trying to catch my breath.

She smiles as she pulls her hair back into a ponytail. "Much. Thanks, Lexi."

"Anytime."

We wander into a few stores. I run my fingers over the beautiful clothes hanging from the racks. Carolyn tries on a really cute purple rhinestone headband, but she doesn't have enough money for it, so I give her the rest of my field-trip allowance from Kaylee, which she finally takes after a lot of convincing.

After a while, we stop to rest in a park. The bench we sit on has a little plaque on it that says *For Julie. There's no other person I'd rather share a pizza with. Love, Marco.* It's in the shade and about ten degrees cooler here than it is in the sun.

"So now that you know my whole miserable history," Carolyn says, "I feel like I can ask. Whatever happened with you and Zoë?"

Hearing Zoë's name from Carolyn's lips is just too weird. "What do you mean?"

"After that day in her room. Did anything else ever happen with you two?"

"Nope." I sigh. "That was it. We didn't even speak to each other after that." I think for a second. "Actually, that's not true. She did tell me how sorry she was when my dad died. But so did everyone else, so I don't really count that." I shrug. "At least she kept my secret, as far as I can tell. That's something, I guess."

Carolyn turns sideways to face me and rests her temple—the one with the birthmark—on the back of the bench. "You must miss him."

"My dad? You have no idea."

"That thing that Mr. Martin made you do during your Father Wound session was pretty messed up," she says. "I don't know how you got through it."

"I just made myself say whatever I needed to say to get out of there." I fidget with my bracelet. "It didn't work anyway. My last memory of my dad is still intact." I look at Carolyn and she's just watching me, waiting for me to continue. "The real last time I saw my dad was the day before Thanksgiving. He was in a hospice. That's a place where they, um, send people to die." Carolyn nods. "My mom picked me up from school in the middle of the day. He knew he didn't have much time left, and he told her to get me. I don't know how he knew, but he did. I guess it's just one of those things that you don't really understand until it happens to you.

"When I got there, he asked my mom to give us a few minutes alone and then he said, 'Lexi, you are the best thing I ever did in my life.' I'll never forget that. He said it right away, like he was worried if he didn't say it right then, he would never get the chance. And then he smiled this huge smile that I didn't understand—he should have been sad. Or scared. He was about to die, but he looked happy. But I think now I get that he wasn't thinking about what was about to happen; he was thinking about what had already happened in his life. And he was proud." I take a breath. "And I almost told him right then, Carolyn. The truth. About me. I'd tried to tell him before and always chickened out, but this time I thought I was really going to do it. Use one of the last moments I had with him to be completely honest. I sat there, the room closing in on me as I concentrated on building up the courage to do it. And then he said, 'Promise me you'll take care of your mother,' and the moment was gone."

"I'm so sorry, Lexi," Carolyn says.

I shake my head. "It's okay. It's actually better. After how my mom reacted when she found out, I'm glad I didn't tell him. I don't know what I would have done if he reacted the same way."

"Do you really think he would have?"

"I don't know."

She looks down at her lap. "I guess I have the opposite problem. My parents have been so cool with it that they refuse to even try to understand why I wanted to come here. They've been really down on me about this whole camp thing."

"Yeah." I want to tell her that she doesn't know how lucky she is, that almost any of us at New Horizons would trade places with her in a heartbeat if we could, but I don't. I understand, maybe better than anyone in the whole world, why she's here. She's trying to move past the hurt. "Did they give you the money for the camp?" I ask.

She nods. "They never said I *couldn't* come; they just asked me to reconsider about a hundred times."

We sit there in silence for a while, watching the people go by, and I try to reason through my thoughts. Eventually I break the silence. "Since we're being honest…"

"Yeah?"

"I think Zoë was part of the reason I came here. It wasn't just about my mom. I mean, it was *mostly* about my mom, but…I think I also thought that if New Horizons could help me get Zoë out of my head once and for all, everything would be better."

Carolyn looks at me with those big blue eyes. "Did it work?"

"Well, I *have* been thinking about her a lot less than I used to…" I drift off.

"That's good!" she says.

But the rest of my unfinished sentence is that I've been thinking about Zoë a lot less than I used to because I've been thinking about *Carolyn* instead. And I can't exactly tell her that.

We walk back to the Capitol to meet the bus and face the music.

And it's the funniest thing: I know I can't tell Carolyn the truth, but in this moment, I can't remember *why*.

It's like the rule my parents drilled into my brain a long time ago: don't talk to strangers. Don't do it, Lexi. It's the worst possible thing you can do. Bad things will happen if you try. It was a certainty in my life—no matter what, I could never, should never, *would* never talk to strangers. But then I grew up. Things changed—the world changed—and suddenly, somehow, I knew that I was *supposed* to talk to strangers. That's how you meet people. That's how you make new friends.

This is the same thing: don't tell Carolyn how you feel. It was the one thing I knew for sure—until it wasn't.

Carolyn and I just spent this amazing, magical day together. We clearly have a connection. We've shared some moments. And up until Natalie broke her heart, she was fine with being gay. More than fine—she was out and happy. She doesn't have a moral or religious objection to it, and her parents are totally cool with it. So maybe…maybe she *doesn't* really want to become straight. Maybe she just needs to be in love again. Maybe she just needs someone who will treat her the way she deserves to be treated.

Matthew was right: I'll never know for sure until I try.

I decide to test the waters. "Have you been thinking about Natalie less since you've been at New Horizons?"

She smiles. "Yeah, actually. I have."

What does that smile mean? Could she be trying to say that *I'm* the reason she hasn't been thinking about Natalie as much? What if the only thing that's standing between us right now is our fear?

Oh God, I want to tell her.

It's an hour walk back to the Capitol, every step a huge effort through the thick, sticky heat, and I war with myself the whole time. Tell her. Don't tell her. Tell her. Don't.

And then the Capitol dome lies ahead, and it's almost six o'clock, and I'm out of time. If I don't tell her now, that's it. We'll be thrown back into the world of watching eyes and prying ears, and I'll never get another chance.

Mr. Martin said I have to make a choice. And I'm finally choosing—I'm choosing my *own* gray area. Why can't I be both a Christian *and* gay? What would be so wrong about that? And instead of working so hard to be something I'm not for Mom, why can't I put all that energy into talking to her, helping her to understand me? I haven't even really tried that yet. Maybe, someday, I can have both a girlfriend *and* my family. Carolyn came to New

Horizons even though she's an atheist, even though her parents didn't want her to, simply because that was what she wanted—proof positive that there are no rules. We make our own destinies.

Screw utopia.

"Hey, Carolyn," I say. "Hold back a second?"

Chapter 25

She stops walking. "What's up?"

"Um…" We're right in the middle of the sidewalk at a busy intersection. We can't have this conversation here, with people brushing past us like this. There's a bus stop a few yards away with an empty bench. I motion for her to follow me.

"What's going on?" she asks once we're sitting. "We're going to be late."

"We have a few minutes," I say, my heart galloping unevenly. "I, um…I wanted to say something."

She looks at me, curious. "Okay?"

A new sprinkling of freckles has cropped up across the bridge of her nose. She must have forgotten to put on sunscreen this morning.

"I wanted to tell you…um…" I stare at those adorable specks. "I think you're beautiful."

Whoa. I've actually said it. I make my body take a deep breath, because it seems to have forgotten how to breathe on its own.

She blinks. "What?"

"I think you're so beautiful," I say again and laugh at how easy it is to say the words. "And smart and funny and brave and strong and…well, unlike anyone I've ever met."

A vaguely familiar crease forms between her eyes. But I don't stop to think about what it means. I need to get this all out, and we're almost out of time already.

"I feel a…a connection to you, Carolyn. And it's different from what I felt for Zoë. It's more…whole. Stronger. And I know we're at New Horizons for another few weeks and that it's a pretty impossible situation, but I was wondering if maybe you felt it too? Because if you do, I think I would do pretty much anything to be with you." Oh my God, I can't believe I'm saying all this. But now that I've torn the fence down, I can't stop what's rushing through. "I honestly think I would give up on the camp and the de-gayifying and let the pieces fall where they may with my mom. I never thought I'd say that, but it's true. Because at this point, I don't feel like I have a choice anymore. Or it's more like I *do* have a choice, but it's a *different* choice than it was before." With each word I say, I feel emptier—but the *good* kind of empty. Like there's nothing holding me back anymore. "I don't know how it would work, but maybe after camp is over, we could, I don't know, see each other or something? I mean, I know Connecticut and South Carolina aren't exactly close, but we could figure it out—"

Carolyn holds up a hand to cut me off. "Lexi, stop," she says.

I gasp for breath and wait for her to say something else, but she just hangs her head in her hands, her hair forming a fortress-like wall around her. Her headband twinkles in the sunlight like a tiara.

After a few excruciatingly long moments, I have to ask. "Carolyn? Can you look at me, please?"

She raises her head wearily and turns to me, her expression... troubled.

Oh God.

I finally remember where I've seen that crease between her eyes before. It's the same one that was there after she fought with her parents on Sunday. They wanted her to come home; she wanted to stay. Because the de-gayifying was—is—the most important thing in the world to her.

I'm such an idiot.

I nod, to let her know that I get it. But I have to bite my lip to keep from crying.

Slice, slice, slice. The cuts and cracks in my heart burst back open.

"Sorry," I mumble. "I guess I misread things." I get up and start walking down the sidewalk.

"Lexi!" Carolyn calls out. Her footsteps close in behind me.

"Don't worry about it, Carolyn. It's fine." I can't turn to face her. "Let's just get back to the bus."

I can't believe this is happening again. I promised myself I wouldn't let history repeat itself. And yet here I am *again*, pouring my heart out to someone who has never looked at me as more than a friend. I'm so incredibly stupid.

"It's just…I thought you understood," she says as we speed walk back to the Capitol.

"I did. I do. Whatever. I really don't want to talk about it anymore," I say. *Keep looking straight ahead. Don't look at her.*

"You said you wanted to change too," she continues anyway. "I thought we were on the same page. Were you lying?"

"Of course not," I snap. "I just changed my mind. Maybe *you* can control your feelings, Carolyn, but I can't."

The bus looms in sight now. Mr. Martin is there on the sidewalk, along with several of the other counselors and campers. Kaylee, Matthew, and Daniel don't seem to be there yet though.

I'm a few steps ahead of Carolyn, so when I get to the intersection on a yellow light, I make a run for it. I make it across the street just in time, but Carolyn has to wait for a green signal. It feels good to put physical space between us.

"Hello, Lexi," Mr. Martin says, his face confused. "Where's the rest of your group?"

"Carolyn's right there," I point at her, stranded on the other side of the street.

"And Kaylee, Daniel, and Matthew?"

This is really the last thing I need right now. I knew we were going to be found out, and I knew we were going to get in trouble, but I'd really rather someone else handle the explaining. All I want is to get on the bus and pull my hood over my eyes and sleep for a very long time.

"Um…" I try to figure out what to say. "We lost them. It was an accident."

Mr. Martin's expression turns angry. "What do you mean you *lost* them?"

How do I explain this without selling Matthew out? "We were getting on the Metro to go to the zoo and Carolyn and I accidentally got pushed off."

"Who pushed you?" he asks.

"Uh…"

"It all happened so fast," Carolyn says, joining us. "It was a really crowded train. We didn't see who did it."

Good. She doesn't want to get Matthew in trouble either. But I still refuse to look at her.

Mr. Martin looks from Carolyn to me. "So you two were alone together in the city all day?"

"Don't worry," I say, the open wounds in my heart stinging. "Nothing happened." And I get on the bus.

Carolyn gets on a few moments later. I fix my stare out the window, but out of the corner of my eye, I see her hover by the empty seat next to me. But then she moves on and sits somewhere behind me.

From my window seat, I watch as Kaylee, Matthew, and Daniel arrive and talk to Mr. Martin. I can't hear them, but there's a lot of angry gesturing and what appears to be yelling. At first, Mr. Martin's rage is directed at Kaylee, but then she tells him something and points to Matthew. Mr. Martin turns on him.

Daniel gets on the bus while it's all still going on.

"He's in big trouble, isn't he?" I ask.

Daniel looks worried. "Yeah."

Matthew stands there on the sidewalk, looking smaller than I've ever seen him, staring down at the ground, nodding as Mr. Martin shouts in his face.

This is all my fault. Matthew pulled that stunt on the Metro as a favor to me. And it was all for nothing.

When Mr. Martin finally exhausts his rant, Matthew gets on the bus and sits in the empty seat beside me.

"Are you okay?" I ask.

"Yeah. Mr. Martin's just a little upset. He'll get over it." He shrugs like it's no big deal.

"Are you sure?"

"Don't worry about me." He flashes me a grin. "How was *your* day?"

I turn back to the window. "I don't want to talk about it."

"Uh-oh. What happened?"

"Nothing happened." But my tone clearly says otherwise.

Matthew puts a hand on my arm. "Lexi?" His voice is quiet now, concerned.

My eyes well up. "Please, Matthew." The tears quietly overflow. "Can we just not?"

There's a moment of silence. I don't turn away from the window to see what he's doing. He's probably looking for Carolyn. But then he says simply, "Okay."

Chapter 26

The Great Gatsby sits on my dresser, filled with the soured evidence of whatever it was Carolyn and I had. I can't bring myself to open it.

The little sleep I do manage to get is tainted by an awful dream of being stranded, all alone, on an island version of Washington, DC. There are no boats or bridges or tunnels, and every time I try to swim to civilization, a strong current pulls me back. I go to the statue of Abraham Lincoln to plead for help, and the only response he gives me is a line from *Gatsby*: "There are only the pursued, the pursuing, the busy, and the tired."

The next morning, I pull Matthew aside on the walk to the dining cabin.

"Okay with you if I join team New Horizons Is Bullshit?" I whisper, cranky from my night of sleep deprivation.

He raises his eyebrows. "Really?"

"Really."

"What *happened* yesterday, Lex?"

"What do you think happened?" I mumble.

"I have absolutely no idea," he says. "You guys are acting so weird."

I look at him, my eyes—and heart—heavy. "I told her how I felt and she shot me down."

Matthew's face falls. "Oh no."

"Oh yes."

"God, Lexi, I'm so sorry. I thought if you guys just had a chance to be alone together…"

"Yeah, well. Don't worry about it. It wasn't your fault."

"It kinda was though—I'm the one who pushed you off the damn train."

I look at him. "Yeah, what happened with Mr. Martin, anyway? He looked really mad."

"He's not thrilled, that's for sure. I'm supposed to meet him in his office after breakfast. He's probably gonna kick me out. Three strikes rule." He actually looks worried.

"Well, that's okay, right?" I say hesitantly. "I mean, you hate it here…"

He nods. "That's true." But his expression doesn't change.

Why do I get the feeling I'm missing something?

"Matthew? Is everything okay?"

But then we're at the dining cabin, and there's no more time to talk.

After breakfast, Matthew heads off to the main cabin for his disciplinary meeting with Mr. Martin, and the rest of us go to the carpet cabin for more reparative therapy exercises.

Now that I know for sure that I have absolutely zero prospects for real love, I might as well stick with the pretend-to-be-straight-for-Mom plan. But it's a lot harder today than it was two days ago to act like I care about this stuff. That stupid fantasy yesterday ruined everything. Allowing myself to imagine, even for just that one moment, that Carolyn and I could really be together has made the whole plan seem a lot less doable. Even though I was flat-out rejected, I can't seem to let the *hope* go. Not hope that I'll get to be with Carolyn—that's clearly not going to happen—but more like the way I *felt* when I thought there was hope for us. I felt… optimistic. For the first time in a long time, I felt like there was at least one outcome, in a long list of possible paths, where everything might actually be okay.

It's like there's some part of me deep in my subconscious that's saying, *Hey, remember how good it felt to think that you might actually get to live an honest, happy life? Yeah, we want more of that.*

I really don't have the energy for this de-gayifying stuff right now. I watch the exercise going on, but all I want is to be in bed with the covers pulled all the way up over my head.

It doesn't help that in addition to being completely exhausted and dealing with a head full of thoughts that are more tangled than a ten-year-old ball of Christmas lights, I'm also feeling more alone than ever. Carolyn is acting like a stranger; Matthew is up at Mr. Martin's, probably arranging his flight home at this very moment;

and Daniel is still super gung-ho about the exercises after what happened on our date.

So when Brianna asks for a volunteer to bring Mr. Martin a note, I jump at the chance.

I take my time moseying through the woods. When I get to the part of the path that's hidden from both the main cabin and the field, I sit on a big rock, take off my shoes, and dig my toes into the dirt path.

The rich soil threads between my toes and burrows under my nails. So much for Brianna's pedicure. I dig down deeper into the earth with my heels. The soil underneath the top layer is cool and moist and soft. It reminds me of the sand on the beach back home.

I lean back against a tree trunk and gaze up at the intricate web of branches above me. I wish I could stay here forever.

But it's only a matter of time before someone will come looking for me, so after a few more minutes, I brush the dirt off my feet, slip back into my shoes, and carry on with my errand.

Mr. Martin's office door is closed when I get there, and I raise my hand to knock but freeze when I hear the voice through the door.

"Please," Matthew is begging. "I can't go home."

Can't go home? But I thought he couldn't wait to get out of here?

Curious, I lower my hand and press my ear to the door.

"So you said," Mr. Martin says. "But you have disobeyed me and disrespected my camp, Matthew. There are rules."

"I know. I'm sorry," Matthew says. "Please just give me one more chance. I'll do anything."

There's a long stretch of silence…and then a few footsteps.

"Well," Mr. Martin says, his voice low, "there is *one* thing you could do for me."

Chapter 27

"Wh-what are you doing?" Matthew stutters.

"Oh, don't play dumb with me, Matthew. I've had my eye on you for a long time. I know what kind of boy you are."

What kind of boy he is? What is going *on* in there?

"What the hell…what are you talking about?" Matthew says, his voice shaky now.

"You don't believe in my teachings. You've been very clear about that."

"So?"

"So…you like boys. You like to touch them, don't you?"

"Uh…"

"I know you do. But, Matthew, have you ever been with a *man*?"

Oh my God.

"*What?*" Matthew shrieks.

There's another brief pause and then a chair skids across the floor followed by some sort of a scuffle. There's a loud thump on the door, and I leap away and press my back against the wall next to the doorframe. The door doesn't open, but when Mr. Martin speaks again, his voice is a lot closer. It sounds like he's blocking the door from Matthew.

"Oh, don't tell me you've never thought about it," Mr. Martin says. "All those times you came to my office…"

"Are you *crazy*?" Matthew shouts. "I would *never*…I can't believe this is happening. Let me out of here."

"No."

What do I do? There's no one else around; everyone is down at the field cabins. I have to get Matthew out of there. I have to let my presence be known. Mr. Martin can't do anything to Matthew if he knows I'm here.

But terror has me frozen in place. What would Mr. Martin do if he knew I overheard this? He's clearly capable of some pretty crazy stuff…

"Let me out!" Matthew says again.

"You have two choices, Matthew. Do what I ask right now, or call your father and tell him you've been asked to leave the program."

Another silence.

Just call your father, Matthew! I want to shout. *Don't go anywhere near this monster!*

"Well? What's it going to be?" Mr. Martin says, sounding pretty confident that he's about to get exactly what he wants.

If that happens, I tell myself, I'll do something. I'll stop it any way I can.

I stand there, flat against the wall, waiting.

"You know, I spoke with your father before you came here. I know what you're facing if you go home early." Mr. Martin's voice is eerily gentle. "I had a father like that too. But mine was worse, so much worse."

"I can't call my father," Matthew mumbles resignedly.

What? No!

"What do you want from me?" he asks miserably, his voice drawing closer to Mr. Martin.

"Take your shirt off."

Matthew sighs. "Okay." Another pause. "Now what?"

"Come here."

Matthew's footsteps come closer.

"Now kiss me," Mr. Martin says.

That's it. I'm going in.

I step in front of the door and raise my hand to pound on it.

But then something happens. Mr. Martin cries out in pain and there's a large crash. The door flies open, and suddenly I'm looking into Matthew's frightened eyes. He's shirtless, his face ghost-white. We just stare at each other in shock for a never-ending second.

There's another moan of pain from within the office, and I look down at Matthew's hand to see that he's gripping a large metal stapler.

Go! I mouth silently. *Get out of here!*

He stares at me for a second longer, as though he's still not quite sure what's happening, and then takes off.

I know what I need to do. I wait outside the door for a few more moments and collect myself. Mr. Martin is groaning and muttering a garbled string of cuss words inside the office. That's good. As long as I know he's alive and conscious, I can take my time.

I wait until Matthew's had plenty of time to get away, and then I take a deep breath and enter the office.

Mr. Martin is lying on the floor across a chair he must have broken when he fell. There's a deep gash over his left eye, and blood is streaming down his face.

Matthew got him good. *Well done, buddy.*

"Mr. Martin!" I exclaim, feigning alarm. I rush over to him. "Are you all right? What happened?"

"Lexi," he groans. "Call for help."

"Should I go get Barbara?"

"No! Call a doctor."

"What doctor?"

"911." He moans in pain again. "Call 911."

"You need to apply pressure to your head," I say, my first aid and CPR training from my job at Hard Rock kicking in. Matthew's shirt is still lying on the floor. I wad it up and hand it to Mr. Martin. "Use this." Then I grab the phone off his desk and call an ambulance.

Mr. Martin is losing a lot of blood. While we wait for the paramedics, he fades in and out of consciousness, and I have to keep shaking him and slapping him to wake him up. If he has a concussion, he can't go to sleep. He might be the world's worst kind of scum, but I still can't let him die.

During a brief moment of clarity, he asks why I'm here.

I show him the note. "Brianna wanted to know if you were still planning on doing a Bible study session after lunch or if they should start setting up for something else."

He mumbles something incoherent and drifts off again.

"Mr. Martin!" I shout in his face and pinch his arm, maybe a little harder than I need to. "No sleeping!"

Finally, the EMTs rush in.

"He was hit in the head," I explain, "and then he fell. I've been trying to keep pressure on the gash and keep him from falling asleep."

"Good work," an EMT with big teeth says. "What happened?"

"Uh…I don't know," I lie. "I just found him like this."

"Okay, we can take it from here."

I start to leave but Mr. Martin's voice stops me. "Brianna!"

"No, I'm Lexi." God, he really is far gone.

"No. Get Brianna."

"Oh. Okay," I say and break into a sprint.

• • •

"I don't understand," Brianna says as we run back toward the main cabin together. "How did this happen?"

I stick with my lie. "I don't know. I just got there and he was on the ground."

"Bleeding from the head?"

"Yeah."

"I don't understand," she says again. Then she starts praying. Out loud. She's really upset, even though I told her he was going to be fine.

The EMTs are wheeling Mr. Martin into the back of the ambulance when we get there.

"Jeremiah!" she cries and jumps into the ambulance too.

Jeremiah? Is that Mr. Martin's first name?

Then the doors are closed, the siren is turned on, and within seconds, there's nothing to show that the ambulance was even here except a thin cloud of dust floating over the gravel road.

I turn back to the main cabin and run up the front steps.

I need to find Matthew.

Chapter 28

He's in the boys' dorm, curled up on his bed.

The boys' dorm is pretty much exactly like the girls', except there's blue everywhere instead of pink, and instead of vanities, they have desks and a shelf filled with sports books.

"Hey." I sit beside him.

"Hey."

"He's going to be fine. He's on his way to the hospital right now."

"Great." He doesn't seem happy about it though. He looks at me. "How much did you hear?"

"Enough."

He buries his face under his pillow.

"I'm proud of you, Matthew," I say gently.

"For what?" His voice is muffled.

"For fighting back. For not...you know, doing what he wanted you to do."

He slides the pillow off his face and stares up at the ceiling. "I thought I was going to have to. I took my shirt off for him. And I kissed him."

I gasp. "You kissed him?"

"It was the only way to get close enough to hit him without him seeing it coming."

"Oh." I think about what I would have done in a similar situation. I don't know if I would have had the guts to do Matthew did. "Matthew, why didn't you just call your father?"

"Not an option. He wouldn't understand."

"Whatever happened to, 'Lexi, this is *your* life, not your mom's. You have to do what makes you happy too.' Sound familiar? I could say the same thing to you—just substitute the word *dad* for *mom*."

"It's different."

"How?"

He looks at me with sad eyes. "Before I left to come here, my dad told me that if I didn't stick with the program for the entire summer, I wouldn't have a home to come back to."

"You mean…he'll kick you out?"

"Yeah. He was serious about it too."

"But he can't do that—you're his kid. He's responsible for you."

He gives me a *can you really be that naïve?* face. "It happens all the time, Lex. There are homeless shelters *just* for LGBTQ kids, for this exact reason."

It's pretty sobering to think that some kids might actually have it even worse than I do. No matter what my mom might be feeling about me being gay, and no matter how damaged our relationship might be because of it, I don't think she'd ever actually throw me out on the street.

"Do you have other family you could stay with?" I ask. "What about Justin?"

"My dad's parents would never take me, and my mom's live in Canada. Justin lives in the dorms at UCSD. They don't let you have guests for more than three nights in a row. I could probably stay with friends for a while, but how long can you really do that for? I'd be pretty much homeless."

"What about your mom?" I ask. "Wouldn't *she* let you come home?"

He lets out a little humorless laugh. "My mother doesn't do anything my father doesn't want her to."

So the perfect family that Matthew painted during his Father Wound session isn't so perfect after all.

I have a sudden flashback to the very first time I saw Matthew. "Did you know I saw you that first day, before we met at the carpet cabin?"

He shakes his head.

"You were coming down the stairs from the dorms. You must have checked in just before I did. You looked…" I trail off.

"Petrified?" Matthew supplies.

I give a little chuckle. "Well, yeah. Was that because of your dad?"

He nods. "He'd just dropped me off. And before he left, he

made sure to reiterate his point: finish the program or else. So I thought I would get through the summer, go home, and go back to normal. My father never said anything about kicking me out if the program didn't work; he just said I had to finish the full eight weeks."

I'm not sure that makes much sense—if Matthew went home at the end of the program acting exactly the same way he used to before New Horizons, something tells me his dad wouldn't be so thrilled about that either. But I guess we've all been leaning on a crutch of denial this summer.

"Matthew…not that I'm blaming you or anything, believe me, I love that you are who you are, but…if you knew all along what your dad was threatening you with, why didn't you try a little harder? Why did you always have to challenge everything?"

He digs his palms into his eyes. "Honestly, Lexi, I never thought they would *actually* kick anyone out. Places like this thrive on their reputation. That's all they have going for them, you know? They're a total scam; they can't actually deliver what they promise for most people. So the only way for them to stay in business is if people *think* they can. If they kick campers out before the summer is over, it would be admitting failure. And then the smokescreen comes down. I saw through it all from day one—or, at least, I thought I did. Clearly, I was wrong."

There's silence for a minute, then Matthew groans and says, "What the hell was I thinking, attacking Mr. Martin like that?"

"You were thinking you had to defend yourself."

"Yeah, but I did it so I wouldn't have to call my dad and tell him I got kicked out. But I'm definitely kicked out now. It was all for nothing."

"You don't know that…" I say. But he's probably right. There's no way Mr. Martin is going to let him stay now.

"I *knew* there was something off about that guy," Matthew says.

"Yeah, but did you know it was *that*? I had no idea."

"I knew from the moment I met him that all that talk about overcoming his SSA was bullshit. But it never occurred to me that he was screwing his campers."

A little gasp escapes my throat. "Wait—you think this has happened to other people too?"

He gives me a wary look. "He knew exactly what he was doing in that office, Lexi. He's no amateur."

"Do you think he's done it to other campers who are here *now*?" I immediately think of Daniel. Matthew might be able to defend himself, but Daniel? No way.

Matthew thinks for a second. "Nah, probably not. I'm the only one he ever calls to his office. And even with me he didn't try anything until today."

I exhale. "But other campers from other summers?"

"No doubt in my mind."

Mr. Martin and Brianna return from the hospital a few hours later—I guess his injuries weren't very serious after all. Matthew and I are still in the boys' dorm when the taxi rolls up the gravel road. He didn't want to go face the rest of the camp, and I didn't want to leave him alone. Funny how with the two head counselors gone, no one came looking for us.

Brianna appears in the doorway, an ominous silhouette in the darkened room. "You two. Classroom cabin. *Now*." She spins on her heels and marches down the stairs.

Matthew and I look at each other. Why are we going to the classroom cabin? Shouldn't they be making arrangements to send Matthew home?

We follow Brianna in silence and get to the classroom cabin to find the whole camp already assembled there. Including Mr. Martin. A thick bandage over his eye is being held in place with a few yards of gauze wrapped around his head. But the scariest part is the look on his face—there's fire in his eyes.

"Lexi, find a seat, please," he says so calmly it's almost menacing. "And Matthew, please join me up front."

Matthew sits in the chair Mr. Martin has pulled out for him at the head of the classroom.

I automatically glance at Carolyn, forgetting in the moment that we're not friends anymore. Her face is distressed. Yeah, whatever's going on here, it's not good.

Mr. Martin wastes no time getting to the point.

"Ladies and gentlemen," he says. "It's no secret that over these past five weeks, Matthew has been lacking in his commitment to the work we do at New Horizons. Though he hasn't taken to the reparative therapy process as quickly as we would have liked, we have nurtured his need to find his own way on this journey."

That is such a lie! But the other counselors are nodding sympathetically.

"But his waywardness reached a new level today. Matthew has disgraced this camp, its teachings, and most of all, himself. We had hoped that, given enough time, Matthew would give himself over to the Lord Jesus Christ, but it's now clear that the devil is more firmly rooted in him than we first thought." He points to his bandage. "Matthew attacked me today."

Gasps and cries of shock ripple through the room.

Mr. Martin looks sad. "I was just trying to give him some extra attention and help him get on track with the rest of you—who are all doing so wonderfully in your therapy, I might add—by giving him some one-on-one tutoring, when out of nowhere, he came at me with a weapon and sent me to the hospital." He stops and looks Matthew in the eye. "Isn't that right, Matthew?"

Matthew stares back at him, his Adam's apple bobbing as he swallows. I desperately want him to disagree, to stand up and tell everybody what *really* happened, but I know he won't. He won't for the exact same reason that I'm not jumping on top of my desk and shouting *Liar!*—we're scared.

And for whatever reason, Mr. Martin hasn't kicked Matthew out yet. We can't risk doing anything that would change that.

"Isn't that right?" Mr. Martin repeats.

Slowly, Matthew nods. "Yes," he whispers.

A brief smile flickers across Mr. Martin's face. It's so quick that I doubt anyone else even notices it. But its meaning couldn't be clearer: he knows he's back in control.

"Yes, what?" he demands, sure of himself now.

"Yes, sir."

Mr. Martin turns back to the group. "Even though I was assaulted unprovoked," he says, "and had to receive eleven stitches in my forehead, I have decided not to press charges against Matthew or send him home early. After all, it's not his fault that the devil lives so loudly inside of him."

There are more sympathetic nods, mostly from the counselors.

"I've been thinking a lot about what to do to help Matthew get rid of that darkness inside him, and after what happened today, I've come to a conclusion." He pauses and looks down at Matthew. "We are going to have an exorcism."

Chapter 29

An *exorcism*? People actually *do* those?

The silence in the classroom breaks at last, and everyone starts talking at once. From what I can tell, the reactions are a mixture of confusion and actual *excitement*.

I lock my eyes on Matthew. He's sitting as still as a statue, his face blank, his eyes glossed over. I think he's in shock.

Mr. Martin gets everyone to quiet down before continuing. "We've only had one other exorcism in the history of New Horizons, but that young individual turned out wonderfully. I truly believe this is the best thing for Matthew at this point in time. It's extreme, yes, but this is an extreme case." He gestures to his head again, as if to remind us that he's just an innocent victim. "We still have three weeks left of the summer, so there will be some time after the exorcism to all work as a team to help Matthew get up to speed with the progress the rest of you have made thus far. Of course, the sooner we expel his demons, the better, so Brianna has made arrangements for the healer to come tonight. I would like for you all to join me as witnesses to this important event in Matthew's life."

Tonight? My mind is racing all over the place. What happens at an exorcism? I saw that movie at a sleepover in middle school and some of those scenes are forever seared into my brain…but I'm pretty sure Matthew's head isn't going to do a full 360.

Mr. Martin squats down so he's eye to eye with Matthew. He speaks softly, like he's talking to a small child who's sad that his best friend has moved away. "Matthew," he says. "Do you willingly agree to this course of action?"

Matthew gives a huge, defeated sigh. "Yes," he says, looking down at his lap.

Mr. Martin tries to clap him on the shoulder, but Matthew shrugs him off. "You've made the right decision."

Mr. Martin dismisses us for our pre-exorcism dinner, but he pulls me aside.

"Thank you for helping me this afternoon, Lexi," he says.

I hate him. I hate what a disgusting, rotten liar he is, and I hate what he did to Matthew in the office, and I hate what he's doing to him now. I refuse to look him in his disgusting, rotten, liar eyes, so instead I stare up at the thick, white bandage. "No problem," I mutter.

"The doctor said I was lucky you got there when you did."

"Oh. Well, good."

"When *did* you get there, anyway?" he asks.

My ears perk up at the practiced casualness of his voice. Does he suspect that I overheard what was going on in the office? He can't know that I know. If he thinks his secret is out, he'll take it out on Matthew for sure. I decide to play dumb. "Do you mean, like, what time?"

"No. What did you see?" He shakes his head and tries again. "I'm just wondering how long I was there before you found me. Did you see Matthew?"

I search his disgusting, rotten face. I wonder, if I didn't already know what he was asking, would I catch on to something fishy now? Probably not. He's a very good liar. I'm sure he's fooled a lot of people with this holier-than-thou, soldier-of-God crap.

"No," I say. "You were all alone when I got there. I have no idea how long you'd been lying there."

"And did Matthew tell you anything about what happened? What made him attack me like that, out of nowhere?"

"No. He said he didn't want to talk about it."

Mr. Martin nods, satisfied. "Well, in any event, thank you again."

"Sure," I say and hurry away to the dining cabin.

Matthew is sitting alone at our table, his forehead resting on the tabletop and his arms covering his head. Carolyn and Daniel are in line for food.

I sit down and bring my face close to his. "You don't have to do this, you know," I whisper.

He looks up slowly, his face all red and lined from the table markings. "You know I don't have a choice."

"Well…" I try to think of some way out. "What about Justin? Can he move off campus or something and then you can move in with him?"

Matthew shakes his head. "He's on a full scholarship, covers his dorm expenses."

"And there are really no other friends you can stay with?"

"For a whole *year*, until I can go off to college? Even if someone offered to take me in, I wouldn't want to be a burden on anyone for that long."

I guess he's right—he's pretty stuck. It's either go through with the exorcism (God, even just the *word* sounds creepy) or leave the camp early with no home to go back to. "Well, it will be fine," I say, though it sounds like I'm trying to convince myself more than anyone. "You'll let the healer, or whatever they call him, bless you and pray for you and excise your demons or whatever and then move on. It can't be that bad."

"Famous last words," he says.

• • •

Dinner goes by way too quickly. As the overcooked meatloaf, biscuits, and apple juice gradually vanish from our plates and cups, the mood in the room shifts from jittery excitement to acute somberness. I guess everyone's dealing with the suspense of what's about to happen in their own way.

After dinner, Arthur and John take Matthew away to go "get ready" for the exorcism, while Mr. Martin leads the rest of us in prayer.

"Dear Lord, we ask that you shine your love on our friend Matthew today. He is standing on the brink of salvation, and he needs your help now more than ever to cross that finish line. Please, Lord, wrap Matthew in your loving arms and carry him away from the darkness. Amen."

"Amen," the room echoes.

Mr. Martin has everyone right where he wants them, but for the first time, it occurs to me that maybe his belief in God is a lie too. He knows better than anyone that Matthew isn't *evil*—he knows exactly why he was attacked. Which means his prayer for Matthew was for show, just like everything else he says.

As we make our way to the carpet cabin, a faint whisper brushes my ear. "What happened?"

I spin around to find myself dangerously close to Carolyn. Her face is just inches from mine. "What?"

"I know something weird is going on," she whispers. "And I know you know what it is."

It hurts to look at her. I turn around and keep moving. "Nothing is going on." I can't tell her the truth—the more people who know, the more dangerous it is for Matthew. And she wouldn't want to hear it anyway—not with how much she *loves* Mr. Martin and New Horizons.

"Matthew wouldn't just attack Mr. Martin for no reason," she insists.

"Carolyn, please," I snap, thrusting a hand through my hair in irritation. "Stop. It's nothing. Just…leave me alone."

I catch a fleeting glimpse of her face before she walks away—she's stunned and hurt. Serves her right.

The exorcism guy is waiting in the carpet cabin. He's wearing all black and a clerical collar and is younger than I expected—maybe thirty or so. He's a large man. Not fat, but tall—well over six feet—with muscles bulging under his shirtsleeves.

Matthew's there already too. He's standing alone at the back of the room, dressed in a shirt and dress pants and tie. I wonder where he got them from—they're obviously not his. They're unflattering and bland, and he keeps tugging at his collar like it's too tight.

Daniel, Carolyn, and I go over to him.

"You're going to do great," Daniel tells him. "God is good."

Carolyn just gives him a hug and a reassuring smile.

Once the two of them are gone, I grab Matthew's shoulders and look him square in the eye. "Listen to me," I say. "You're going to be fine. Whatever happens, it can't be worse than the Father Wound sessions, right?"

He nods.

"All you have to do is get through it. Then you'll be able to stay for the rest of the summer and you'll go home to your family and everything that happened here will be in the past." I hope he was right about his father being satisfied with his just completing the program, regardless of whether it worked or not, and letting him stay at home.

He nods again.

"I'm here for you. And so are Carolyn and Daniel. You're not alone."

"Thanks, Lexi."

I give him a quick hug, and then he goes up to the open stage area of the room.

The exorcism guy introduces himself to us all as Brother Wilson. "Thank you for being here," he says.

Like we had a choice.

"Through prayer and the power of Jesus Christ, *together* we will heal this young man."

And then he gets down to business. He exchanges a few words with Mr. Martin that are too low for me to hear then turns his attention to Matthew, who is standing awkwardly.

"Have you truly given your life to Jesus Christ, Matthew?" Brother Wilson asks.

Matthew stares up at him. He shrugs.

"I need an answer," Brother Wilson says.

Matthew stays silent. He looks as if he's deciding whether to tell the truth or just say what Mr. Martin wants him to say. *Just cooperate*, I think at him.

Finally, he says, "I'm not an atheist or anything…"

"Yes or no, Matthew."

"No, sir."

I hold my breath. *Please.*

"Would you like to?"

"Yes, sir."

I exhale. *Thank you.*

"What is the nature of your possession, Matthew? What are you seeking freedom from?"

"Um…"

"It's okay," Brother Wilson says. "We are here to help you, not judge you."

"I, uh…I'm seeking freedom from…being gay, I guess." He cringes, like every word is causing him pain.

Brother Wilson nods. "The homosexual demon. When was the first time you noticed the existence of this demon inside you?"

"When I was young."

"Do you know *how* the demon got inside of you?" Brother Wilson asks.

Matthew shrugs again.

"Actually," Mr. Martin interjects proudly, "we have done quite a bit of work on this very matter." And he explains about Matthew's Father Wound and his growing up in the theater environment.

Matthew just stares at his feet, listening to the disgusting, rotten liar talk about him like he isn't standing right there.

"Before we go further," Brother Wilson says when Mr. Martin

is done speaking, "you must close that doorway forever. There is no use expelling the demon from your soul if he will just be able to return as soon as we're done. Do you promise to keep that doorway firmly sealed, Matthew? Do you renounce your life in the artistic world?"

Lie, Matthew. Lie with everything you have!

Matthew nods. "I do."

"Very good. Now, Matthew, are you personally aware of any false religions in your family?"

Matthew looks up. "False religions?"

"Witchcraft, Satanism, Universalism, Islam?"

"No."

"Good. Are you a faithful Christian, Matthew?"

"Um. Yes."

But Mr. Martin clears his throat to get the healer's attention and then shakes his head slightly.

"I see," Brother Wilson says and purses his lips. He turns to the rest of us, sitting quietly in our neat little rows, like perfectly programmed schoolchildren. "I need your help, my friends. While I prepare Matthew for the acceptance of Jesus Christ into his life, I need you all to pray and bind the demon. Please, begin now."

I look around the room—Daniel and several other campers, plus all the counselors, bow their heads and start praying, some at full volume, some fiercely whispering to themselves, some just moving their lips.

I glance at Carolyn and find that she's already looking at me. She's only two seats down from me, but the prayer-infused environment prevents us from speaking even a single word. So she just raises her eyebrows questioningly, as if to ask *Why the hell is Matthew going along with all of this?* I just shake my head. There's no way to explain now, even if I wanted to.

While everyone prays, Brother Wilson asks Matthew to call upon Jesus for salvation.

"Um," Matthew says, confused and miserable. "Jesus? Save me. Please."

"May I place my hands on you, Matthew?"

Matthew nods. Brother Wilson looks to Mr. Martin for permission, and he nods as well. Brother Wilson rests one hand on Matthew's forehead and one on the back of his head. "Jesus will save you, young Matthew! Jesus will set you free! I anoint you in the name of Jesus Christ!" he proclaims.

Hands still on Matthew's head, he turns to us again. "Louder!" he orders. "Pray louder! Now is the time to cast this homosexual demon out once and for all!"

The prayers grow from whispers to shouts. The muddled sound of overlapping words surrounds me, combining to form a sort of dissonant, chaotic symphony. The room is loud and vibrating with passion and tension and uninhibited faith.

"Keep going! More! He needs more!"

Even though there are a few of us, me and Carolyn included,

who don't participate, most people are feeding into the whole scene, wailing and raising their hands to the air and stomping their feet and shouting out.

An English class lesson on *Julius Caesar* flashes back to me—my teacher was trying to explain the concept of a "mob mentality," and I never really understood it. I got the logistics, of Brutus joining the conspirators and killing Caesar because he got so wrapped up in the excitement of the moment, but I never understood how someone could truly get to the point of doing something that they wouldn't normally do just because the group was doing it. But now I think I get it.

The cabin is filled with a noise so loud I have to cover my ears. The floor is pulsing, and the air is buzzing with energy.

I mean, yes, most of these campers are religious anyway. This *is* a church camp. And yes, we've all become accustomed over these last five weeks to doing whatever the counselors tell us to do without question. Even I still do that. Even *Matthew* is doing that right now.

But still. For these usually mild-mannered kids to suddenly transform into a bunch of howling, beseeching demon-casters who are actually taking the task of binding Matthew's "homosexual demon" (something that, theoretically speaking, we *all* have) seriously…well, it all makes better sense now, the "power of the mob" thing. And it sucks.

While the praying grows stronger and louder still, Brother

Wilson dives into the meat of the exorcism. "*You*, homosexual demon, come out in Jesus's name!" he shouts, still gripping onto Matthew's head. Matthew stands there, eyes squeezed shut, arms straight down at his sides, his hands pulled into tight fists. His chest heaves unevenly, his breathing ragged. I know he's saying a prayer of his own right now—for this all to be over soon. "Homosexual spirit," Brother Wilson continues over the cacophony, "I command you to vacate this young man's body!"

It goes on like this for a long time. The crowd prays and the healer "casts the demon."

And Matthew just stands there, letting it all happen.

Just when I'm starting to feel like it's got to be over soon, that it can't possibly get worse, Mr. Martin shouts out, "The demon is still inside you, Matthew, but he has been weakened! It's time to expel him forever!"

He nods to Brother Wilson, and Brother Wilson nods back. "Pray!" Brother Wilson commands the group, and everyone picks up their chanting with even more energy. "The blood of Jesus will clean the spirit!" he shouts, and then, with no warning, he hits Matthew.

Hits him. Punches him, with his large fist, in the stomach.

For a moment, I'm stunned. That didn't really happen, did it? It couldn't have. It doesn't make sense.

But Matthew is on the floor, curled in the fetal position, gasping out in pain.

I finally find my voice. "*NO!*" I scream, in control of myself at last. I launch myself out of my seat and climb past the laps and legs of the people in my row. "Don't hurt him!" I cry. "Somebody stop this!"

My shouts ring throughout the room because—I'm only just realizing—the crowd went silent at Brother Wilson's blow. Instead of chants and stomps, the room is now filled with ghost-white faces frozen in shock and a sense of incompleteness as gasps are held in but not released.

Oh, thank God. They're not as brainwashed as I thought. But they're still just sitting there.

"Homosexual demon, be gone!" Brother Wilson yells as Matthew lies there, trying to get his air back. "I force you from this body!" And he kicks him—just once, seemingly strategically placed in Matthew's middle section, but hard.

When I reach the aisle—still shouting for somebody to help—I'm immediately restrained by two of the counselors. I don't pay attention to who they are—all I can focus on is Matthew, writhing on the plushy blue carpet, sobbing.

I flashback to the first day of the Father Wound sessions, when Ian was hitting Gabe with the Nerf bat. That was the worst thing I'd ever seen—scary and violent and cruel. But that was nothing compared to this. This is *real*. This time, there are no soft foam bats or counselors monitoring to make sure no one gets hurt.

This time, the counselors *want* him to get hurt.

"Spirits of homosexuality, *get out*! I compel you to leave!"

"Matthew!" I scream.

Matthew rolls over and vomits.

A strange, irrelevant thought pierces through my rage—they're going to have to replace the carpet again. There's no way they're going to get the stain out.

Is this why the carpet seemed so new at the beginning of the summer? Does this type of thing happen often at New Horizons? Mr. Martin said they've only had one exorcism here before, but maybe there have been other beatings and attacks that weren't attached to exorcisms? The counselors don't seem at all surprised by what's happening, and no one is doing anything to stop it.

I try to get away from my captors, but their hold on me is unbreakable. So I just keep screaming and crying until I exhaust my air supply. I break off, gasping, and only then, in the gap in my own shouts, do I hear the others.

Other people are yelling too, pleading for them to leave Matthew alone. I blink through my cloudy vision. It's Jasmine and Ian and Gabe and Rachael and this guy named Chris who I've never really spoken to but who is all of a sudden one of my favorite people in the world.

And one voice is louder than all the others. I whip my head around to find the source of the sound. And then I see her—in the opposite aisle, across the cabin, Carolyn is being restrained by John and Brianna. Her face is red and splotchy, and her eyes are overflowing with tears. "*Stop!*" she cries. "*Please, stop!*"

We lock eyes. Past the tears and puffiness and utter horror, her gaze burns with strength, and I know that no matter what's happened between us in the past, right now we're on the same side.

It gives me the clarity I need to see this whole situation for what it truly is.

The exorcism isn't just for Mr. Martin to assert his power and control over Matthew—it's *payback*.

Matthew embarrassed Mr. Martin, so Mr. Martin is embarrassing Matthew—in front of everyone.

Matthew hurt Mr. Martin, so Mr. Martin has found a way to hurt him right back.

I didn't think it was possible to hate that man any more than I already did.

I spot Daniel in the crowd, clutching his wooden cross to his chest. His mouth is hanging open, and his eyes behind his glasses are as huge and round as oranges.

I clear my throat as much as I can, take a deep breath, and call out, "Daniel!"

He jumps at the sound of his name and looks around, confused.

"Over here!" I say, and he finally turns my way.

I look at him desperately, and he stares back. He looks terrified and confused, like he still doesn't quite comprehend what's happening.

"Help," I croak.

There's no way he can hear me over the shouts of the others and the continuous bellowing of Brother Wilson, but his face registers with understanding. He knows what I'm asking. He nods his head quickly, faces forward again, and bends his head over his cross.

While Daniel prays for Matthew, and Carolyn hopes or wishes or does whatever her version of praying is, I relax in the arms of the counselors, making it clear that I'm giving up. They loosen their grip on me right away, probably glad for a rest. I count to three, take a long, deep breath, and gather my strength. And then I make a run for it. I bolt away from the counselors, sprint down the aisle, and dodge Mr. Martin.

Just as I get to Matthew, Brother Wilson gives another kick, his third and final blow, and Matthew passes out.

I throw myself down and cover his body with my own anyway, protecting him. But it's too little too late.

Brother Wilson steps back, wipes the sweat off his brow, and says, "In the name and authority of the Lord Jesus Christ, we forbid you, homosexual spirit, from operating in any way within young Matthew ever again. Praise be to God."

Chapter 30

They won't take Matthew to the hospital.

He regained consciousness shortly after the exorcism finally came to an end. Barbara looked him over right there in the carpet cabin—the other campers had already been ushered back up to the dorms, but I refused to leave his side until I knew he was okay. He was badly bruised and in pain, but Barbara assessed that there were no broken bones or anything life-threatening. So Mr. Martin said there was no need to call a doctor.

And Matthew agreed.

Yesterday, I would have been surprised about that. Today, not so much.

If a minor showed up in the hospital in this kind of shape, the authorities would immediately be called. It would probably lead to an investigation of New Horizons and maybe even arrests. Bad news for Mr. Martin.

And at the very least, Matthew's parents would be called, and Mr. Martin would spin it just so, and Matthew's dad would find out all the reasons why his son was on the verge of being kicked out of the camp. Bad news for Matthew.

So, for both their sakes, they're keeping the whole thing under wraps.

The next day, while Barbara and Kaylee tend to Matthew in the infirmary, the other counselors keep us occupied. The boys play another baseball game; Brianna leads Bible study; the girls take turns practicing threading the sewing machine. There's no down-time, and meals are rushed. It's like they're trying to prevent us from actually having time to think about what happened last night.

Like that's even possible. I've been threading sewing machines for years, but now every time I try, I break the thread or prick my finger. I can't concentrate.

Carolyn and I share a lot of looks. All this waiting and worry has got to be even worse for her because she still doesn't have any idea why Mr. Martin did this to him.

That night, as we're getting ready for bed, I finally get the chance to talk to her.

"Lexi," she whispers as soon as I come over to her area. "We have to do something! We have to go check on him."

"I know," I say. "But how?"

"We could ask."

I give her a *yeah, right* look.

"Okay, okay. We'll have to sneak out then. After everyone's asleep."

I raise an eyebrow. "Seriously?"

"Seriously. We have to make sure he's okay."

"But what if we get caught?" I ask, unsure.

Carolyn bites her lower lip, thinking. "I don't know. All I know is that I can't just stay here doing nothing."

I sigh. "I know. Okay, let's do it. Eleven o'clock? Everyone should be asleep by then."

She nods. "Eleven."

Even though the lights are turned out as usual at ten, I can't sleep. I'm too worked up worrying about Matthew, replaying the whole thing in my mind, nervous about sneaking out. If we get caught, that's it. We'll be shipped back home before the sun comes up.

And then where would I be? I was ready to give up the fake-being-straight-for-Mom plan when I thought I would have Carolyn to help me through it, but she's made it perfectly clear that she doesn't want me. So I would be kicked out with nothing to show for my time here at New Horizons—not turned straight, no chance to go forward with the fake-it plan, and no girlfriend. I'd be right back where I started.

But Matthew is my friend. I need to make sure he's okay. I need to let him know we're here for him.

And there's also the tiny issue of *guilt*. All of this is because of me. Because Matthew wanted to give me the chance to spend the day with the girl I liked. This is *my* fault. I can't turn my back on him now. No matter the consequences.

I watch the digital alarm clock next to Deb's bed.

10:58.

10:59.

11:00.

The room is very still, the girls' breathing deep and rhythmic.

As quietly as I can, my heart hammering in my chest, I slip out from under the sheets and grab my sneakers from under the bed. I tiptoe across the room, past a snoring Deb, and meet up with Carolyn near the door.

Are you sure you want to do this? I ask her with my eyes.

The moonlight streaming through the window catches her face. She nods once.

I twist the doorknob slowly and silently, and we leave the dorm. The door closes behind us with a muted thud.

We stop at my rock to brush the dirt and grass from our feet and slip our shoes on.

"Barbara or Kaylee will probably be down there, you know," I say. Even my whisper sounds loud in the dark woods.

Carolyn nods. "I know. We'll have to peek through the window when we get there to see if they're awake."

"And if they are?"

"We won't be able to go inside. But at least we'll be able to see Matthew through the window. Hopefully it'll be a good enough view to be able to see how he's doing."

"Okay," I say. We resume walking.

Then Carolyn says, "About the other day…"

I flinch. Why is she bringing that up now? Don't we have enough tragedy to deal with at the moment?

"I really don't want to talk about it," I say. It comes out harsher than I mean it to.

"Oh," Carolyn says. "All right."

"It's just…with everything going on with Matthew…"

"No, I understand. Sorry."

The field looks different at night. It looks smaller somehow, and the moonlight casts unfamiliar shadows across the grass.

The infirmary is the only cabin with a light on.

"I guess they're awake," I whisper.

"Yeah." She looks at me. "Well, it's now or never." And she takes off across the field.

I follow close behind, being careful not to step on any crunchy leaves or twigs.

We're about halfway across the field when a thought occurs to me.

"Wait." I grab Carolyn's arm and she stops short. I can't help noticing how soft and warm her skin is.

"What?" she whispers.

"Let me go to the window first."

"Why?"

"What if Kaylee or Barbara happens to be looking out the window when our faces pop up in it? We'll be in a lot of trouble."

"Yeah, but we knew that was the risk."

"But it doesn't have to be *both* of us who get in trouble," I say. "If the only face she sees is mine, I'll be the only one who gets caught. You'll be safe. I can give you a signal to go hide before they come outside."

Carolyn stares at me. "But why should it be you who sacrifices yourself? This was my idea—*I* should be the one to take the fall."

I shake my head and allow myself to look into her eyes. They're twinkling with the reflections of the stars above. "I think we both know I'm not exactly getting anything out of the program. If one of us has to go home, it should be me."

She hesitates.

"So we're agreed then," I say. "Good. Now come on."

I'm almost at the infirmary window when the door swings open and Carolyn and I find ourselves face to face with Brianna.

Chapter 31

We stare at each other, stunned, for an eternity.

We're caught. We're both going home—I didn't even get the chance to be noble and save Carolyn. I wonder if they'll let us see Matthew before we leave.

I open my mouth to say something, though I have no idea what, when Brianna snaps into action. "Follow me," she whispers and unlocks the door to the carpet cabin.

Carolyn and I exchange a glance and follow her inside. My stomach turns over when I see the large brownish stain on the carpet.

Brianna keeps the light off and leads us over to the far corner, as far away from the infirmary cabin as possible.

"What are you two doing?" she demands.

"We, uh—" I begin. I look to Carolyn for help.

"We wanted to see Matthew," she says unapologetically.

"You realize you're breaking about fifteen camp rules by being here right now?" Brianna says.

We nod. "We were worried about him," I say.

Brianna slides down to the floor, suddenly tired and sad. "I know," she says. "You're good friends."

My jaw drops. Did Brianna just *compliment* us? Even though she just caught us breaking fifteen of her precious camp rules? Did we stumble into some sort of alternate universe?

I look at Carolyn. She just shrugs.

I sit beside Brianna on the floor. "Is he okay?" I ask gently.

"He's doing as well as can be expected. He's in a lot of pain, but he'll make a full recovery."

The knot in my chest loosens a little.

"Are we in trouble?" Carolyn asks, sitting now too.

"Did anyone see you leave the dorm?" Brianna asks.

"No."

"Are you sure?"

"Yes."

"Then no. If someone had seen you, I would have had to report this to Mr. Martin. But I'm fine with keeping it between us if you are."

Okay, we've *definitely* entered Bizarro World. Brianna's actually being *decent*. But I'm not going to question it.

"Thank you," I say. Brianna looks at me, and I see a hint of the smile I saw that day so many weeks ago in the rec cabin—proof that there's a real person in there somewhere. Looking at her here, sitting on the floor, her pigtails coming loose, her face exhausted, it dawns on me how young she really is.

"Why did Mr. Martin do this to Matthew?" Carolyn asks. I guess she figures that we've already been caught breaking the rules and we've been given a rare moment with an open, honest Brianna, so she might as well take advantage.

"Because Matthew attacked him yesterday. Mr. Martin told you all that."

"But it doesn't make sense!" Carolyn says, frustrated.

"Matthew is troubled," Brianna says. "But now that his demon has been released, hopefully he'll be able to turn his life around." But the words lack her usual passion.

I run my fingers over the carpet, thinking. The fact that Brianna isn't dragging us to Mr. Martin's office right now means she's kind of on our side in this. She cares about Matthew too. And she believes, on some level, that what Mr. Martin did was wrong.

I decide to take a chance.

"Mr. Martin made a pass at Matthew," I say.

Brianna and Carolyn gape at me.

"Actually, it was more than a pass," I continue. "He tried to black-mail Matthew into having sex with him. He said that if Matthew didn't do what he said, he would kick him out of New Horizons."

Brianna shakes her head. "No."

"Yes. I was there."

"When?" Carolyn whispers, her eyes filled with rage.

"Yesterday. When I went to bring Mr. Martin the note. I heard everything through the door. Matthew hit Mr. Martin with the stapler because it was the only way to get away. I think the exorcism was payback—and a way to scare Matthew into keeping quiet about what happened."

Brianna's covered her ears, but I know she can still hear me. "It's not true," she says. "You're lying."

"Why would I lie about something like this, Brianna?"

She keeps shaking her head in denial.

"I know there's a part of you that knows what I'm saying is true," I say softly. "If you had as much faith in Mr. Martin as you say you do, we wouldn't even be having this conversation."

It takes a long time, but Brianna's headshaking gradually slows. She lowers her hands from her ears. She looks ragged and pale, like her whole world is shattering around her.

"How long have you worked here?" I ask her.

"Ten years," she mumbles.

"Since the camp first opened?"

"Yes."

"So you've known all the campers who've come through the camp?"

She nods.

I twirl a piece of the carpet material between my fingers and glance at the dark stain across the room, remembering Matthew's certainty that he wasn't the first camper Mr. Martin has hit on. "Has anything like this happened before?"

Brianna hesitates, but I can sense it—I'm *this* close to finally uncovering the truth about this place.

I glance at Carolyn, half expecting her to be lost in her little world again, remembering Natalie and reminding herself of all the reasons why New Horizons is good. But she's right here, watching Brianna closely, waiting for her answer.

"It's okay, Brianna," I say. "You can tell us."

"I can't though," she says, her voice full of anguish.

"Why not?"

"Because I don't know anything for sure. It's just suspicions I have. And what if I'm wrong? I can't go around slandering my brother like this!"

"*Brother?*" Carolyn and I exclaim at the same time.

"Yes, Jeremiah is my brother. My last name is Martin too."

Okay, things are starting to make sense.

"But…you're so much younger than he is!" Carolyn says.

Brianna nods. "There are nineteen years between us. There are a lot of kids in our family. He's the oldest. I'm the youngest. He left home before I was even born."

"So how did you end up working together?" I ask.

"Oh. Well, he needed to come home—he'd had an accident and had almost died. My parents took him in, but only on the condition that he attend church and Bible study with them and give up his homosexual lifestyle. At the time, I wondered if he only agreed because he had nowhere else to go to recuperate. He and my father…I don't know. They never got along. And I grew up hearing such terrible things about my brother from my parents and my older siblings." She pushes back the frizzy tendrils of hair that have escaped from her pigtails. "Anyway, the change in him was almost immediate. He was so grateful to God for saving his life, for giving him a second chance. He was saved. So when he asked me if I wanted to start New Horizons with him, of course I said yes. I was almost done with high school, and I thought it was a wonderful idea—my own calling from God."

"But then you started having suspicions?"

She lowers her eyes and shakes her head to herself. "I really shouldn't be talking about this with you," she whispers.

"And your brother shouldn't be sexually and physically abusing teenagers!" I snap back.

"Lexi…" Carolyn says, wordlessly warning me that if I lose my cool, we'll lose any chance of getting Brianna to tell us what she knows.

But I've gotten through to Brianna. I see it. The way she's looking right at me now, I actually think she's relieved to finally have the chance to get it all out. She just needs a little push.

"I really can't…" she says, shaking her head weakly. "I shouldn't…"

I steel myself to do probably the worst thing I've ever done. I hate myself for manipulating her this way, but getting this information out of her is important. "Brianna," I say. "Even if you don't tell us another word, I already have a lot of information I'm sure the police will be interested in. The other campers might have kept your secrets in the past, maybe because they were scared of what would happen or intimidated into believing giving this place up would ruin their chances of becoming straight, I don't know—but believe me, I'll tell them everything."

She gasps and stares at me, openmouthed and wild-eyed. "No, you can't—"

"But I'm wondering if maybe it's not as bad as I think it is. Because if the information you have is really that terrible, you would have told someone a long time ago. So, maybe if you tell us what you know, it will help us understand, and we won't have to go to the police."

Carolyn looks at me like I've lost my mind, but Brianna gets it. She understands my threat perfectly. Don't tell us anything, and New Horizons is done for. Tell us what she knows, and she's got at least a chance.

"Promise me," she says.

"Promise you what?"

"Promise me that if I tell you, you won't call the police."

I chew on the inside of my cheek, thinking. Mr. Martin deserves to be locked up for the rest of his life. But I need to know what Brianna knows.

"I promise," I say, and then silently add the qualifier, *Until after the summer is over*. I'm pretty sure he won't try anything with any other campers this summer, so there's some time to work with.

Brianna asks Carolyn the same thing.

"Um…I don't know…" she says, glancing at me worriedly. Of

course. She's a victim of abuse herself—of *course* she'll want to call the police immediately. But in order to have a real case against Mr. Martin, we need to know what Brianna's seen. I nod, letting Carolyn know it's okay—I won't let Mr. Martin get away with this.

She takes a deep breath and then says, "All right. Yes, I promise."

Brianna's shoulders sag with surrender. "At first, he was as earnest as could be. His motivations were pure; I know they were. He was so eager to prove himself to God—and to our parents. He was doing everything right. But then…"

"But then?" I nudge.

She sighs. "I first noticed it after the first year or two. He would always choose one boy to pay special attention to. It's always one who's resistant to the reparative therapy, like Matthew. At first I thought what he was doing was wonderful—spending extra time with the kids who needed the most help—but after a while, I noticed some strange trends."

"Trends? What kind of trends?" I ask.

"Well, even during the years where we have quite a few resistant campers, Mr. Martin would only choose *one* to give special lessons to. And it would always be the most handsome one. And the boys would usually act strangely after a private session in Mr. Martin's office. They would be quieter, more withdrawn."

"You never actually caught him with a boy?" Carolyn asks.

"No. Like I said, it's just suspicions."

"If this has been going on for so many years, why haven't you ever done anything about it? Why haven't you confronted your brother?" I say.

"And how was I supposed to do that, Alexis? I didn't want to get him in trouble. I didn't want to believe he hasn't actually been cured of his sickness. I didn't want to destroy things with my family after they're all so glad to have him back. And honestly, I didn't want the camp to get shut down. I love this place." She holds her arms out, gesturing to the interior of the cabin. "I've dedicated my life to this. And I truly believe the work we do here at New Horizons is right. It's God's work. And if Jeremiah were exposed, New Horizons would be gone."

"So what you're saying," Carolyn says, angrier than I've ever seen her, "is that our friend is lying in that infirmary in agonizing pain because you don't want to lose your job? Because somehow his life and his dignity, and the dignity of all the other boys who Mr. Martin has hurt, are a small price to pay for your precious *camp*?"

Brianna looks shell-shocked. Carolyn is right; that's exactly what she's saying. But I bet Brianna's never thought about it in those terms before. She's been living in a happy little bubble of blind denial. "No, I—"

"I want to see Matthew," Carolyn demands. "That's why Lexi and I came here, and I want to see him. Now." She's on her feet. I join her.

Brianna sighs. "All right. Let's go."

Chapter 32

Barbara and Kaylee jump when Brianna opens the infirmary door. Clearly they weren't expecting her back so soon. And when they see me and Carolyn behind her, they look even more bewildered.

"What are they doing here?" Barbara asks.

"I asked them to come," Brianna lies smoothly. "They're in his group, and I thought it would help Matthew to have his friends here with him."

"Well then, where's Daniel?" Kaylee asks.

"I couldn't very well go into the boys' dorm at this time of night, could I, Kaylee?" Brianna snaps.

Kaylee's face turns red. "No, of course not. I apologize."

I still can't see Matthew. His cot is hidden behind the open door. It's so hard to be patient, standing here waiting for all the formalities between the counselors to be over. I just want to see him.

"Now, I would appreciate it if you would give Alexis and Carolyn a moment alone with their friend."

"Yes, of course," Barbara says, and she and Kaylee duck out of the cabin.

Brianna opens the door wider, and Carolyn and I rush inside. Matthew is lying on the cot, the blanket in a bunch by his feet. He's wearing a white T-shirt pulled up to his chest and loose-fitting gym shorts. His face, arms, and legs look fine, but his middle is covered in bruises—dark ones, purple and black. There are bags of ice on his ribs and propped up against his sides. His eyes are closed, but judging from the contorted expression on his face, he's in pain, even as he sleeps. My strong, funny friend is broken.

"I'll give you a few minutes," Brianna says and closes the door behind her. The three of us are alone.

Carolyn and I kneel beside Matthew and look at each other. I feel like I'm about to burst into tears, but her expression is hard, seething. She holds my gaze, and I know she understands. She finally sees this place for what it truly is. And she's done.

My pulse quickens.

I tell myself that just because Carolyn's seen what Mr. Martin did to Matthew and learned that Mr. Martin isn't any better than Kenny or any other abusive scum out there and that New Horizons isn't what she believed it to be doesn't mean that anything has changed. She can still be done with this place without wanting to be with me. She's still haunted by what happened with Natalie, and besides, she's never officially said anything that should make me think that she likes me. Matthew was the one who put that idea in my head, not her.

But still. The way she's looking at me right now…

Matthew rolls over in his cot and groans with pain as his wounds press against the thin mattress.

Carolyn tears her eyes away from mine. "Should we just let him sleep?" she whispers.

"No," I say. "If it were me, I'd want to know that you guys were here." I reach over and brush the hair back from Matthew's sweaty forehead. "Hey, Matthew?" I say softly. "Wake up. It's Lexi and Carolyn."

He mumbles something unintelligible.

I place my hand on his arm and shake him slightly. "Matthew."

His eyes fly open, and he sucks in air. He looks around wildly, trying to get his bearings. Then his eyes settle on me, and he relaxes.

"Hey," I say and make myself smile. "How you doing?"

"Peachy," he says, his voice gravelly with exhaustion. "Can't get enough of this place. I'm thinking of investing in a timeshare."

I laugh in relief and smile at Carolyn. She grins back. Same old Matthew. Bruised, yes. But not broken after all.

"Are you in pain?" Carolyn asks.

Matthew grimaces. "Yeah. Bruised ribs. The pills Barbara gave me are helping though."

"Oh, Matthew," I say. "I'm so sorry."

"What are *you* sorry for?" he says. "You didn't do this to me."

"No, but you were in trouble because of me in the first place. This really is all my fault."

"Are you crazy? None of this is your fault."

"But in DC—"

"Lexi, this was going to happen no matter what," Matthew says. "It was always about me. I think from the very first day Mr. Martin met me, he knew it was going to end one of two ways. And honestly, between this and what he *wanted* me to do, I'll choose this every time."

"Don't worry." I keep my voice low, just in case Brianna is outside listening. "He's going to get what's coming to him. Brianna told us some stuff. You were right—he *has* done it before."

Matthew raises an eyebrow. "What do you mean *Brianna* told you some stuff?"

Carolyn and I explain what happened and what Brianna told us about her brother. Matthew's eyes grow wider and wider the longer we talk.

"I cannot *believe* that she told you all that," he says when we're done.

"I kind of backed her into a corner so she had to. But honestly, I don't think we gave her enough credit. She lied to Kaylee and Barbara just so we could come see you."

"Unreal," Matthew says.

"So when does Barbara think you'll be able to get out of here?" Carolyn asks.

"She guessed a week. I just have to wait until I can get up and walk around without crazy pain. It's okay. I actually don't mind being here. It's better than having to face all those people who watched that asshole beat me up and didn't try to stop it."

"I'm so sorry," I say again, my heart aching.

"Lexi! Stop apologizing!" Matthew says. "I would slap you, you know, if I could move."

"Okay, okay, sorry."

He shoots me a look.

The infirmary's creaky screen door swings open, and Brianna enters the room. "It's after midnight, girls. You need to be getting back to the dorm."

Carolyn and I stand. I lean over and give Matthew a light kiss on the forehead. "We'll be back," I tell him.

"I know. Thanks, you guys."

Brianna comes closer and looks down at Matthew like she wants to say something but can't find the words.

"Brianna?" he says. "You okay?"

She nods. "I…um…I just wanted to say I'm sorry for what Mr. Martin did to you. I think…maybe…he sometimes goes too far."

It's a half-ass apology, but coming from her, it's huge. "Thank you," Matthew says.

Brianna keeps standing there, staring at him.

"Was there something else?" he asks.

"I was just wondering…did it work?" she asks.

"Did what work?"

"The exorcism."

Carolyn and I exchange a look, but I have to give Matthew credit. He keeps a straight face. "Yes," he says, deadpan. "I think it just might have done the trick."

Brianna's face breaks into the biggest smile I've ever seen from her. "I'm so glad to hear it. You're going to be just fine, Matthew." She turns to me and Carolyn. "I'm going to sit with Matthew until Barbara gets back. You two go ahead."

We wave good-bye to Matthew. While Brianna's back is still turned, he rolls his eyes at her. Brianna's right—he's going to be just fine. Thank God.

As we walk back through the quiet woods, Carolyn says, "What was Matthew talking about back there, Lexi? Why do you think this is your fault? What happened in DC?"

"You caught that, huh?"

"It was pretty hard to miss."

There's no point lying now. "He pushed us off that train because he knew I liked you and he wanted to give us the chance to spend the day alone together."

She takes her eyes away from her path to look at me and in doing so trips over a root sticking out of the earth. I grab her arm just in time to save her from hurtling face-first to the ground. Her hand flies to her chest, and she steadies her footing and catches her breath.

I'm still holding on to her. I can't seem to let go.

She meets my eyes and my heart pounds. "Thanks," she says. "You saved me."

"Anytime." I smile.

"So Matthew knew?" she asks.

"Yeah." We're alone, in the dark, my hand is on her arm, and we're actually talking about my feelings for her. Whoa.

"What did you tell him?"

I shrug. "I don't know. Nothing."

She takes a step closer and smiles. "I don't think he would have gone through all of this for *nothing*."

I can't speak. I can't think. She's so close. She smells incredible. I stare at her mouth—one corner is turned up ever so slightly. I glance up and find that her eyes are on my mouth too. I'm pretty sure we're feeling the same thing.

But then the unmistakable sound of someone walking down the path pulls us apart. My hand leaves Carolyn's arm and she leaps away, putting several feet of space between us. She starts walking again, and I follow, left with only one thought: *what just happened?*

The source of the noise was Barbara. We run into her on her way back to the infirmary from the main cabin. "Go get some rest, ladies," she says. "It's been a long couple of days."

"We will," Carolyn says. "You too. And thanks for taking care of Matthew."

"Of course, dear. Good night."

Carolyn and I don't say anything else for the rest of the walk. The closer we get to the main cabin, the more dangerous it would be to pick up our conversation where we left off. When we get back to the dorm, Carolyn wordlessly grabs *The Great Gatsby* off my nightstand and goes over to her area. I get into bed, and just as I'm about to drift off to sleep, the book lands with a *thump* on the foot of my bed.

It's too dark in the room for me to see Carolyn, but there's just enough moonlight streaming through my window for me to see that she's dog-eared a page. It's page 28—the end of chapter one. Most of the page is blank for the chapter break, and Carolyn's drawn something in. It looks like a map. *Tomorrow morning,* she's written underneath. *6 a.m.*

Chapter 33

It's still dark when I get out of bed. Carolyn's already gone, off on her run. And today I'm joining her. I don't have time to take a shower, but I brush my teeth and wash my face quickly and throw on some clothes. Everyone is still sound asleep when I sneak out.

I grip the book tightly and follow Carolyn's map as best I can. Instead of making a left out of the main cabin to go toward the field like I have every day for the past month and a half, I turn right. I tiptoe across the grass, keeping close to the side of the building in case anyone happens to look out any of the second-floor windows as I go by. Going to meet Carolyn like this is even more dangerous than sneaking out last night to go see Matthew. Our reasons for doing that were honorable, as far as Brianna was concerned. But meeting Carolyn alone, in the early hours of the morning—well, there's only one reason for us to do that. I try not to think of that reason as I half walk, half run to meet her.

The map Carolyn drew from memory in the dark is surprisingly detailed. I know exactly where to enter the woods, exactly which trail to take when I reach a fork. She knows this place well—it's her own little private world that no one else at the camp has seen. And she's invited me into it.

I round the next bend and there she is. She stands in the middle of a little open, grassy area, stretching. She's in her running clothes, her hair pulled away from her face, beads of sweat sprinkling her collarbone. She smiles when she sees me. "You found it," she says.

"Yeah," I say, suddenly incredibly nervous. "You run here every day?"

"Yup. Beautiful, isn't it?"

I'm sure it is. But I can't keep my eyes off her. I take a step closer. She holds my gaze and takes a step of her own.

And then, like two magnets that have suddenly entered the same force field, we come together.

He knew that when he kissed this girl, and forever wed his unutterable visions to her perishable breath, his mind would never romp again like the mind of God.

Electricity explodes through every part of me as my mouth meets hers. *This* is what a kiss is supposed to be. There's no one else around, no party games, no boys to be putting on a show for. Just me and Carolyn and the lightning between us.

I drop the book and pull her closer to me. Her hands are in my hair, one of mine is on the small of her back, the other caressing her face. It's the best moment of my life.

Far too soon, we break apart. Carolyn grins at me, her face flushed, her eyes full of…*something*. Something good. She threads her fingers through mine and we sit together in the grass. We stay like that for a while, holding hands, just staring at each other. And then I can't take it anymore—I close the distance between us and crush my mouth against hers again. We topple over onto the grass, giggling and kissing and happy.

• • •

"We have to be getting back," she whispers. It's the first thing either of us has said. We're lying in the grass, her head resting on my chest. I run my fingers through her hair and breathe her in.

"I don't want to," I murmur.

Carolyn laughs and props herself up on her elbows to look at me. "Me either." She gives me a soft peck on the lips. "But it's seven o'clock. Kaylee's alarm is going to go off in thirty minutes, and you need to be back in your bed by the time that happens."

She's right. But I hate the reminder that the real world actually exists. I want to just stay here, lying in this patch of wild grass with Carolyn forever.

"Okay," I say with a sigh and push myself up to standing. "Let's go."

We hold hands as we walk back through the woods, and I slip back into bed just in time.

Chapter 34

I can't believe this morning really happened. I finally kissed Carolyn, after all this time. And it was perfect. I keep catching myself staring at her as we get ready for the day, grinning like a giant dope.

But she's acting like nothing happened. She barely even looks at me, and when she does, her eyes hold no hint of the magic that happened between us.

I know she has to act that way, to play it cool so we're not found out, that I need to be acting that way too, but I can't help but feel a little twinge of worry when I see her impassive face. Maybe she changed her mind at some point between our time together in the woods this morning and now. Maybe she's freaked out by what happened and decided to reaffirm her commitment to the de-gayifying. Maybe I did something wrong...

I wish I could talk to her, but there's just no way.

"Has anyone heard anything about Matthew?" Daniel asks at breakfast.

Carolyn and I look at each other. *Do we tell him?* she asks silently. I shrug.

"What's going on?" Daniel says, suspicious now.

"Okay. Don't tell anyone," Carolyn says, her voice low, "but we went to see Matthew last night."

"You did?"

"Yeah."

"Well, how is he? Is he all right?" He looks really worried.

I nod. "He's going to be okay. He's pretty shaken up and in a lot of pain though. Barbara said he should probably be able to join the rest of us in about a week."

"Can I go see him? How come you guys got to?"

Carolyn and I share another look, and this time I see a hint of the sparkle from this morning in her eyes. "It's a long story," she says and squeezes my hand under the table.

That one small touch is everything.

I try not to smile, but it doesn't work very well. My skin sizzles where her hand meets mine and it takes everything I have to stop myself from jumping on her right here. God, I want to kiss her again.

Daniel looks back and forth between the two of us, like he knows there's something going on but he doesn't know what. But he doesn't get to ask because Mr. Martin claps his hands to get everyone's attention.

"I've invited some very special guests to speak to us today," he announces. "This is one of my favorite sessions of the entire summer—it's alumni day! New Horizons campers of the past are here to share their success stories with us!"

The carpet cabin is set up similarly to the way it was on the very first day of camp: the chairs are arranged in a big circle. But there are even more chairs in the circle this time to accommodate all the counselors as well as the five "very special guests."

The guest speakers are all pretty young. The youngest looks about nineteen, the oldest maybe twenty-five or so. They are all dressed pretty similarly too, in New Horizons chic—the girls are wearing skirts and dresses in pastel, Easter-egg shades, with long hair and delicate jewelry. The men are in crisp, collared shirts and ties. Every single one of them has a wedding ring on his or her finger.

They sit up straight in their chairs, looking at Mr. Martin like he still holds some power over them, like they're all frightened fifteen-year-olds again, on their first day of camp.

Pieces start to click into place—the campers' almost God-like worship of Mr. Martin, even years later. What he said to Matthew in the office yesterday about *I had a father like that too. But mine was worse, so much worse.* His lies, his coercions. Brianna's story about his past. There are still so many holes in the plot, but I think I have enough to at least sketch a pretty coherent outline. And I think what it all adds up to is *power*. Somewhere along the way, Jeremiah Martin lost control of his life. I don't know how or when or why, and I don't want to. He can keep his Father Wound to himself. But what I do know is this is how he's trying to get that control back—by demanding our obedience, respect, attention, even our love. Or what he thinks is love, anyway.

Mr. Martin introduces the guests, and they each tell a brief version of their story—they're all variations on the same theme: "I led a misguided youth, but through the guidance of New Horizons and the support of my church, my SSA is buried far in my past. I'm now married with two wonderful children and happier than ever, living the life God intended for me."

After the opening statements are over, we get to ask questions. It's too bad Matthew is missing this—he would be having a field day right now. But without Matthew here to ask the hard-hitting questions, the Q&A is just as safe as the speakers' stories:

"How did you meet your husband/wife?"

"Do you ever worry about your children having SSA?"

"What do you do to ensure your SSA never comes back?"

"How did you stay away from temptation in college?"

"In what ways is your life better now than it was when you had SSA?"

Blah, blah, blah.

I watch Carolyn carefully throughout the session, trying to read her expression. But her face is so carefully arranged for the counselors that even I can't see past the mask.

It's torture, being so close to her but not being able to do anything about it. In some ways, it's worse than when I loved her in secret. At least then I didn't know what I was missing.

A crazy impulse comes over me, and I make the split-second decision to do what Matthew can't. I raise my hand and ask, "Do any of you still find yourselves attracted to members of the same sex?"

The guests look at each other, but no one volunteers an answer.

Kaylee is suddenly very interested in her manicure. John stares out the window, and Deb's face is as blank as always. Mr. Martin is the only one looking at me.

"Of course not, Lexi," he says with a pleasant smile. "God has cured us."

"Sorry, I guess I'm just a little confused," I say just as congenially. "The work we do here at New Horizons consists mainly of learning the techniques to resist our SSA, right? To keep making the right choices, even after we leave New Horizons."

"Yes."

"So that means that our 'cure' depends on our actively choosing to not be gay every single day. That's a lot of work. And I'm not saying it's not worth it or that it's not right or anything like that," I add, "but it's got to be tiring. So I'm just wondering if any of you ever find yourselves letting your guard down and letting the SSA creep back in, even just for a moment. If you ever experience any of those old feelings."

There's a moment of silence as Mr. Martin studies me, trying to figure out which road to take here. I blink back at him innocently, my posture perfect and my legs crossed delicately at the ankles, just like Brianna taught us. Finally he turns to the guests.

"Please, don't be shy," he says to them. "Do you ever experience any of those old feelings?"

The guests answer exactly the same:

"No."

"No, sir."

"No."

"No."

"No."

Mr. Martin turns back to me. "Does that answer your question, Lexi?"

"Yes. Thank you, Mr. Martin."

"Good. Moving on."

I'm not even sure what the point of pushing him like that was, but the tiny smile curling the corners of Carolyn's mouth made it worth it.

That night, as we get ready for bed, I catch Carolyn's eye across the dorm room. I raise my eyebrows questioningly and she gives a tiny smile and nods. That settles it—I'm going to meet her again. Luckily, sleepy, old Barbara is on dorm duty tonight.

• • •

The instant Carolyn and I see each other in the woods the next morning, we throw ourselves at each other. It's amazing how her touch, her kiss, is already something I need so desperately. Now that I've had it, I can't live without it.

"Lexi," she whispers and brushes her mouth across my lips, my jaw, my neck. She pulls my body tight against hers, and then her hands are slowly traveling up my shirt. I'm not wearing a bra, and it's only a matter of seconds before we cross over into new territory. I want it. I want her, so badly...but I have to press pause.

"Wait," I gasp and make myself pull away.

"I'm sorry," she says quickly. "I didn't mean to—"

I smile and shake my head. "No, believe me, you didn't do anything wrong." I give her a quick peck on the lips to reassure her. "I just think...we need to talk."

Carolyn looks disappointed, but she nods in agreement. "You're probably right."

We sit in the grass and study each other. It's pretty clear neither of us knows where to begin. But we only have a finite amount of time before we need to go back to camp, so I decide to jump right in. "Have you changed your mind about wanting to become straight?" I ask point-blank.

To my surprise, Carolyn laughs. "I would have thought that was pretty obvious," she says.

"Well, not entirely," I admit. "You just seemed *so* into the idea, even after I told you all that stuff in DC..."

She takes my hand. "I was trying to convince myself that I

didn't have feelings for you," she confesses. "When I first realized I liked you, I wanted to believe more than ever that the reparative therapy could work. I was so scared of what would happen if I let myself go where my heart wanted to take me. And then after we talked about Natalie in DC, those fears kind of renewed themselves. I was being stupid. I'm so sorry."

"When did you realize you liked me?" I ask, thrilled that she's finally said the words.

"Honestly?"

I nod.

"The first moment I saw you," she says, "across the circle in the cabin."

I squeeze her hand. "That's when I knew I liked you too."

She squints, remembering. "It was really strange, actually. There was like this…*connection* I suddenly felt with you. Like a spark or something."

"Like lightning," I say.

She smiles. "Yeah. Like lightning."

"So," I say, just to be sure, "you're done with the de-gayifying?"

"I'm *so* done." She shakes her head. "I can't *believe* I actually wanted it to work."

"You had your reasons," I tell her. "We both did."

"Well, now that I know who Mr. Martin really is, I don't want anything to do with him or his camp ever again."

A terrible thought occurs to me. "You know, you could go home now. Your parents want you to. Now that you don't have any reason to stay, you could leave."

"But I *do* have a reason to stay…" She reaches over and brushes her thumb lightly across my lips.

My heart swells. "I won't hurt you," I promise. "I'm not Natalie."

"And I'm not Zoë," she says, still staring at my mouth.

"I know."

And then she kisses me.

This time, I don't stop her.

Chapter 35

At breakfast later that morning, I take Brianna aside and ask her if we can go visit Matthew again. She purses her lips, considering.

"Please," I say. "We didn't get to see him yesterday."

She sighs. "All right. But Daniel has to come too. I'll present it to Mr. Martin as a supportive group thing. He won't be able to say no to that."

"That's fine. Thank you so much." I resist the urge to hug her. That probably wouldn't go over so well.

The day carries on, but the workbook exercises mean nothing to me. Every time I think about this morning in the woods, I feel a flash of heat and a flutter in my stomach. I'm probably blushing like crazy. The way Carolyn touched me, the things she showed me...I simply had not known that kind of bliss could exist.

Of course, that makes it even *harder* to act normal in front of the counselors and campers. How am I supposed to act normal with her sitting two feet away from me and *those* memories flashing through my mind?

Brianna comes over to our group at the end of the classroom

session, and I snap out of my daydream. "Mr. Martin has given his permission for you to spend your rec hour this evening visiting Matthew in the infirmary if you'd like," she says.

Guilt falls on top of me like a heap of bricks. How can I be so happy when Matthew's in so much misery?

"Yes," Daniel says. "Yes, of course we want to see him!"

So after dinner, we go to the infirmary.

Matthew looks a million times better than he did the other night. He's alone in the cabin, sitting up in his cot, reading a book. His bruises have faded to a putrid yellowish color—it looks really gross, but it means they're healing. His face lights up when we enter the room.

"Hi, guys!" he says.

Suddenly Daniel bursts out in tears and throws his arms around Matthew, forgetting the no-touching rule. "You're really okay," he says between sobs.

Matthew winces. "I'm okay," he says, patting Daniel's back gingerly. "You don't have to worry."

Daniel pulls back, sniffling. "I was praying for you."

"Thanks, buddy." Matthew smiles.

"You look so much better," I say as Carolyn and I join them.

"I feel a lot better," he says. "I'm starting to go a little stir-crazy in this room though. I've resorted to reading this fine selection from the New Horizons library to keep me occupied." He gestures to the book in his lap.

I pick it up. "*The Gift*," I read aloud. "A story of faith, choices, and waiting for marriage." I raise an eyebrow.

"It's either that or stare at the ceiling all day," Matthew says with a shrug. "So what have I been missing? Any good gossip?"

Carolyn and I automatically look at each other. She's all smiley now that we're away from the babysitters, which makes me all smiley too, and a fresh wave of memories from this morning rushes over me, and my cheeks get warm, which makes her smile even bigger.

"We had an alumni day yesterday," Daniel says. "They were so inspiring. They're all married and happy…" He goes on about what the guest speakers said yesterday, but Matthew isn't paying attention. He's looking at me and Carolyn, a massive grin on his face.

He waits until Daniel's recounted all the details he could think of about the alumni day and then says, "Spill."

"Huh?" Daniel says.

"You two." Matthew points to me and Carolyn. "I want details. Don't leave anything out."

That, of course, makes me blush all over again. There are some details that Matthew is just not going to get.

Daniel is looking back and forth between the three of us. "What did I miss?"

"Nothing," I say quickly. "Matthew's still a little delirious."

Matthew pouts like a three-year-old who was just told he can't have any ice cream. "Fine," he says. "Don't tell me. I'll just carry on my miserable existence in this tiny cabin with nothing to keep me entertained except a book about protecting your virtue."

Way to make me feel even more guilty. Thanks, Matthew.

I look to Carolyn for backup. She's much better at this playing-it-cool stuff than I am. But she grins and says, "I say tell them."

My jaw drops. "Really?"

"Sure. Why not?"

"Okay, *what* are you guys talking about?" Daniel says.

"Please, Lexi?" Matthew pleads. "I would do it for you."

His words pierce straight through me, putting a major hole in my will. Of course he would do it for me. He would do anything for me. He already has. He really does deserve to know that everything he went through wasn't for nothing, and it seems like we're never going to get another chance to talk without Daniel being present, so…

I throw up my hands in defeat. "All right."

Matthew claps excitedly.

"But it doesn't leave this room, okay?"

"Of course," Matthew says.

"Daniel?" I ask. "Can you keep a secret?"

He nods. "Yes."

"Carolyn and I are…" I realize I don't know how to finish. What are we? Girlfriends? Dating?

"In love," Carolyn says.

I catch my breath, and Carolyn's gaze meets mine as if to say, *Aren't we?* Her eyes are hopeful.

"In love," I say, surprised at how comfortable the word feels on my tongue. After all the times I've thought it, it's the first time I've actually said it out loud.

Daniel's mouth falls open.

"Oh my God, oh my God, oh my God!" Matthew squeals. "This is amazing! Tell me *everything*. Start at the beginning."

We don't tell them *everything*, but we tell them enough. By the time we're done talking, Matthew's eyes are shimmering with unshed tears.

"What's wrong?" I ask.

"Nothing! I'm just so glad," he says. "All of this"—he gestures to his bruises, and then out the window to the camp—"was actually worth something."

Daniel looks at Carolyn's and my hands, clasped together. "You both seem really happy," he says. But I think he's wondering whether that's a good thing or a bad thing.

"We are," Carolyn and I say in unison.

Matthew heaves a giant sigh. "I miss Justin."

• • •

Brianna's on dorm duty the next morning. It'll be infinitely riskier to sneak out with her on guard than it was with Deb and Barbara. But not going to meet Carolyn in the woods is just not an option. I need that time with her.

It's not until I've slipped out of the dorm and am on my way to our meeting spot that I realize that Carolyn and I never actually made a plan to meet today. Maybe she assumed that Brianna days are a no-go. She's probably off running somewhere, not expecting me to come looking for her.

But I keep walking anyway. If she's not there, I'll go back. But we only have less than two weeks left at New Horizons, and then she'll go back to Connecticut and I'll go back home to South Carolina, and I'll regret every single moment I could have been with her but wasn't. So on the off chance that she is there, I keep going.

And there she is, lying in the grass. I slide my body over hers and kiss her deeply.

"Good morning," she murmurs.

"Morning."

"I didn't know if you were going to come."

"I didn't know if you were going to be waiting."

She brings her mouth to mine again by way of an answer.

A while later, as we lie together in the tall grass, half-dressed and limbs tangled together, I tell her, "This was my wish."

She strokes the hair out of my eyes. "What wish?"

"When you held out that speck of glitter on your fingertip and told me to make a wish. This was it."

"Making out in the woods?" she says, laughing.

I playfully pinch her arm. "No. You and me. Together."

She looks at me, all traces of joking vanished. "What's going to happen after the summer?" she blurts out.

I swallow. "What do you mean?" I say slowly. But of course I know what she means. It's the question that's been gnawing at the back of my mind ever since our first morning here in the woods.

She sits up. "I'm just wondering where you're at, like, with your mom and everything. Are you going to tell her about us?"

"Um…I don't know. I haven't really thought about it." It's kind of a lie. I *have* thought about it. I just didn't let myself think about it long enough to come to a conclusion. There were too many other feelings, too much *goodness* going on.

"But you said in DC that you would tell your mom the truth…"

Yeah. I did say that. But that was when Carolyn and I were still a pipedream. Now it's all so…real.

As I try to iron out my wrinkled thoughts, I'm distracted by the sight of Carolyn hastily standing up and readjusting her clothes. Her movements are clipped, tense. What happened?

"What's wrong?" I ask.

"Nothing."

I grab her hand. "Carolyn."

She stops moving and looks at me.

"What's going on?"

"You clearly don't know what you want, Lexi." She crosses her arms as if trying to protect herself from me.

I stare into the blue of her eyes. "Of course I do. I want to be with you."

She stares back at me, searching, and after a long moment, her expression softens. "I want to be with you too."

I breathe out, relieved. "Good."

"But that means you're going to have to tell your mom." She sits down again. "If we're going to do this, we have to do it for real. I can't be with someone else who isn't a hundred percent committed. I can't do secrets anymore."

I nod. "I know."

She slides closer to me and slowly leans in, her eyes never leaving mine. My heart speeds up with anticipation. And then, just as our lips are about to touch, we hear it.

"Stop right there, ladies."

It's Mr. Martin.

Chapter 36

Carolyn and I move apart so fast it's like a grenade was set off between us.

I scramble around like a fumbling idiot, my heart leaping every which way around my ribcage. At least I still had my bra on.

I pull my shirt on as quickly as possible and avoid all eye contact. The longer I put off facing Mr. Martin, the longer I can extend the calm before the hurricane.

But when I hear Carolyn whisper, "Daniel," I know the time for denial has passed.

I look at her and follow her gaze across the grass to the edge of the trees. Behind Mr. Martin stands Brianna, her expression wiped clean of any of the friendliness it may have formerly held...and Daniel. He looks distraught. He's gripping Carolyn's and my copy of *The Great Gatsby* tight against his chest.

The map. That's how they found us.

"Daniel, how could you?" Carolyn says.

He just shakes his head slightly. His eyes are apologetic, but he doesn't speak and he doesn't move away from the counselors. He's chosen his side.

"Daniel did exactly what he was supposed to do," Mr. Martin answers for him. "Well, not *exactly*—he went to Brianna first instead of coming directly to me." He shoots Daniel a disappointed look. "But he spoke with us last night and told us what was going on between the two of you. He was worried for your souls. And well he should be. It's not just the reprehensible act itself, but the lying, the sneaking around, the act you put on for the camp. You are *sinners*."

I stare him down, calmer than I thought I would be when this moment arrived. "Look who's talking," I say, each word clear and biting.

Mr. Martin blinks. "Excuse me?"

"You know *exactly* what I'm talking about. And so do you, Brianna."

Brianna opens her mouth but seems to change her mind about speaking. Instead, she turns slowly away and walks back the way they came.

Mr. Martin's confident façade falters for a fragment of a second. I don't back down—I hold his stare, letting him know that I know everything. And then, still staring him down, I reach my hand out to my side. After a moment, I feel Carolyn's soft hand slide into it and hold on tight.

We stand like that for a long time, us against them: the boy who's beginning to realize he's been kept in the dark about a lot more than just me and Carolyn, and the man who's beginning to realize that his days of getting away with all this are coming to an end.

But there's nothing Mr. Martin can do now except continue with the script. He says, "You are aware of the penalty for this type of transgression—"

"We know," I cut him off. "Come on, Carolyn. Let's go home."

• • •

Carolyn goes into Mr. Martin's office first. I wait outside with Deb, who's watching over me like a stone gargoyle. Brianna's nowhere to be seen. She's probably off praying, trying to convince herself that everything is going to be fine.

But no amount of praying is going to save New Horizons now.

I listen through the door as Mr. Martin explains to Carolyn's parents over the phone what happened and that they must come pick her up immediately. The conversation is short. "They'll be here in six hours," he tells Carolyn, hanging up the phone. He sounds disappointed that her parents weren't more upset.

The door opens and Carolyn and I lock eyes as we switch places. "Good luck," she whispers as the door closes and our connection is broken.

Thanks, I think. *I'm going to need it.*

Mr. Martin dials my mom's number. As he hits the last digit, I say, "Can I tell her?"

He looks at me, receiver to his ear. It's probably already ringing.

"You can supervise," I say. "I just want to be able to tell her myself. It's all the same in the end, right?"

Mr. Martin thinks for a moment and, probably deciding that he'd better get on my good side while he still can *just in case* I actually really do know what I said I know, hands the phone over to me.

"Hello?" my mother's distant, small voice comes through the earpiece.

I bring the phone to my ear and take a deep breath.

"Hello?" she says again.

"Mom?"

"Lexi! What a wonderful surprise!" She sounds just as cheerful and dynamic as she did during our last phone conversation. I don't want to ruin it. Oh God, what if I tell her this and she down spirals? What if things get bad again?

But I have no choice. Mr. Martin is staring at me, waiting to get to the punch line, and Carolyn is somewhere in this cabin, depending on me to do the right thing.

"Mom, I have something to tell you."

"Oh? Is everything all right?"

"Yes and no. I, um…" Mr. Martin is watching me closely. "I need you to come pick me up."

"Yes, next Sunday, right?" Mom says. "I have it marked on the calendar."

"No. Today. Now."

There's silence down the line.

"Mom?" I say, worry building up in my chest. "Are you there?"

"Yes, Lexi," she says quietly after a moment. "I'm here. What happened? What did you do?"

I immediately feel defensive. Why does she assume it was something *I* did? Why does everything automatically have to be my fault?

I mean, okay, it *is* my fault. But she doesn't know that yet.

"I tried, Mom," I say. "I really, really tried. I just…It didn't work. I'm so sorry."

I hear some sort of clanging through the phone, like Mom's angrily putting away pots and pans or something.

"Mom? Say something, please."

The clanging cuts off. "I'm leaving in five minutes. See you in a few hours." The line goes dead.

I hand the phone back to Mr. Martin, my mother's voice repeating in my ears. "She's on her way," I say.

Chapter 37

When I leave Mr. Martin's office, Carolyn's not there anymore.

But Deb is waiting for me. "Come with me," she says, and I follow her into another room, one I've never seen before. It's a small bedroom, with a single bed and modest furnishings. There is a Bible on the desk and a photograph of Deb and a dark-skinned man with a mustache and his pants pulled up way too high. This must be her room for when she's not on dorm duty.

"What are we doing in here?" I ask. "Shouldn't I be packing or something?"

"You won't be allowed back into the dorm until the other campers are safely down at the field cabins."

Safely. Of course. They don't want to risk me and Carolyn infecting the other girls with our sickness.

And then, way too late, it dawns on me that it's not just the other campers they're keeping us from—they're keeping us apart from each other too. This tiny room is a cell, and Deb, standing there in front of the door with her arms crossed, is the prison guard. A bud of panic sprouts in my stomach. "Where's Carolyn?" I say cautiously.

"With Kaylee."

"Can I see her?"

"No."

"Why?"

"Why do you think?" she retorts.

I stare into Deb's flat eyes and sink down into the desk chair, suddenly sick to my stomach.

They're keeping us separated. I'm not going to get a chance to say good-bye.

Oh my God—I don't even have her contact information. All I really know is her first name and that she's from Connecticut. That's pretty much the same amount of information she has about me. How are we ever going to find each other again?

Think fast, Lexi.

"Is that your brother?" I say, pointing to the picture. Maybe if I can somehow get Deb to open up, she'll help me.

"That's my husband," she replies flatly. "Now be quiet."

"You must miss him," I say. "Do you get to talk to him much while you're here?"

She shoots me a look that says, *I told you to be quiet.* That's the only answer I get. Her face closes off even more, like she's a robot powering down.

I sigh and lay my head down on the desk like I used to do in study hall. Or I guess I *still* do that in study hall. It seems like years since I was in school, but I'll be back there in a matter of weeks.

Senior year. Back to my boy-crazy friends and Zoë acting like I don't exist and senior pranks and homecoming and planning for college. But even with all the tedium, it won't be the same as it was. Because I'm different. I'm not going to hide anymore.

I just really need Carolyn to help me through it.

Why the *hell* didn't we exchange our contact info?

• • •

About an hour later, Arthur knocks on the door. "Lexi can pack her things now," he says.

I follow Deb up the stairs and to the girls' dorm, where Carolyn's bags are already packed and waiting on her neatly made bed. She's not there though.

It's going to be okay, I tell myself. Even if I have to call every single sixteen-year-old Carolyn in the entire state of Connecticut, I'll find her.

I get to work neatly folding my clothes and wedging them all in my suitcase. Deb insists I take all the makeup and beauty products I've accumulated over the course of the summer, so they go in next, followed by my shoes. The suitcase is heavy and full, near bursting at the zippers, but it feels empty. Because it's missing something.

"Hey, Deb?" I say.

She comes over to my area. "Yes?"

I say a quick, silent prayer. I need this to work. "Daniel has my book. Would you be able to get it back from him for me?"

She purses her lips, considering. I don't know if she knows about the map or Carolyn's and my notes to each other inside or not, and she doesn't let on now.

I look at her, pleading. "Please? It's really important."

Finally, she nods. "I'll be right back. Do not leave this room."

I nod. Where would I go anyway? Wherever Carolyn is, she's being guarded.

After Deb leaves, I rummage through Carolyn's stuff, looking for anything that might help me find her. There are clothes, a half-completed sweater still attached to her knitting needles, running shoes, her purple rhinestone headband, but nothing helpful.

I hurry back to my bed, tear a blank page from my journal, and write—as neatly as I can—my address, email address, and cell phone number.

Then I add: I'm not sorry we got caught. I'm going to tell my mom everything. I love you.

I fold the paper into a neat square and slide it into the side pocket of Carolyn's duffle bag.

Satisfied, I go back to my own area and settle in to wait.

Fifteen minutes go by then thirty. Deb's taking a lot longer than she should. Was she lying? Maybe she had no intention of getting my book back for me after all. Or maybe Mr. Martin or Brianna confiscated it as, I don't know, *evidence* or something.

I'm beginning to give up all hope of ever seeing the book again when Deb comes back in. She hands the tattered paperback over to me. "This took forever to find," she says, annoyed. "Daniel didn't have it."

"He didn't?"

"No, Matthew had it with him in the infirmary."

He did? That's weird. Daniel had it in the woods with him only a couple of hours ago. How would Matthew have gotten ahold of it? And why?

"Oh," I say. "Sorry about that. Thanks for getting it back."

Deb nods and settles into her chair to resume the Great Watch. My mom's due to arrive in about three hours.

I'm itching to open *Gatsby*, but I force myself to wait a suitable amount of time so Deb doesn't get suspicious. It seems she didn't open the book on her way back to the dorm—she doesn't know all the secrets it contains. After about twenty minutes or so, I casually open the book as if I'm planning on reading for a while. But I discreetly flip through the pages, searching for a hint as to why Matthew would have had the book.

And there it is, on page 169, in the chapter-ending blank space just after Gatsby is shot.

Hey, Lex—

Matthew has scrawled.

Daniel told me what happened. For what it's worth, he feels really bad about ratting you guys out. And even though he used the map to find you, he never let the book out of his hands. So no one else has seen what's in it. Maybe that's a sign that he's on his way to changing his mind about all this crap. Or maybe not. I don't know. Anyway, I guess I'm not gonna get a chance to say good-bye, so I just wanted to tell you what a great friend you've been to me this summer and that you better keep in touch or else!

I'm so happy for you and Carolyn—you guys are perfect together. When you get married, I want to be your maid of honor.

Talk to you soon, Lexi. Love ya! And remember, don't let the man get you down.

Xoxoxoxo Matthew

matthew.hilson8@mail.com

I smile, tuck the book safely away in my suitcase, and curl up on the bed, taking in the pink dorm room for the last time.

• • •

I'm jolted awake by Mr. Martin's voice. "Lexi."

I rub my eyes and sit up. "Yes?"

"Your mother is downstairs." He spins on his heels and walks away.

This is it.

Time to face my mom.

Chapter 38

She's in the lobby, sitting in one of the sleek leather armchairs. I see her before she sees me, and a knot forms in my throat when I get a good look at her—she looks great. Her old color is back in her face, her cheeks are fuller, her eyes are bright in a way that feels much more permanent than it did before. She's the mom I knew years ago.

"Hey, Mom," I say.

She stands up when she sees me, and her face bursts into a huge smile.

All the emotions that have been brewing inside me finally come to a boil. I drop my suitcase handle and run into her arms. She holds me and rocks me and I cry into her shoulder. "I missed you," I mumble.

"I missed you too, Lexi." She strokes my hair like she used to do when I was a little kid and home sick from school.

Mr. Martin clears his throat. "Follow me, please," he says and leads us into his office like he did that first day. "Mrs. Hamilton,

I'm sure you're wondering what Lexi has done to force us to ask her to leave our camp," he says.

My mother nods.

"She was caught sneaking off with another female camper," he says. He pauses, waiting for my mother's reaction. But her face is unreadable. "She and this other young woman have had a blatant disregard for the rules and teachings of New Horizons," he continues, "and I'm afraid we have no choice but to expel them both."

My mom sits there for a minute, absorbing the information, and then says, "Thank you for letting me know."

Mr. Martin looks surprised that that's her only response. And honestly, so am I. What is she thinking?

Mom signs my release papers and shakes Mr. Martin's hand, and before I know it, I'm walking out of the main cabin and driving back down the gravel mountain road.

We don't speak until we're on the highway.

"Your cell phone is in the glove compartment," Mom says. "It's fully charged. I thought you might want to call your friends to tell them you're coming home."

I have nine new voicemails and 138 emails. I'll look at them later.

"Mom…" I begin. But I don't know what to say. I search her face, looking for some kind of answer.

The corners of her mouth turn down. "I'm not going to tell you this is all okay." She keeps her eyes on the road.

"I know," I say quietly. That would have been too much to hope for.

"I worry about you. So, so much. This life isn't what I would have chosen for you."

No kidding.

"And I really wish we were going back home on different terms. But that's only because I want what's best for you."

"But this *is*—"

"Let me finish," she says, finally darting a glance over to me. "I really missed you, Lexi. More and more as the summer went on. And as much as I wanted you to get help, I was also incredibly mad at myself. You're my daughter, and I sent you away." She takes a deep breath. "I'm not so sure I should have done that."

I stay silent. I never thought I'd hear my mother say any of this.

"I spoke with Pastor Joe quite a bit. We talked a lot about family and priorities and letting our faith guide us instead of our fear. He asked me if I love you, and I said of course. Then he asked me if I love you *unconditionally,* even if this part of you never changed."

I hold my breath.

"And I admit I didn't answer that question as quickly. I really thought about it, because I did know it was a very real possibility, not just a hypothetical. And I realized there was only one truthful answer—of course I love you unconditionally."

I let the breath out and realize I was digging my fingernails into the flesh of my thigh. I move my hands away and stare at the ten tiny commas etched into my skin.

"So," Mom says, her hands tightly gripping the steering wheel, "I may not agree with it, and I'll never *approve* of it or stop praying for you, but I'm really going to try to learn to live with it. Because we need to be in each other's lives. If there's anything this summer apart from each other has proven, I think it's that."

I take a breath to try to steady my voice. "Okay," I manage.

"Can I ask a favor though?" Mom asks, her voice a little bit lighter now.

"Sure…"

"I don't want you to lie to me anymore. Please don't do that, but…maybe just bring up things on a need-to-know basis? At first, anyway. While I get used to the idea."

I smile. "Okay, Mom. I won't make you march in the parade until next year. But I think we should stop on the way home and pick up a rainbow flag for the front porch."

She shoots me a look. "That's not funny, Lexi." But she's smiling. Sort of.

We drive past a farm—black and white cows dot the green hills like sprinkles on an ice cream cone. I can't wait to get back to the beach.

"You know," Mom says after a minute, "your father always suspected."

My heart stops. "Suspected?"

She nods. "That you were…this way. We talked about it. Well, *fought* about it."

My head is spinning. "What…what did he say?"

"He thought we should tell you it was okay, that we'd support you no matter what. I couldn't do it though. I didn't want to believe it was true." She looks at me out of the corner of her eye. "I made him promise he wouldn't say anything to you."

I knew *he didn't know what he was talking about.* That's what Mom said on the phone when I told her I thought the de-gayifying was working. She'd been talking about Dad.

Dad knew. He knew the whole time. And he loved me anyway.

Sneaky, unstoppable tears rush to my eyes.

We drive on in silence for a while.

After a couple of hours have gone by and I'm sure Carolyn's left New Horizons, I clear my throat and say, "Mom, I have to make a call."

"Go ahead."

"It's about something pretty serious. I think you should pull over."

She looks at me questioningly but pulls off at the next exit and parks the car at a gas station.

I dial.

"911, what's your emergency?" says the voice on the other end of the line.

"It's not exactly an emergency, but I need to report several counts of child abuse and sexual harassment," I say. Mom gasps, and I give her a little headshake to let her know that I'm okay, that I'm not the one who was victimized.

The dispatcher puts me in touch with the local law enforcement and I tell the police officer everything I know. It's a long, difficult conversation, but by the end, I'm pretty confident that Mr. Martin is going to get everything he deserves.

• • •

We're almost home when my phone rings. The number flashing on the display is unfamiliar. My heartbeat speeds up.

"Hello?"

"Lexi?" It's Carolyn. She found my note.

I glance at Mom. She's diligently watching the road, but we're about two feet apart from each other, and the radio's off—of course she's going to hear every word I say. I wish I didn't have to have this conversation, my first one with Carolyn away from the confines of New Horizons, in front of her. But I also promised Carolyn I wasn't going to hide from my mother anymore. So here goes. "Hey," I say softly.

"Hey. I miss you already." There's a muffled sound in the background, and then she says, "My parents say hi."

I laugh. "Hi back."

There's so much to talk about. What my mom said. How things went with Carolyn's parents and Mr. Martin. What she's told her parents about me. My call to the police. Matthew's note in *Gatsby*. The good-byes we never got to say in person. What the hell I'm going to tell everyone at school. How she and I are going to make this long-distance thing work.

But there will be time for that later. Right now, all I want is to sit here on the phone, knowing that even though Carolyn and I are driving further and further apart at this moment, we're closer than we've ever been. Right now I want to just *be*.

"So," I say.

"So," she says back, and there's a smile in her voice that makes my heart explode with heat and fire.

It actually feels a lot like lightning…only way better.

Acknowledgments

It might sound crazy, considering I don't actually *know* her, but I must start this long list of thank-yous by sending an enormous shout out to Lady Gaga, whose song "Hair" is the reason this book exists. Thank you, Gaga, for inspiring me in such a profound way, and for giving a voice to all the teens in the world who just want to be loved for who they are.

Thank you to Leah Hultenschmidt, my wonderful editor, for being so smart, insightful, patient, enthusiastic, and all around cool. Major props and thanks to my publicist Derry Wilkens for working tirelessly to bring *The Summer I Wasn't Me* and *My Life After Now* to the world. And thank you to Aubrey Poole, Jillian Bergsma, Cat Clyne, Abbie Digel, the Sourcebooks cover design team, the sales and marketing team, the copyeditors and proofreaders, and every single person at Sourcebooks who worked on this book.

In case you didn't know, Kate McKean is the best agent *ever*, and I am so lucky to have her on my side, from Lucy to Lexi and beyond.

This book was my creative thesis for my MFA, and I absolutely won the thesis advisor lottery with Sarah Ketchersid. Thank you, Sarah, for your unparalleled wisdom, and for making me rewrite the first fifty pages more times than I can count. You were always right.

Thank you to David Levithan for not only being an incredible professor and inspiration, but for doing all you do to help little guys like me find a real place in the NYC YA author scene.

The Lucky 13s—including Alison Cherry, Mindy Raf, and Lindsay Ribar—is just the coolest group of kid lit authors ever, and I'm proud to be one of you.

To my creative writing instructor Sarah Weeks and my New School peeps Amber, Jane, Kevin, and Molly, thank you so much for your encouragement as I was drafting the early chapters of this book.

To my beta readers, critique group, and kickass thesis group—Caela Carter, Sona Charaipotra, Dhonielle Clayton, Alyson Gerber, Corey Ann Haydu, Riddhi Parekh, and Mary G. Thompson—you're all a bunch of geniuses. You were more integral to the creation of Lexi's world than you probably realize, and I love you for it.

Thanks to the fam—Susan and John Miller, Jim Verdi, and Robert and Alyssa Verdi—for being so excited about my books. Thank you to my sister-in-law Emily Chiles for writing me a letter of recommendation for my grad school application! Thank you to the Petrie family at large—and Cynthia Farina and Rachel Leigh Smith in particular—for being so supportive and so cool with the topics I choose to write about. I would have written the books anyway, but, you know, it's really nice to know you've got my back.

Paul Bausch, thank you for being such an awesome guy and for putting up with me all those times I couldn't go out on the weekends because I had to work. Love you, homie.

Amy Ewing, this book was dedicated to you basically before it was even written. Thank you for reading and re-reading, for talking it all through, for squealing with me in South Africa when I got the happy news email from my agent, for loving this quirky little band of four like they're real people, and for reassuring me that Carolyn is, in fact, super hot. You are my champion!

About the Author

Jessica Verdi lives in Brooklyn, NY, and received her MFA in Creative Writing from The New School. She loves seltzer, Tabasco, TV, vegetarian soup, flip-flops, and her dog. She will choose Spike over Angel and Jess over Dean *every single time*, and has tattoos of a book and an elephant—two of her favorite things—on her arms. Jessica is also the author of *My Life After Now*. Visit her at www.jessicaverdi.com and follow her on Twitter @jessverdi.

If you liked *The Summer I Wasn't Me*, check out these other great titles from Sourcebooks Fire.

MY LIFE AFTER NOW

Jessica Verdi

What now?

Lucy just had the worst week ever. And suddenly, it's all too much—she wants out. Out of her house, out of her head, out of her life. She wants to be a whole new Lucy. So she does something the old Lucy would never dream of.

And now her life will never be the same. Now, how will she be able to have a boyfriend? What will she tell her friends? How will she face her family? Now, every moment is a precious gift. She never thought being positive could be so negative. But now, everything's different… because now she's living with HIV.

PRAISE FOR *MY LIFE AFTER NOW*:

"Debut author Verdi paints Lucy's devastation and her tangled emotions with honesty and compassion…telling Lucy's story with realism and hope." —*Publishers Weekly*

"Verdi forces her readers to face Lucy's dilemma with unflinching honesty and unfaltering compassion. A gem of a novel." —*RT Book Reviews*, 4½ Stars, Top Pick of the Month

IF HE HAD BEEN WITH ME

Laura Nowlin

"If he had been with me, everything would have been different."

Finn and Autumn used to be inseparable, but middle school puts them on separate paths going into high school. Yet no matter how distant they become or who they're dating, Autumn continues to be haunted by the past and what might have been. While their paths continue to cross and opportunities continue to be missed, little do they know that the future might separate them forever.

PRAISE FOR *IF HE HAD BEEN WITH ME*:

"Friendship, love, secrets, hope and regret…this book has it all! *If He Had Been With Me* is a page-turner that you won't be able to put down." —*Girls' Life*

"This sweet, authentic love story masks complex characters dealing with complex issues…First-time author Nowlin keeps the story real and fast paced." —*Booklist*

16 THINGS I THOUGHT WERE TRUE

Janet Gurtler

Heart attacks happen to other people #thingsithoughtweretrue

When Morgan's mom gets sick, it's hard not to panic. Without her mother, she would have no one—until she finds out the dad who walked out on her as a baby isn't as far away as she thought…

5000 Twitter followers are all the friends I need #thingsithoughtweretrue

With Adam in the back seat, a hyper chatterbox named Amy behind the wheel, and plenty of Cheetos to fuel their road trip, Morgan feels ready for anything. She's not expecting a flat tire, a missed ferry, a fake girlfriend…and that these two people she barely knew before the summer started will become the people she can't imagine living without.

PRAISE FOR JANET GURTLER:

"Just right for fans of Sarah Dessen and Jodi Picoult." —*Booklist* on *I'm Not Her*

"The characters breathe with life." —*Kirkus* on *Who I Kissed*